Bright Fire
Maya Hess

BLACK LACE

Black Lace books contain sexual fantasies.
In real life, always practise safe sex.

First published in 2007 by
Black Lace
Thames Wharf Studios
Rainville Road
London W6 9HA

Typeset by SetSystems Ltd, Saffron Walden, Essex

Printed in the UK by CPI Bookmarque, Croydon, CR0 4TD

The paper used in this book is a natural, recyclable product made
from wood grown in sustainable forests. The manufacturing process
conforms to the regulations of the country of origin.

ISBN 978 0 352 34104 4

1

Brogan stood before the priest. The southerly wind broke through his long hair, entwining with the locks of his bride-to-be as she waited beside him on the exposed hill crest. The sky was loosely striped – a salad of tangerine and early morning indigo, creamed with light cirrus clouds. The air was fresh and prepared, hung with the ripeness of spring and the promise of summer.

'In the joining of hands,' the priest began. Laymar had overseen as many hand-fasting ceremonies as there were clovers in the ankle-deep grass. Brogan and Cailla linked fingers, ignoring the warm wind that rippled their clothes. Their eyes locked, making certain that their future was assured, and temporarily making them unaware of the many attending guests that approached to tie the colourful knots of fabric around their entwined hands.

'Brogan and Cailla,' Laymar continued, 'as the fire burns through Beltane, so shall it burn through the days of your union . . .'

Two more guests approached and knotted bright, hand-crafted fabric around Cailla's slim joint and the tense strap of Brogan's wrist. Laymar walked around the magic circle, reinforcing the existing charge in order to summon the gods to bless the year-long union of the village's ripest couple.

Since childhood, Brogan and Cailla had been destined to come together. Within hours, the consummation would be complete and Cailla would fold beneath her new husband's keen body while the rest of the village danced and feasted and burnt fires throughout the night. But before the couple were allowed privacy, they would take part in a sacred fertility ritual.

The ladder of muscle in Brogan's back tensed involuntarily and as he thought of the two women that waited for him – the pleasure, the indulgence – he couldn't help it that his chest swelled and his chin tilted up to the partially cloud-covered sun. He was a lucky man, he thought, although the divine woman beside him was nothing he didn't deserve. Brogan squinted up at the unusual sky.

What was this – a storm at Beltane?

'Creature of fire, creature of light...' Laymar spoke his magic, glancing briefly at the hilltop fire that had been kept burning for seven days. If the skies delivered the storm they were currently promising, there would be no fire for the ceremony. '... hear my will addressed unto thee. Make the Beltane fire burn bright...'

Laymar broke from his spell and threw back his head. His long hair flagged like ripped cloth around his shoulders. Above him, the sky had become liquid slate and churned with a spiral of blue-green froth. Laymar had once been to the edge of the land and the sight above reminded him of the winter seas. Unnerved by the unusual happening, he gathered his thoughts before the gods could steal them clean from his mind.

'... make the Beltane fire burn bright and bless the lovers for –'

Cailla suddenly screamed as a ball of fire split the sky in two. The thin veil of cerulean sky that dragged across the rapidly darkening eastern horizon was doused by smoke and flames. The brilliant light ripped the heavens at the seams and tore through the increasing whirlwind, its tail lashing down at the ground.

'The fire,' Laymar cried, breaking the hand-fasting verse. 'The sacred fire must be traversed by the couple.'

He looked up again, frowning, as the opened sky burned luminous. 'Quick!' he insisted. 'The union must be sealed before the anger of the gods rains upon us.'

Brogan wrapped his free arm around Cailla's narrow waist, forcing her breasts against the shaped metal of his ceremonial armour. He liked the bend of her body melding against the needy splint of his. 'Ready?' he asked.

'Ready,' she said uncertainly, locked into a trusting gaze with her betrothed. Once they had leapt through the waist-high flames – a beacon to the surrounding settlements that a union was taking place – their coming together would be complete and irrevocable for a whole year. Aside from the promised fertility rite that was traditional in their village, Brogan and Cailla would remain faithful to one another until their next hand-fasting the following spring, when Cailla would be with child.

'You're beautiful,' Brogan said. 'And nearly mine.' He felt his body stirring beneath his clothing but doubt was riding on the sudden deep breath that he drew in. He couldn't be entirely sure if it was Cailla's proximity or the prospect of dipping into the ripened body of Iona and then watching Cailla do the same that made him stiffen. He could think of no better way to assure the gods gave them a child.

Suddenly, a deafening noise arced across the thunderous sky. The circle of hand-fasting guests screamed and scattered, the women and children mapping out crazed circles of panic as they ran terrified around the hillside.

'Now!' Brogan ordered, tugging on his frozen partner. He had to secure his woman, knowing how many other men in the village were keen to take her if he didn't. 'Run with me through the fire.'

But it was as if Cailla had turned to stone and despite the wrenching he gave her arm and shoulders, she would not move. She simply stood straight and followed the ball of fire as it streaked across the sky above them, her face lit both by fear and the flames licking at the strange falling object.

'Flee for your lives,' Laymar ordered. 'The gods are upset by this union and are punishing us!' The priest gathered his ceremonial robes and beckoned to Cailla and Brogan. 'Return to your houses, if you have any sense.'

Brogan drew his dagger from its sheath and sawed it through the bands of fabric that bound his wrist to Cailla's. If she wanted to face the gods alone, that was her decision, but he didn't want to be on the hillside a moment longer. 'Cailla?' he yelled. 'Will you come with me?'

The woman was silent. Her long auburn hair flicked around her pale face and neck, whipping before her eyes as she stared blankly into the sky. Briefly, her gaze veered to Brogan and she saw the grim expression of the man she loved. She had never seen him scared before.

'No,' she said simply and turned her attention back to the menacing whirlwind in the sky.

Brogan cursed angrily before joining the exodus that covered the hillside like flowing lava. As he fled from the sacred place, running now for all he was worth, thankful that his hunter's legs carried him from the danger faster than any of the other villagers, he felt the ground jolt beneath his feet. Then, simultaneously, there was a thunderous crash, as if all life was ending or the dome of the sky was cracking and permanent night would fall down upon them. He wouldn't look back; he couldn't look back. Sweat drove channels of fear down his chest and soaked the clothing beneath the decorative metal of his breast-plate as he tore down the hill. Away from Cailla.

Seconds later, it was all over. The valley echoed with the remnants of the gods' anger and the bending trees gradually straightened and their leaves merely rippled in the residual breeze. Hardly daring to look up, Brogan noticed that his shadow was slowly returning, a good sign that the precious sun hadn't fallen.

Without a thought for Cailla, he ran between the village huts and strode to the sacred roundhouse that was saved for fertility rites, healing and other important ceremonies. If the gods were angry, then he would appease them by sacrificing his body to the beautiful Iona.

Brogan stepped into the darkness of the round mud and straw hut. A small fire flickered in a central pit and the smoke wound up through a hole in the roof in a spiral similar to the vortex he had just seen in the sky. He needed to rid his mind of the terrible scene just witnessed.

'Brogan,' Iona whispered.

As his eyes adjusted to the darkness, Brogan could see that the woman was waiting for him, as expected, on a bed of furs and straw. He reached for the strapping on his heavy armour and removed the metal. Already, his spirit felt lighter.

'Did you not see the anger of the gods?' Despite his fitness and reputation for being the hardest warrior and hunter in the entire valley, Brogan's breathing was laboured. He wiped at the sweat on his forehead. 'A great fireball came travelling through our skies on the back of a grey beast.'

'Oh, Brogan,' Iona laughed. 'You have seen nothing but an unusual storm. It passed soon enough.' She propped herself on her elbows, her body surrounded by swathes of animal fur. 'Tell me now, are you and Cailla united? Did Laymar seal the knot?'

Brogan sighed. 'We didn't travel through the fire.' He

removed the dagger sheath that was slung around his hips and loosened the ties on his tunic. It was warm in the roundhouse and the air smelled of earth, smoking logs and of Iona. He breathed in the sweet scent of her musk and felt himself stiffen beneath the loose cloth. He felt safe and secure in the peaceful hut where the air was still. He knew that Iona would soothe him.

'Then where is Cailla?' Iona frowned and pulled herself up from the straw. She arranged the folds of the pale cloth around her body.

'She wanted to stay behind, to see the gods.' Brogan stepped towards Iona, the sight of her already banishing storms and gods and Cailla from his mind.

'You left her out alone in a storm?' Iona and Cailla had grown up together, shared everything from their clothing and jewellery to their passionate belief in the forces of nature. 'Brogan, how could –' Iona walked to the roundhouse entrance but Brogan stopped her. His hands gripped her shoulders, longing to slip down to cup her heavy breasts.

'She wanted to stay. She wanted me to come to you. Even though the ceremony wasn't complete, Cailla told me to continue with our rite.' Brogan grinned and relaxed his grip as Iona retreated in thought. He followed her back to the fur bed and helped remove her woven shawl. He pressed it to his face and inhaled the scent of her body.

'Very well,' she said. 'I will be yours but on one condition.'

Brogan's eyes narrowed, his mouth breaking into a wide grin. He knew that Iona had noticed the rise in his cloth braecci by the way her jade eyes threaded between his groin and his leer. 'Name it.'

'You must allow Cailla the same freedom between now and when she finally becomes yours.' Iona pressed her hands on her hips. She knew that Cailla wouldn't welcome the arrangement but the expression on Brogan's face was worth the bargain.

'Freedom?' He strode around the fire, considering the unthinkable. Cailla was his; she had always been his.

'And you must allow it without interfering,' Iona added, knowing she was pushing him way beyond the limits of any self-respecting warrior. Brogan defended their settlement fiercely, hunted for much of the winter food. He believed he had earned the right to any woman he chose.

'I agree,' Brogan finally said, kicking at the dusty earth beside the fire. He didn't like bargains, much less when they came from a woman like Iona who held herself in far greater esteem than she deserved. Her job was simple – to provide fertility to the village's couples and ensure there were warriors, hunters and women for generations to come. That the silly woman insisted on delving into the spirits and forces of nature – such territory best left to Laymar and the Druids – was just another annoying indicator of her frivolous character. And the sexual bargain she had just offered typified her need for danger and control.

'Remove your tunic and skirts,' Brogan demanded, realising that her offer excited him like the thrill of taking down a wild pig. He would deal with his end of the bargain later.

Iona pulled the drape of blue and green dyed fabric from her pregnant body. She wore nothing beneath her skirts and aside from the curved bronze torc around her slim neck, she stood completely naked beside the fire pit.

'Do you know how long I've waited for this?' Brogan dragged his rough hands across the mound of her ripe belly. There were so many curves on this woman, he didn't know where to begin. He reached for her breasts, knowing that he had taken them too hard when she gave a little cry. Brogan didn't care. He dipped his head and nipped their brown ends, stretching the tips of her nipples as he pulled away. 'My turn,' he said, kicking off his leather shoes before removing his own tunic and braecci.

'I see you are ready for me,' Iona giggled.

Brogan took himself in one hand. 'This has been waiting to enter your body since the day you became a woman.' He grinned, pushing back the curtain of wind-swept hair from his face. He eased his hand up and down his erect shaft like he was preparing his weapons for battle. 'Get down into the furs,' he ordered, his voice shaking from the power welling in his groin. He would take Iona roughly, how he liked, without care for her pleasure. There would be plenty of time to do things her way afterwards. He planned on having her over and over again, throughout the day and the next night – the time that had been set aside for his and Cailla's fertility celebrations.

Iona lowered herself into the sheepskin and fox furs, the firelight dancing over her smooth, pale skin. She arranged herself comfortably, unaware that Brogan had other plans for her body. 'I am ready for you,' she laughed, winking at the tall figure above her. She was pleased that he had come to her. Her need for a man, in her condition, would have caused her to seek relief elsewhere if he had not sought her out in the roundhouse.

Brogan dropped to his knees and touched Iona's head. 'Your hair is the colour of the sky I just witnessed,' he confessed. 'And as silken as the river flowing through our valley.'

'My hair is black,' Iona said, puzzled.

'And that was the colour of the sky before the fireball –'

'Sshh about your silly fireball and tell me what you

think of this.' Iona spread her legs to reveal a neat patch of glistening hair beneath her huge belly. She reached down and tentatively dipped a finger between her buttocks, drawing a line through the seam of wetness and up onto her flattened-out navel. She left a silver trail, which Brogan wasted no time in devouring before licking his way down to the place he truly believed to be the centre of all human pleasure.

'Oh, Brogan,' Iona cried. 'I cannot bear the feelings you give me.' She writhed in the fur, needing to pull away from the bolt of bliss that drove through her as Brogan's tongue dug deep inside. Iona was gripped by ecstasy but also by guilt as she allowed the man that had long been promised to her best friend to take her without the protection of Laymar's fertility rite. If Cailla had been united with Brogan as planned, if Laymar had given his approval, if the couple could enjoy her body between them and receive her fruitful magic . . .

'Turn over,' Brogan barked. When Iona made no move, he hoisted her up and onto all-fours, like she was an animal in the pen. His whole body was veined and rigid and pumped from fear and excitement. He'd wanted Iona for so long that not even a storm to wipe out the entire village would prevent him taking what was his.

He reached around Iona's distended girth as it hung down beneath her and guided her buttocks back onto his erection. His hardness held its position as Iona's slick body eased onto him, allowing him to finger her weighty breasts.

'You are like no other I have had,' Brogan said, gasping as she clenched around him. 'You are like a heavy fruit about to drop from the tree in summer. I have never felt a woman this way before.'

'It's my pleasure and my job, dear Brogan,' Iona said cheekily. She turned her face sideways, tempting Brogan to sink his teeth into the stretched skin of her lithe neck. As he did so, he gripped her wide hips and eased her up and down on his shaft. With him kneeling and Iona half sitting, half on all-fours, he had a splendid view of his cock as it was swallowed time and time again by Iona's cherry-red lips.

'Is it true that by the time you have had forty summers, every man in our village will have possessed your body in this way?' Although Brogan was a possessive man and when he took a woman, he meant to keep her, he couldn't help it that the thought caused his heart to pump faster. At that moment, he would have given up his entire armoury of swords to witness Iona being ravaged by the men of the village. When she thought it was over, when she was dripping with a hundred different kinds of seed, he would step in and take her to the highest place she knew. Brogan was well aware of his power as a lover.

'At least,' she giggled, 'and perhaps many from the settlement across the valley, too. I have heard tales of their virile men.' Then her laugh changed to moans as her buttocks slapped against the fuzz of Brogan's groin.

'You are dirty and immoral,' he spat, still revelling in the image of men queuing up for the woman who was squeezing him with unimaginable skill. 'You think you are so clever but . . .' Brogan slowed and eased himself in and out of Iona as gently as he could manage. Never before had he taken a woman and not felt her powerful, pulsing clench around his girth seconds before he came. He couldn't stand for his reputation to be questioned. Cailla was expecting the best.

'Harder, Brogan, now please, harder.' Iona was writhing helplessly, her body searching for his cock but Brogan had withdrawn. He had other ideas.

'Lie back,' he demanded and was surprised that she

did so without question. Iona was known for being stubborn and strong-minded. 'Open your mouth,' he said and guided his burning erection between her lips.

Iona devoured him. From the tight sacs hanging beneath his tireless cock to the uncharted skin behind and up to the eager, exposed head that by now could only tolerate the tiniest most feminine of licks – Iona ate it all like she had suffered a winter of starvation. In fact, it was quite likely that she had.

Brogan gripped an oak post that formed part of the frame of the thatched roundhouse. He dug his short nails into the grain as he cried out and slammed himself deep inside the woman's throat. He would fill her up; he would make it so that she was never hungry again.

In a dozen or so strokes, he spent himself deep inside her mouth in a noisy, frantic climax comparable to the thunderous crash sent from the gods. Brogan jerked and shuddered and every muscle across his lean body pulled together, creating a formidable sight. He was a powerful man with a powerful need.

'And how did you find that?' Iona was beside him, rubbing his shoulders. Later, she would douse him with scented oils and groom his hair. Then, she hoped, he would take her again. A woman could never get enough of a man like Brogan.

'Adequate,' he said coldly. Then he turned on his side in the fur and grinned. He stole a deep kiss and tasted himself on her tongue.

'Aren't you forgetting something?' Again, Iona spread her legs and exposed the trim line of her pretty sex. Brogan didn't need any more reminding. Hungry as ever, he pressed his face into the musk of her hidden folds and teased and licked at the crest of her mound until she too bucked her heavy, full body by the warmth of the fire.

Even after this, Brogan wasn't nearly finished with her.

Cailla was frozen by fear and wonder as the lightning ball ripped across the sky, its trajectory on course for the sacred hilltop. Briefly, she glanced at the villagers, Brogan included, as they ran down the hill and away from her hand-fasting ceremony. For Laymar to flee, this must be a message from the gods and therefore something that no mortal should witness.

Cailla raised her hands up to the light – a signal that she was willing to take whatever punishment was forthcoming – and began to chant the verse that Laymar used to protect the village from enemy warriors. Tears welled in her narrowed eyes as the whirlwind swirled and dragged above, the lower tip of it just touching the treetops as it swept over the forest in the valley.

'*Take not my heart –*' but Cailla was prevented from continuing as the bright fireball emerged from the whirlwind and hurtled towards the crest of the hill. Within seconds, there was a loud crack and bang and the earth shook beneath her feet. She threw herself to the ground in fear and pulled her wool cloak over her head.

Cailla sweated and trembled, muttering all the words she had learnt from Laymar in a desperate jumble. Only when the thunderous noise quietened to a dull roar could she uncover her head and peer up at the thing that had fallen onto their hillside. She felt the heat from the burning fireball.

Slowly, she peeled back the pretty woven cloth that was to be the garment she wore when Brogan took her for himself. Cailla squinted and gasped as she saw the black smoke and flames coming from the god-like beast that sat upon the most revered site in the surrounding land. She stood without removing her gaze from the creature as it rested upon the grass, breathing its heavy breaths of fire and gently growling from its long journey.

With her heart thumping in her chest as it did when Brogan took her in his arms, Cailla stepped towards the strange sight. She fingered the bronze amulet in her belt pouch for luck.

Suddenly, the beast burst open and the commotion caused Cailla to stop in her tracks. She couldn't have been more than fifteen feet from it and marvelled at its bright coat and shiny nose. Strangely, it appeared to be made from a similar material to Brogan's swords and armour although there was no mistaking the living, breathing capabilities of this animal. In case it was a hunter, Cailla froze. She searched its skin for a beady eye.

'Damn fucking weather forecast!'

The beast not only opened but spoke words that Cailla could not comprehend. She begged her body to stop shaking.

'Where for the love of God am I? Some bloody Hicksville field and not a road in sight.'

The beast spewed forth what appeared to be a woman. A woman unlike any in their village and only determined as female by the familiar curves that were easily viewed through thin clothing. The beast-woman's face was blackened and her hair wild, as if she had prepared for battle. A female warrior!

The she-warrior jumped from the beast and then winced in pain. 'Ouch! My ankle.' She hopped about and rolled up her battle garment. Her leg was bleeding. Cailla stepped forwards from the cluster of bushes in which she was sheltered. A twig snapped.

'Who's there?' The she-warrior stood straight again and glanced around.

Cailla, always honest – even to her detriment –

emerged from the covering and made herself known. 'My name is Cailla,' she said. 'And I give myself to you as a sacrifice to the gods. Take no one else from our village, I beg you.' Cailla thought of Brogan; how she loved him and wanted nothing more than to protect him.

'Whoa,' said the she-warrior, laughing. She started to walk but stopped, wincing and limping. 'Look, can you tell me where I am exactly? The rescue services will want a pretty exact location out here.' The woman laughed hysterically and winced and hopped about and squinted all around the valley with her hand shielding her eyes. 'Bloody weather report.'

'Yes, you are on the sacred hilltop. It is a very special place.' Cailla fell to her knees as the she-warrior removed two blackened discs from her head and placed them over her eyes.

'No shit. So I tell rescue that I'm on the sacred hilltop. Y'know, guys, that sacred hilltop, the special one.' The she-warrior paced about the hill as much as her ankle would allow. She slapped her hands against her legs. 'OK, how about you tell me the nearest road, you know, the A403 or whatever. A town would be cool, too. Perhaps York or did I nearly make it to Darlington?'

'I am so frail in your great presence –'

'Look please, lady. Just give me a fucking clue where we are? I'm not talking precise grid refs here. Even a county would do to get started, huh?'

The she-warrior approached Cailla, her head cocked to one side, waiting for a reply. But when the great beast behind them began to stretch and give out more fire, the woman yelled a verse and hobbled back to the sleeping creature. She reached inside the thing's head and in a moment there was much commotion as a white spray as ferocious as any the flooding river puts forth came out of a pot the colour of blood.

'At least they made sure the fire extinguishers worked, even if they couldn't get the weather right. Jees, look at my landing gear, will you? Crumpled and fit for the wreckers.'

Cailla fell to the ground again, wishing that she had fled with Brogan. She could be by his side, gazing up the hill at the strange spectacle from a safe distance.

'Look, can you just get up and help me? My ankle's knackered and my plane's just crashed. I've got priceless cargo in there that, if I don't deliver by tomorrow, then I'm dead meat. My landlord's about to evict me and to top it all, I think my fiancé's shagging my best friend. It's not been a good day, y'know? So cut the re-enactment crap in your silly clothes and tell me where I am!'

Cailla began to cry.

'Oh, hell.' The she-warrior sat down on the grass beside Cailla. 'I'm sorry, OK? Here's what I'll do. I'm going to call the airport first, let them know where I ditched because I'll have dropped clean off their radar, and then you can speak on the phone and tell them exactly where I am. Does that sound reasonable?'

Cailla flinched as the she-warrior touched her back. 'Whatever you say, I will comply,' she murmured, hardly able to view the close-up image of the she-warrior.

'Fine. Shame Hugh isn't as amenable as you, hon.'

The strange woman removed something shiny from her pocket but in a moment was standing and pacing about with her limp. 'Oh that's just great. That's just my sodding luck today. I knew I should have stayed in bed. No fucking reception.'

Cailla glanced up as the she-warrior performed a slow dance on the hillside that involved raising her arm and touching the shiny object before yelling strange words.

'Does Orange cover this area, do you know?'

Cailla was confused but she stood up, which seemed to please the visitor from the gods. She reached out and dared to touch her auburn hair – and she was going to speak, she was going to be helpful – but the land and sky began to spin and she had no choice but to faint to the ground.

2

'You know what?' Jenna suggested down the phone as she clicked on the aviation weather website. 'Why don't you sort it out, huh? You make sure the champagne's Bollinger not Moët and the canapés are Beluga not salmon. You check that the correct numbers are being catered for and that the extra photographer is booked in case the first one loses his camera. Don't forget to see that the newspaper's been tipped off and Aunt Agnes or whatever she's called is told the wrong date so she doesn't come because you know she'll get drunk and destroy the wedding cake or grope the best man and, and . . .'

Jenna refreshed the weather page as she spoke but it still read the same. Fine and clear between London City Airport and Dundee. 'And don't forget the bloody Australian prawns,' she yelled into the dead handset. Hugh must have been passing through a tunnel. Suddenly he wasn't there.

Jenna pushed her laptop aside and slumped back on her bed. 'So the weather's OK, my plane's fixed, the cargo pick-up is arranged and the rich man in Scotland is expecting me at his fancy castle.' She rolled over and fumbled on the night stand for her cigarettes. The packet contained only one. 'Note to self. Buy more smokes and take shotgun to Scotland. I hear it's roebuck season.' She grinned and clicked her Zippo.

Finally, Jenna plumped up the pillows, inhaled deeply on a Marlboro and pressed all the buttons on the remote. She settled on a Western at the same time she remembered that last night's Chinese takeaway was still in the fridge. She couldn't have planned a better night. Then she remembered her wedding and her toes curled and her fingers went numb.

'Oh god,' she wailed. 'Why me?' Ignoring the television, she called her best friend. She was always good for a dose of face-slapping reality.

Come on ... You're about to marry one of London's most eligible bachelors and you're complaining about the mother-in-law or the size of his dick? Do you realise just how rich and powerful this guy is?

And on it would go. Just what Jenna needed in her one-bedroom apartment with her cold Chinese balancing on her knee. She couldn't bear fried rice on the duvet.

Someone answered the phone but no one spoke. 'Hey, Mel? It's me.' Jenna paused as she heard heavy breathing. 'Mel, are you there?' Then there was a moan and a slapping sound followed by another moan and a man's voice.

'Get yourself back on my cock now, you little bitch.'

There was yelping and panting and then, at the precise moment she dropped the carton of Yangchow special fried rice onto the quilt, Jenna recognised the voice.

'Hey, you, wait. There's someone on the phone. Ouch!' More giggles. *'Hello?'*

Hugh – her fiancé – was at Mel's house. Fucking her.

Just as the aviation weather forecast promised, the day dawned clear blue with a light south-westerly, ten knots max. Jenna had taken care of the pre-flights in a sleepless daze, her mind having tumbled all night like a load of dirty washing in the machine.

Hugh at Mel's place?

She shook the thought from her head and allowed

the gathering breeze to ruffle her long auburn hair. Her friend would never do that to her, right?

'Do you have a licence for that machine, Miss Bright?'

Jenna turned, her hand caressing the line of the aileron. 'Vic,' she said smiling, knowing it always riled him but now he had his hands on her ribs and was threatening to tickle.

'Don't Vic me,' he replied, digging his fingers into Jenna's tense body. Five years ago, Mark was flying for British Airways. Then he saw the light and became a priest. Ever since, his friends had called him Vic. 'Father or Your Holiness or even God will be fine.'

'Right,' Jenna said, laughing. 'Look, I have to get my checks done then I'm off to Dundee. To a fancy castle.' Jenna postured and made a face.

'And what about the husband-to-be?'

Jenna froze, the increasing breeze tearing at her loose jacket. 'He's fine, thanks, and perfectly capable of managing without me for a few days.' Her throat constricted at the thought of leaving Hugh alone.

'A few days? Are you staying up in Scotland long?' Vic shielded his eyes against the early morning brightness. Jenna's billowing hair was like a sunrise against the harsh tarmac.

'I've been invited to a shooting weekend by my client. A perk of the job, I guess.'

She was keen to get off. Even though the weather forecast predicted clear skies, high pressure and low to moderate breeze, Jenna could feel something brewing by the way the wind had suddenly switched to the north-east.

'I'll see you soon, then,' Vic said slowly. Jenna always had time for him; always saved a place for him in her heart. He turned and walked away.

'Wait,' she said without knowing why. 'What are you doing at the airport?' It was something to say; bought her another bitter-sweet moment with the man that she once thought could have been hers.

'Just catching up with old friends.' Mark smiled.

For a moment, Jenna thought he'd said *checking up on old friends* but then realised she was mistaken. They'd first met at this airport, several years ago.

'Don't fly today,' Jenna blurted out. 'Watch the weather,' she continued and couldn't for the life of her think why. She was finishing up her pre-flights and about to fly to Dundee, for heaven's sake. All met reports checked and double-checked.

'Weather looks fine to me,' Mark said, upturning his palms as if checking for rain. He licked a finger and stuck it in the air. 'Fine and clear all the way, Miss Bright. Enjoy your flight.' This time he turned and carried on walking.

'Tower, this is bravo mike holding at runway two-eight and waiting to taxi. Requesting clarification of London City QNH and QFE. Over.' Jenna tapped a long nail on the cover of the altimeter. 'Don't play up today. I really want to go to Carrickvaig Castle for the weekend. I *have* to get away.'

'Golf bravo mike. London City QNH is one . . .' But the radio connection to the tower was suddenly like a rustling paper bag in Jenna's headphones and the noise hurt her ears so much that she turned down the volume. 'Oh not today,' she muttered, attempting to retune the radio.

'This is golf bravo mike to London City tower. Do you read me? Over.' Again, the small cockpit of the Piper Saratoga was filled with static and crackling but then the radio jumped back to life like a switch had been flicked and the tower came through loud and clear.

'Golf bravo mike cleared for take-off on runway two eight. Exit circuit to the north-east please, Miss Bright and get yourself to three thousand as soon as you can because I have a couple of big ones racking up. Over.'

Jenna smiled. She'd known Dan since she'd learnt to fly. 'I don't wish to know about your big ones, Mr Elliott. Just get me on my way and I'll wave bye-bye when I knock up regional control.' She patted the radio, convinced it was now working fine and released the brakes.

'You shouldn't be knocking up anyone, bravo mike. You're nearly a married woman. Clear for take-off, Miss Bright and have a safe flight.'

Jenna eased the throttle forwards and taxied to the start of the runway. As the peninsula of tarmac stretched out ahead between the docks, she wasn't sure whether to take notice of the knot in her throat as Dan mentioned her impending marriage, or enjoy the fluttering inside her chest at their mild flirting over the airwaves or . . .

She increased the throttle and gathered speed down the runway. Taking off always took her breath away.

'What the –' Jenna briefly turned her head to the four empty passenger seats in the cabin behind. A low rumbling sound droned from the back and as the aircraft sped faster down the tarmac, she briefly considered terminating take-off. She glanced back again and saw that the wooden crate was still wedged and strapped between the seats. Her client's precious cargo, whatever it was.

Fifty knots, fifty-five, sixty . . . if she was going to abort, now was the time. Jenna increased the throttle even further, held her breath and focussed on her long weekend away. Escaping London was the only way to forget that her fiancé was sleeping with her best friend. Life needed re-evaluating.

The vibrations transformed into a doleful whine as the aircraft approached eighty knots but still Jenna pushed on, even though she wasn't entirely sure her altimeter was set correctly or her radio was functioning as it should. She certainly couldn't begin to describe what was causing the unusual noise in the back. The landing gear, a tyre about to blow, a loose cowl? Any sensible pilot wouldn't have got as far as the runway. Today, Jenna wasn't feeling sensible.

'Rotate,' she whispered to herself and eased the stick back gently until the nose wheel of her beloved Saratoga lifted off the tarmac. Seconds later, with all instruments in the green, the single propeller easily hauled the aircraft out of London's Docklands. Jenna kept a grip of the throttle and used her left hand to guide the stick through the slight crosswind. The wind had changed again.

'Bravo mike on her way,' Jenna said to herself, breathing a sigh of relief that the unusual noise had abated and all her instruments appeared to be functioning. 'I'm going to forget about weddings and best friends and lousy fiancés and just concentrate on having a good time. Oh, and maybe learn how to shoot.' Her words were hung with a touch of anger and remorse but were flattened away when she heard a strange whispering. The words were indecipherable.

'Oh, now what?' she snapped, adjusting the squelch control. 'Golf bravo mike to London City tower, please repeat your last message. Over.'

More static filled with unintelligible whispers. 'London City to bravo mike. No contact was made with you. Repeat, no contact made. Everything OK up there, Jen? You sound a bit stressed.'

'Everything fine, thanks, Dan. I'm fifteen hundred feet and will be breaking soon. I'll be out of your hair in no time.' But Jenna didn't get to hear Dan's reply because the radio hissed and crackled and then went completely dead. No amount of fiddling or re-setting could spark it back to life.

'That's just great,' she moaned, thinking she would have to turn back for sure now. 'Could things get any worse?'

Jenna decided to allow fifteen minutes for the radio to cool down before she began checking fuses and wiring. Worst case, she'd use her mobile to call a local airfield and make an unscheduled stop to get the thing repaired.

'But my client's expecting me early evening and I'll be late and my reputation will suffer ...' Jenna pushed her sunglasses on top of her pony-tailed hair and tried to keep calm but when a voice coming from the rear of the aircraft whispered her name repeatedly, it was impossible to prevent her cheeks flushing, her heart palpitating and the hairs on her neck prickling with fear.

'Who's there?' she squealed, turning around as best she could within her tight harness. She saw the cream leather seats, which were usually filled with paying business passengers, and wooden crate marked FRAGILE. The entire rear cabin was doused in a pale grey mist.

'Oh shit!' she cried but as quickly as she reached for the fire extinguisher, the mist vanished and the whispering stopped.

For the next hour, hardly daring to breathe but also determined not to be fazed by the strange events, Jenna busied herself by studying the map strapped to her thigh, worked out navigation routes and, by the time she spotted the giant tornado approaching, it was too late to do anything but hold on and pray.

'No reply at home,' Mel said. 'Shall I try her mobile?'

'If she's flying then it'll be switched off. I don't get it. The stupid woman always calls me before she leaves.' Hugh paced Mel's apartment in his boxers. He stood in the bay window and lit a cigarette, squinting up at the sky as if he might spot his fiancée circling overhead.

'Nope. I'm getting her voicemail again.' Mel didn't leave a message. She wasn't sure that her words wouldn't be recorded dripping with guilt. She slipped a robe over her shoulders and was about to offer Hugh coffee, knowing that after he had woken properly he would most likely leave.

'Hey, no clothes,' he ordered. 'You know I like you naked.' Hugh slid up behind Mel and strapped his arms around her from behind. He pinched her nipples roughly and bit into her long neck with a smoky mouth. 'Clothes are for when other people see you, not me.'

'Sorry,' Mel whispered, gasping as the robe was torn from her body. Hugh parted her buttocks with his free hand and drove a clenched fist between her legs from behind. His wrist wedged firmly against her butt and his fingers prised apart the lips of her overworked pussy. Roughly, he began to work her up and although reluctant at first, Mel couldn't help but get turned on yet again as her insatiable lover took what he truly believed was his.

'Suck it,' he ordered and Mel dutifully took his fat erection in her mouth. It was a strange recipe of dried semen, her own musky scent and the bitter tang of hair gel that Hugh had insisted she slather over him the night before. And Mel was still turned on enough to finger herself to get to where she needed to be to accompany her lover to yet another climax.

What it was that made her adore him so, she wasn't sure – his wealth, perhaps, or his self-indulgent good-looks or possibly that being the fiancé of her best friend made him completely off limits? Mel supposed it was a combination of everything and as the first rods of impending orgasm circled her belly, she really didn't care. She wanted him, as she'd always wanted him and now, with his tireless cock shoved down her throat, Mel didn't ever want to let him go.

'Faster, faster and bite me,' Hugh growled, breathless and needy. The warm fuzz of his slightly rounded belly bumped Mel's forehead as she sucked and bit and ate every inch of Hugh's cock like she'd starved for a week.

Suddenly, she was lying on the floor with the side of her face rubbing the carpet. Hugh grabbed her buttocks and pulled them up, forcing his way into her tightened hole. It took a few minutes to gain a stronghold of her damp body and the couple of yelps that she let go simply fuelled the man's need to hit home.

'See what you do to me, you dirty bitch?' And Hugh delivered a sharp slap across her pale, round buttocks so that she squealed even more. Again he took a swipe and relished the tightening of her internal muscles around his shaft. Sex with Mel was disposable, like she was his reusable toy programmed not to complain.

Not caring if she actually climaxed or was split in two from his rampant thrusting at her rear, Hugh gripped her shoulders and hammered himself spent. When it was over, he fell forwards and contented himself by coaxing her broad nipples to peaks.

'Do you love me, Hugh?' Mel asked meekly. She always hated herself at this point. Too late to keep her pride, certainly too late to hide from the guilt and however much she promised herself it would never happen again, she knew that the next order Hugh barked at her would have her stripped and begging for him.

'No,' he replied bluntly through the smoke of a cigarette. 'I love Jenna.'

'Oh,' said Mel, wondering why that turned her on so much. She rolled away and reached for her robe but Hugh tossed it aside. Mel grinned.

'You represent the forbidden. The bad. The need. Every man's right, in fact.' Hugh stood up and went into the bathroom. 'You make my life perfect,' he said laughing back at her and spraying well left of the pan.

When he'd gone, Mel cleaned up the mess, showered, tried to concentrate on a movie but ended up dialling Jenna's mobile number a hundred times. It was still diverting to her voicemail.

'Hey, Jen. It's me. Just wondering if you've left for Scotland yet and, you know, if you got there OK. Well . . . call me back and oh, Hugh sends his love.'

It was as she hung up that she realised her mistake. *Hugh sends his love.* As she slipped back into bed, determined to sleep off her guilt, Mel wondered if she had unconsciously intended to alert Jenna that she had been with her fiancé.

She finally slept and the last thing she thought of was the girth of Hugh's erection stretching her lips and the sting of his hand across her buttocks.

3

Jenna stared at the heap of woman at her feet. Her plaid tunic had ridden up her legs to expose pale flesh with a fine covering of light down. The woman's long hair – decorated with small metal objects and flowers – fell across her face. Jenna touched a hand to her shoulder.

'Are you OK?' She prodded her back. 'Please, wake up or we're both lost.' Then, 'Oh god!' as a fresh burst of flames licked at the Piper's front cowl. Jenna lunged for the extinguisher and sprayed for all she was worth, finally allowing her precious aircraft to creak and cool and settle on the hillside.

'Wake up, dammit,' Jenna cried, sorely tempted to nudge the useless woman with her boot. She hoisted her onto her back and saw that she was still out cold. Then she limped over to a rocky crag and painfully climbed up to the top of it to get a view of the surrounding area on all sides of the hill.

'Very special place. Sacred bloody hilltop,' Jenna said bitterly, shook her head and squinted around. Finally, through the trees, she saw several columns of smoke winding vertically up. 'Look at that. The wind's dropped to nothing and yet I managed to get caught up in a tornado. Right, that's where I'm headed. If there's a bonfire in the valley then there must be someone having it.' Jenna climbed back down to the woman on the grass. 'And hopefully it's someone with more sense than you,' she added.

She gathered some belongings from the crumpled Piper and slung them in a bag which she hooked over her shoulder. The cargo, she decided, would be safer in the locked aircraft and the shotgun was definitely best left stowed in the rear locker. Jenna fastened the doors, satisfied there would be no more fires, and limped off down the hillside.

'Bye,' she called back to the unconscious woman but only managed about twenty paces before she stopped abruptly and said, head bowed, 'OK. You win. You'll have to come too.' How, exactly, Jenna didn't have a clue.

She crouched at the woman's side and wound one arm around her shoulders and the other under her knees. Then she tried to stand but with only one good ankle, it was impossible. Jenna took both the woman's hands and tried to drag her but she got only a few paces and saw that her skin would soon become very sore because her tunic was already starting to rip and unravel. It didn't look very well made. In fact – and Jenna gasped – the check wool tunic had crumpled and torn and come loose right up to her hips, showing that the unconscious woman wasn't wearing any underwear beneath her fancy-dress costume.

Jenna slumped down on the grass beside her and was about to cover up the mound of pale hair at the top of her legs when she noticed that something or someone had very obviously and very recently turned this woman on. Jenna couldn't help but notice the tell-tale trace of juice nestling on the edge of her pink lips. Her very pink lips – swollen and engorged from some recent sexual activity or at the very least, the promise of.

The unexpected sight made Jenna's breathing quicken into shallow pants. She found herself aroused at the sight of the woman's exposed body and could easily have reached out and taken a private stroke – a lick, even – if she had so desired. But more than that, more exciting than the silver streak on pink lips was the promise of a man nearby. A man who could help. A man who could lead her back to civilisation and a telephone. Someone had got the woman into this state.

'I reckon you got a bit carried away during one of those historical society's re-enactment displays and wandered off with a gorgeous warrior type and were just about to get it on in the bushes when *bang*, I crashed in on the scene.' Jenna was about to cover the woman's legs but her hand suddenly froze in fear.

'Who dares invade our sacred hilltop? Who is it that takes my woman from me at the moment she is to be mine?' The voice was loud and gravelled and angry and cut through the entire valley before it struck Jenna's ears. 'Who?' it yelled.

Jenna turned slowly, her hand still in position above the unconscious woman's pubic mound. Behind her, towering above her in what looked like full battle dress of very long ago, was a man so convincing in his outfit that Jenna could have almost believed she was in prehistoric Britain.

She smiled nervously. Better get him on side, she thought. She stood up. 'Hi, I'm Jenna Bright and you'll never believe it but my plane's just come down on the hill and I've really hurt my ankle and this lady, well, she just fainted. Probably never seen a plane wreck before.' Jenna held the smile, trying to make out it wasn't such a serious situation. 'Can you help me? Do you have a phone with reception or is there a village nearby?'

The man shifted uneasily and placed his hand on an iron sword that was at least five feet long and must have weighed a ton.

They sure take this seriously, Jenna thought, casting a quick sweep up and down the man's body. She didn't know much about history and costumes but someone had gone to a lot of trouble to make his costume authentic. Probably the limp woman lying at her feet – had he said she was his wife?

'And I'm so sorry to have interrupted you and . . .' she glanced at the woman, 'but there was a freak tornado at five thousand feet. It totally came out of nowhere. Not to mention the crazy whispering from whatever weird cargo I'm carrying.' Jenna inwardly kicked herself. She didn't want the chap telling the aviation authorities that she'd heard voices. She'd have her licence taken away for sure. 'Anyway, if you could just help me then –'

To Jenna's surprise, the man fell to his knees. 'Forgive me, please forgive me.' He withdrew the sword from his belt and stabbed it in the ground only inches from Jenna's feet. She jumped back. 'Your greatness overwhelms me but now I am prepared to suffer by your hand. All I ask is that you kill me with my own sword.'

'Kill you?' Jenna pulled a face. 'Good heavens, you do take this all seriously, don't you?' Jenna hobbled over to a small rock and sat down. 'The only killing going on around here is from my ankle and it's me that's dying. Any idea where the nearest A&E department is?'

Slowly, the man raised his head. His shoulder length hair tumbled across his swarthy face and his broad and obviously very toned and lean shoulders, previously hunched, straightened to their full width. 'You are dying?'

'Well, not really of course. I was bloody lucky though. Look at my plane, will you?' Both glanced at the wreck. 'I think I've broken my ankle, though.'

'Your beast sleeps?' the man asked.

'If that's your way of saying it's knackered, then yes, it sleeps. It'll take someone pretty handy with their metalwork to get my baby airborne again.'

'Your beast is young?' The man was standing again now and Jenna was hardly able to keep a straight face, despite her predicament, but then the sudden roar of his voice sent her reeling back to the Piper as he strode up to the unconscious woman as if her condition was an afterthought. 'What have you done to my Cailla?'

The man reached down to the woman and trailed his hand up her leg, apparently enjoying the feel of her skin over the whimpers of Jenna and her ankle. 'She sleeps, too,' he said quietly now, glancing up at Jenna.

'Yep, she just hit the deck. Not my fault.' She was about to say he should probably cover her up because the soft cleft at the top of her legs was still exposed but Jenna stopped with her mouth hanging open as the man allowed his fingers to continue onto the woman's pubic mound. 'Do you think that's entirely appropriate?' Jenna asked firmly. 'I mean, we both need medical treatment. She should have come round by now. Check her pulse.'

When he made no move to offer medical assistance, Jenna reached forwards and felt for signs of life. 'Her pulse is weak but there. Can you carry her? I can limp down the hill, I think.'

The man appeared not to hear her. His eyes, naturally dark, had taken on a misty hue and paled to an unnerving shade of grey. His muscles started to twitch, especially on his arms and thighs, like he was fighting back emotion or desire or need. But it was the growl that frightened Jenna. That noise coming from deep within his chest.

The sudden whorl of mysterious clouds had dispersed, the wind had dropped and the sun bathed the valley and surrounding forests in a light the colour of syrup. In fact, the sky had never looked so clear and unpolluted. Even in the countryside, Jenna was used to seeing a perceptible band of grime on the horizon.

'It's a beautiful area,' Jenna commented, attempting to break the man's strange trance. 'So many trees.' And it was true. While she couldn't for the life of her think which forest she had crashed near, she was convinced it would be National Trust. Hell, she didn't even know which county she was in.

'Look, she's coming round,' Jenna said but didn't get a reply. 'Make sure her airways are clear ...' She trailed off. He obviously knew nothing of first aid.

'Our ... godd ... ess ...' Cailla whispered with scarlet lips and flushed cheeks. Jenna thought she looked beautiful and strangely calm.

'Take me as ... a sacrifice,' she continued. 'Brogan, look. Do you see our goddess?'

He focussed on Jenna and his eyes narrowed, turning to pure thought. He nodded slowly.

'Do you see, my love? Can you see our goddess?' Cailla lifted her freed hands and pushed them through his matted hair. 'I will wash you and feed you,' she whispered adoringly.

'A goddess,' Brogan said softly. The first pleasant words he had said since his arrival. 'A goddess.' This time slightly louder and then he stood up. It was like he had suddenly remembered that they weren't entirely alone; as if he had been momentarily consumed by such a great need for his woman that the rest of the world didn't exist. '*Are* you a goddess?' he asked, pacing around Jenna and adjusting the wide leather belt that carried his sword and other tools.

'Well,' Jenna laughed, relieved that things seemed to be getting back to normal. Jenna quite liked this. 'Hugh has called me that from time to time. So if you want me to be a goddess, then goddess I am. Now, if you can just tell me where I am, I can radio back to –'

'Prepare for a magnificent feast, Cailla! This is truly a great Beltane for our clan. Laymar must be told immediately and preparations begun for tonight's celebrations.' The man dropped at Jenna's feet for the second time, bowing his head as he spoke. 'And I will be revered for finding and protecting our beautiful goddess. I will be your keeper and your servant.'

Jenna laughed from embarrassment. 'Whatever. Er ... can we just go to the nearest village or town now? I think I can walk OK.'

Cailla was on her feet, arranging her tunic and dishevelled hair and flitting around Jenna like she had never seen another woman before. 'She is our goddess of fire, Brogan. She came to us in a chariot of flames. See?' Cailla gestured to the Piper. 'It is a good omen for our hand-fasting and tonight the ceremony will be repeated and we will finally be united.'

Jenna picked up her belongings and decided to make a move. 'Well I'm off. If you want to point me in the direction of a shop or pay phone, that'd be great. If not, have a nice day. And, oh, don't touch the Piper.' She walked a few paces, stopped, turned and yelled as loud as she could, 'Or the Fire Goddess will get you!'

To her surprise, the couple genuinely flinched at her words but then hurried alongside her. The man easily lifted Jenna's pack off her shoulder and the woman offered up her wool shawl as the sun passed behind a cloud. In silence and awe, the unusual pair guided Jenna down the grassy hillside towards the clearing in the forest with the twists of smoke.

As the slope of the hill rounded out to flat pasture, Jenna started to feel more than a little puzzled. During the descent, she'd scanned around the surrounding countryside for signs of villages or towns or pylons that would lead to civilisation and help. But there was nothing. Aside from forest and a smattering of ploughed areas, there was simply nothing but the green of the land topped by a deep cerulean sky.

'We are nearly there,' Cailla said softly. 'We will make

you comfortable and honour your arrival.' She smiled and lifted a hand to stroke Jenna's auburn hair but thought better of it when Jenna pulled a face.

'Are you, er, camping out or something?' Jenna smelt a mix of campfire smoke and searing meat. 'Having a barbecue?' She wondered what the time was and glanced at her watch, tapping it when she saw it had stopped. 'Damn. It must have broken in the crash.'

'Our goddess speaks from another world.' Cailla smiled proudly at Brogan. It was truly a marvellous Beltane.

Just go along with them, Jenna thought. Get to a house, ask to use the phone, wait for help and get away from these crazy people.

Then, from nowhere, a dizzy, nauseous feeling washed through her. She stopped suddenly and thought she might fall over but the thought of this sexed-up man having his way with her while she was out cold forced her to stay upright, albeit with a wobble.

'Not ... feeling so ... good. Can I get a glass of water?' Jenna leant against a tree. 'Are we at your camp or re-enactment site yet? I could use a sit down. Does anyone have a mobile phone?' The pain in her ankle was worsening and questions were swimming in her brain. The day's events were finally taking their toll.

'Earlier, she said she was dying,' Brogan whispered to Cailla. 'Imagine the shame if it is found that we allowed a goddess to die. We must get her fast to Iona. She will know what to do.'

'We can go to the back entrance of her roundhouse. She will be there waiting for us anyway.' A moment of regret passed across Cailla's face as she recalled her unfinished and unconsummated hand-fasting ceremony. She and Brogan were to spend the day and night with Iona, sealing their love and securing their fertility. Now, they were calling on Iona for help with their goddess.

'Come,' Brogan directed at Jenna. 'We will get you the help you need.'

At first, Jenna thought she had dropped clean to the ground because suddenly the leaves and the moss and the brown velvet forest floor were where the sky should have been. Then she realised that she was still conscious and had been swiftly draped over the wretched barbarian's shoulder.

They moved at a rapid pace and from this angle not much of what they passed was visible. The smells became stronger – roasting meat and a stew of root vegetables mingled with aromatic smoke – and a sudden bustle and orchestra of chatter and children's cries and animals bleating and barking passed through her ears. They seemed to by-pass the centre of whatever kind of settlement this was completely.

'Where are we going?' Jenna asked, but she was ignored. Then she saw the sides of a building, like nothing she had ever seen before. The walls were made of what looked like mud mixed with straw and the roof was made entirely of yellow thatch, again most likely straw. Jenna craned her neck to get a better view and if she had possessed the strength, she would have beaten hard on the man's back to let her go. For now, she had no choice but to remain cast over his shoulder.

'Iona,' Cailla whispered. 'Iona, come quickly to your rear door.' Cailla pushed on the creaky willow door. 'I don't understand,' she said. 'Iona should be here. She should be waiting to receive us both.'

Brogan grimaced, knowing that Cailla would be angry if she knew he had already received his fertility rite without her. But as far as he was concerned, more would be needed later. Both women together would assure his manhood and ability to perform. His mouth curled up at the thought.

They went into the cool, dark roundhouse and allowed their eyes to adjust to the dim light. A fire still flickered in the central pit.

'Iona!' Brogan boomed. Something stirred within a heap of furs the other side of the fire. 'Wake up, Iona. We've brought you a gift.' Brogan's voice was loud and deep and shook the dirt foundations of the hut. His white teeth flashed in the firelight as he held firmly onto Jenna. The woman had relaxed onto his body, making him reluctant to place her down. Brogan liked the weight of her slim form melded around his shoulders as if he had just trapped a rare animal for taming.

'Who's there?' Iona's voice was thin and tired. She emerged from the furs wearing nothing but her under-tunic and her usually plaited hair was in a mess about her shoulders. 'Brogan, is that you back again?' A smile developed on her otherwise expressionless face. She stood and forced her eyes to open.

'Again?' Cailla questioned quietly, but Brogan ignored her and under the circumstances, she didn't press for an answer. It was likely that during the terrible storm – the whirlwind that had brought them their goddess – Brogan had fled to the safety of the nearest roundhouse. Iona's.

'I've brought you a gift,' Brogan exclaimed in a voice that, if he wasn't careful, would alert the entire clan to their discovery. For now, Brogan wanted to keep their catch a secret. 'A goddess,' he announced and unceremoniously dumped the listless Jenna onto the pile of furs. She lay like a stunned animal, curled and twisted with a swollen ankle and smoke-blackened skin and she couldn't have looked less like a goddess if she'd tried.

Iona took small steps around Brogan's prize. 'She certainly looks different to us,' she admitted. 'But are you sure she's a goddess? Is she perhaps a messenger from another clan or indeed a noble woman cast out by her clan?'

'She truly is a goddess,' Cailla interjected. 'Iona, I was the one who witnessed her coming and she flew from the sky in a great fire beast. The creature is sleeping on the sacred hilltop. She is our Goddess of Fire!' Cailla ran up to Iona – always so wise and loving – and pulled her close, placing a head on her shoulder. 'Our hand-fasting was broken by the fire beast. We would have come to you sooner but I fear that for now, our fertility plans have been disrupted.' Cailla looked at Jenna, the cause of the disruption. She stirred and moaned within the pile of fur.

'She is tired from her journey,' Iona commented. And then, turning to Cailla, 'Nothing can disrupt our promised ritual. Laymar will see to it that your hand-fasting is completed and not only will we celebrate that but also the arrival of our goddess. It is a doubly special Beltane this year.' Iona held Cailla firmly by the shoulders and inspected her at arms' length. 'Besides, I see that you have already begun your passage to fertility.' Iona smiled and brushed her fingers against the woven cloth of Cailla's special tunic, allowing them to linger over the peaks of her breasts. 'Your cheeks are flushed as one who has offered herself to a man.'

'Indeed, but not satisfied him,' Brogan said, interrupting the women. He liked to see their closeness but his exclusion was not allowed. 'First, we have to deal with the goddess. Iona, you must attend to her needs and Cailla, you will help. I will guard her while you work and then Laymar must be told. There is much preparation for tonight.'

Jenna suddenly opened her eyes and sat up. 'Where am I?' she asked, having momentarily forgotten the crash. 'Am I in Scotland yet? Did I make it to the castle?'

'She speaks unfamiliar words,' Iona noted as she steered an iron crane off the fire with long tongs. Then, using a wad of old cloth, she grasped the metal cauldron and tipped boiling water from it into a clay pot. Crouching beside the bemused goddess, Iona unfurled leather pouches of dried herbs and made a potent infusion, steeping the roundhouse in the scent of the forest floor after a warm rain.

Then she took a clean cloth, dipped it in the aromatic mixture and washed Jenna's face. The soot and grime melted away, revealing the first signs of the goddess's pale skin.

'Truly she is to be revered with a complexion as fair as this. And when I wash it, her hair will shine like the brightest fire embers.' Iona stroked the tangled strands of Jenna's auburn hair and then attempted to release her clothing in order to bathe the rest of her. 'And what unusual garments are these?' she asked now that Jenna was more alert and gazing at the unfamiliar surroundings. Iona tugged and twisted the buttons on what had been a clean white shirt that morning.

'Hey!' Jenna batted Iona's hand away from her chest. 'What are you doing?'

'Undressing you,' Iona said sweetly. 'We welcome you to our clan and when I have washed you, we will fetch Laymar, our Druid. He will speak with you in ways we do not understand.'

'Like I said to this chap,' Jenna pointed at Brogan, who was standing beside the willow door with his hand firmly around his sword. 'All I need is a telephone and to find out exactly where I am. The name of the nearest village would be fine.'

'Iona,' Cailla interrupted. 'We must wait for Laymar

to translate her strange language. Only one so wise will have any idea what the goddess means.'

'Goddess?' Jenna laughed. 'Heavens, this sure is one hell of a weird day.' She stretched and started to stand but then stopped and dropped back into the furs again. 'Oh, I get it,' she said grinning. 'It's one of those caught on camera type shows or ... oh my god!' And Jenna glanced around the inside of the dim hut, seeing only plaid cloths and bunches of herbs and metal implements hung from the ceiling. 'OK, where are the cameras? It's one of those reality TV shows, isn't it? You all have to live like peasants for six months, try not to kill each other and then the last man standing walks away with twenty grand and a contract for their own show on some obscure Sky channel. Am I right?'

She tried to stand again, ignoring the woozy feeling and the lump on her head that was biting into her skull. 'God, I could use a cup of tea. No, make that a large whisky.'

Shakily, Jenna moved about the roundhouse, looking at the unfamiliar objects. 'They sure went to a lot of trouble to make this realistic, didn't they? Is it Channel 4?'

She trailed her hand over a crude loom upon which was set a half-made piece of tartan cloth. Baskets of sheep's wool stood in the corner and aside from the fire pit in the centre, the remainder of the dwelling was draped in furs and cloth with a vast array of dried flowers and herbs hanging from the thatch.

'Drink this.' Iona offered a clay beaker containing another herbal infusion. Thirsty from her ordeal, Jenna took the drink and gulped it down gratefully.

'Thanks, that was good. Do you have to eat like they did in the old days, too? Don't you get the urge to get in the car and pop to the local Indian? I'd miss my Chinese and what about cigarettes and wine and ...'

The room began to spin and Jenna's head swirled with a colourful vision of everything the hut contained, rather like being on an out of control carousel. 'Oh...' she gasped before falling into someone's strong arms – *the barbarian's strong arms* – and being placed upon the fur once again.

As reality turned to dreams, Jenna was aware of a fuss over her chest and stomach. Nearby voices, fumbling and then a ripping sound and cool air over her skin followed by the warm and wet cloth washing her breasts, her belly and ... more haze, rushing in her ears like she was underwater ... someone pulling on her legs, muted voices, the air on her toes, water on her legs, her thighs, between her legs and then Jenna was lost in a blissful blackout that seemed like a thousand years' sleep filled with the most arousing dreams she had ever had.

4

Vandenbrink Holdings Ltd was one of those companies where no one was exactly sure what it did, even its employees. Rachel, PA to successful, rich, respected boss Hugh Vandenbrink, came closest to having an actual job description. Currently, at four-twenty on a lovely, if not unusually breezy, May afternoon, Rachel was occupied by balancing her butt on Hugh Vandenbrink's desk. Her legs were spread, her skirt hitched around her thighs, her knickers already removed with precise instructions to leave her scarlet stilettos exactly where they were.

'Smile,' Hugh said loudly, not caring who heard or knew what they were up to. He aimed his mobile phone between Rachel's legs and snapped away. 'A new part of you every day as a screen background. Put your finger in and let me take another.'

'Yes, sir,' Rachel replied. In an hour, she would be on the underground headed home. She touched her finger between her lips, allowing it to sit alluringly on the edge.

'Right in,' Hugh demanded. 'Then suck it clean.'

'Oh my,' Rachel chirped. 'You're full of ideas today.' She opened her mouth, leant back her head and dragged a long finger with a painted nail along the length of her lips.

'Slowly,' Hugh chastised. 'I want to take lots.'

So aside from arranging meetings, taking minutes, organising social functions, and taking care of just about every aspect of Hugh's personal life – including buying his underwear, condoms and deodorant, which had been on her lunchtime shopping list – Rachel's job description also included as much sex with the boss as he demanded, whenever he demanded it.

It was printed in black and white and she had signed it. On her very first interview, nearly a year ago now, she was told to strip and pose and answer questions in the nude before being called back for a second time. On her third and final interview, as she lay breathless, sweating and face down on the boardroom carpet, Hugh informed her that she had got the job.

'Fuck me,' he said, snapping the phone shut.

'Where, honey? Desk, bathroom, or corridor in case you want to get caught?'

'No, not fuck me. *Fuck me.*' Hugh grabbed a pile of papers off his leather-topped desk and rifled through a file marked *Urgent*.

'Anything I can do?' Rachel deftly unbuttoned her blouse and slipped it off her shoulders. Her breasts sat perfectly in a cream lace bra, each one a little too full for the cup to completely contain. She knew what Hugh liked to see. It was the details like that – the hint of Hugh's favourite perfume touched between her legs, the body cream that melted her skin under his fingers – that earned her a decent bonus each month. 'Can I call anyone?' She noticed him scanning a list of numbers.

'Get Bob from Wilmot and Bailey on the phone and ask him what the fuck went wrong? Better still, put him on to me and I'll ask him.'

'Yes, sir,' Rachel replied and, without demolishing her provocative position, she reached for the office telephone and dialled the number on file. 'I have Hugh Vandenbrink for Bob Michaels, please.' A pause. 'I don't care who he's with, this is urgent. What? I don't know why it's urgent but it's Mr Vandenbrink, so it must be.' Rachel pulled a face at her boss. 'Thank you,' she said finally.

Hugh lit a cigarette, adjusted the bulge nestling in his

suit trousers and continued to gaze longingly up Rachel's skirt. God, she was delicious. Then he laughed to himself, drawing in a lungful of smoke, thinking that really he should shower before he had Rachel. It was only an hour since he'd left Mel's place.

'Here,' Rachel beckoned, holding out the phone.

'Bob? Yes, good. What the fuck happened? I get distracted by other business for a few days then hear nothing back from you. Is it mine? Did I get it?' Hugh inhaled, paced to the window, glanced at Rachel who was still exploring with her finger, then barked down the phone once more. 'Is it bloody-well mine?'

Rachel cowered when the explosion came. She pulled her legs up onto the desk and covered her head with her hands. She'd never been scared of her boss before but this was probably a good time to respect the temper she knew he had.

'*What?*' Hugh yelled at such volume, Rachel thought the plate glass windows of their eighth floor office suite would explode. 'No? No? You're telling me we lost it?' Hugh stopped shrieking for a moment, stubbed out his half-finished cigarette, lit another, stood in the centre of the room and said, quite calmly, 'How much?' Then his head fell and he breathed out heavily. 'One point two? You're telling me I lost the thing I wanted most in the entire world for a wretched one point two million?' Another pause. 'When I said one was my limit, I didn't mean my *limit* limit.' He was shouting again. 'So which motherfuck has walked off with my statue tucked under his arm?'

Rachel, having unfurled herself, thought she ought to appease her stressed boss and so took it upon herself to slip down his trousers and free the erection that she had seen brewing in there. She found that the rigid cock she was used to handling had slackened to half its usual size.

'Mmm,' she said, looking up at Hugh although he ignored her. 'You can get big in my mouth all over again, honey.' And she pushed the soft head onto her tongue, drawing him all the way down her throat.

'What do you mean *it's not a statue*?' Hugh continued on the phone. 'Of course it's a fucking statue. Of a naked woman with big tits and her legs spread wide. And ... I ... want ... it ... so get it back for me or you can drag your sorry ass to the gutter while I destroy you and your lousy auction house with one phone call.' Hugh threw the handset across the room and turned his attention to Rachel. 'What would I do without you, babe?' And he thrust his hips hard against her face.

'Be completely frustrated and angry all the time instead of just some of it?' she suggested, slipping him out of her mouth for a second. 'Tell me what's happened, honey? Then I can make you all better.'

'I lost it, Rachel.' Strangely, Hugh was subdued. Rachel had never heard him like this before. 'Some anonymous bidder struck me out and my useless man on the inside, Bob, failed to do his job. I would have paid anything for that statue. It was going to be a ...' Hugh trailed off and placed a hand on Rachel's soft hair. 'It was going to be a wedding gift for Jenna.'

'Couldn't we find a similar one?'

Hugh laughed. 'If you got every archaeologist in the world to pick up their trowel, twenty four hours seven days a week for three lifetimes, you'd never find another piece like that. It was two and a half thousand years old. A Celtic fertility symbol carved from stone.' He bowed his head. 'And I wanted it bad.'

'Why not make the new owner an offer he can't refuse? Everyone has a price, don't they?' Rachel thought of her own position, the sexual extras her job as Hugh's PA involved, her salary three times that of her friends.

Hugh smiled. 'You're right and dammit, I will. Bob

wouldn't tell me anything about the winning bidder except that he's from Scotland and some nonsense about returning the piece to its rightful heritage. But I have my ways and I can find out. I'll make him an offer that's so mind-blowing he'll be handing over the statue before I can get my cheque book out.' Hugh plunged his mouth onto Rachel's. 'You're so right that everyone, my lovely, has a price.'

The pair kissed for several minutes. Rachel was relieved to feel Hugh growing against her thigh again and that the silly auction hadn't stripped him of the need to finish what he'd started.

Hugh held onto Rachel's willing body, the span of his arms easily winding around her slim back as he ducked his head to her breasts.

'Take this off,' he said impatiently. He was about to nose-dive into Rachel's cleavage but stopped, his arms rigid and a strange expression on his face. 'Isn't that where Jenna's gone? Bloody Scotland or something? God damn, she could have given me a lift up there. Now she's away, I'll have to trust someone else to fly me up there.'

Rachel sighed and strapped her fingers around Hugh's stop-start erection. 'There are plenty of flights to all the Scottish airports. It will only take a phone call for me to get you on one. Once we've finished here.' She massaged the silken head of his penis and attempted to kiss him again but he ducked away.

'Which city did she go to?'

'I have no idea, Hugh. You should pay more attention to your wife-to-be.' Rachel – although she had only met Jenna once and thought she was pleasant, if not a little too pleasant for a man like Hugh Vandenbrink – did not wish to discuss the whereabouts of his fiancée while she held his cock in her palm. Cold and icy wasn't in her job description and she was only human after all. She didn't like the tug of heart muscle she felt when thinking about Jenna, as if the woman had stitched a line of guilt into her very existence.

'Glasgow or Aberdeen?' Hugh mulled. 'Edinburgh, even?' He planted a thoughtless kiss on Rachel's forehead and, stretching his cock from her grip, he retrieved the telephone from where it had landed and punched out Jenna's mobile number. 'She'll probably be there by now.' And he recalled how, at Mel's house, how they had discussed her and telephoned her but couldn't get through.

'You said she went away for the weekend. Who's she gone to see? Do you even know why she's gone?' Rachel was trying not to sound impatient. It was her job to untangle Hugh's life.

'I don't know the client although I do remember her saying she was making a delivery. Usually, she flies businessmen around Europe and I remember that she wondered why they didn't use a courier. She grumbled about being used as a cargo plane. I think she was more worried about that precious aircraft of hers than –'

'But *where* has she gone, Hugh?' Rachel removed her scrunched skirt to reveal her shapely legs and stockings in the hope that it might make Hugh be quiet and get on with fucking her. Earlier, his advances had been an imposition due to the pile of work on her desk but now he had got her so hot, she was desperate to get on with it.

Hugh thought and shrugged, suddenly realising that his wife-to-be could be up to absolutely anything and he wouldn't know. That made him mad. 'I haven't a clue where she's gone and, apart from what would have been a convenient flight up to Scotland, the relevance of her being there is purely coincidental. My prime concern is to find the thief that stole my statue.'

'Your prime concern should be this.' Rachel reclined

on the leather settee at one end of Hugh's large office and spread her legs. What Hugh saw was so inviting that he clumsily stripped off the rest of his suit and pumped up his own erection right in front of Rachel's face before sticking it inside her.

Rachel let out a whimper as he filled her up and pulled him deeper still by wrapping her legs around his back. She slid further down the leather chair and, crumpling into an awkward position half on and half off the chair, Rachel consumed her boss as greedily as she could.

'You ... could ... come with me,' Hugh said, breathless with effort. His neck was veined and his arm muscles rigid as he propped himself over his PA.

'You know we always come together, Hugh,' Rachel giggled in his ear.

'I mean to ... Scotland.' And Hugh buried his face in Rachel's neck while he drove himself faster and faster to climax. When Rachel opened her mouth to reply, he pushed his hand over her lips. Whatever she had to say could wait. He was busy thinking – about ancient fertility statues, about what Jenna was up to on her own in Scotland, and imagining that he had a queue of women waiting to get a piece of him. Really, if he didn't find sex several times a day, usually from different women, he was no good to anyone.

Suddenly, Rachel stopped moving and her entire body turned to steel. Her lips thinned and her neck lengthened and her spine arched. It was going to be a big one. She slowed and hovered on the brink of feelings she wanted to last for ever and yet it took all her mental strength not to plunge headlong into orgasm.

'Wait, wait,' Hugh ordered, never pleased if his woman climaxed before him. He demanded the tight grip and pulse of a woman's orgasm to coincide with his own, ensuring maximum pleasure for himself. That was what it was all about, after all. If Rachel or anyone else gained satisfaction from his body, then that was up to them. Judging by his lovers' post-coital comments, he could safely say that the bliss they enjoyed was the best ever.

Hugh rammed himself home, stopping for nothing to build the heat within his groin. 'I'm ... coming,' he said, allowing Rachel time to hurl herself over the precipice of climax with him.

For a few seconds, nothing existed for Hugh or Rachel. Neither of them in love with each other, or ever likely to be, the selfish use of their bodies culminated in the centre of an all-consuming orgasm.

'God ...' Hugh slackened and felt his semen pooling inside Rachel. For a moment, he believed it was Mel, no Jenna, no that other woman at the club ... whoever ... and he loved the delicious damp layer sticking them together at the chest and groin. His cock was drowning in her pussy and his sweat was clinging to her breasts and belly and legs and every part of her so the current that had briefly passed between them conducted at its best.

'Yes, God, indeed,' Rachel sighed. She kissed Hugh on the shoulder but he backed away like she had stuck him with a pin.

'You're coming with me. To Scotland,' he finished. Rachel frowned.

'Really?' Job description, paragraph two: Drop everything when boss says.

'What do you expect me to do? Not have sex while I'm away?' Hugh slithered off her and pulled on his shorts and trousers. 'If I knew where my fiancée was in Scotland, I'd drag her over to join me but she's not answering her bloody phone. Still, she's the least of my problems.' Hugh lit another smoke. 'Rachel, get me Bob on the phone again and tell him I want the purchaser's details *immediately*!'

'Yes, sir,' Rachel chirped. She felt good now, as if she'd been on a drip of hot spices. Her body buzzed and tingled and she couldn't wait for the next time Hugh made her job that little bit more challenging. Several times, she'd been taken to his home to entertain him for the weekend – a thrilling experience and a chance to try out the plethora of toys he possessed. How Jenna hadn't found out, she didn't know. She jabbed the keypad, still wearing only her stockings and high-heels.

'Hello, Bob Michaels, please.' Rachel scooped back her blonde highlighted hair while she waited.

Hugh cast an approving eye over her body. She obviously worked out regularly and took care of herself and, sexual skills aside, Rachel was a darned good PA. She'd got him out of a number of sticky business situations not to mention organising his entire schedule as well as keeping on top of his home life and organising his personal staff. Rachel was a gem to be protected.

Ten minutes later and the woman ranked pretty close to all-time perfect females in his life. She slid a piece of paper across the desk. Hugh turned his gaze from the wedge of clipped blonde hair between her legs, not sure which was a better sight – seeing his own deposit glistening in the overhead light on the edge of her sex or the name of the man who stole the statue from him by a piddling two hundred thousand. The name won by a whisker.

'Euan Douglas. Hmm, well, Mr Douglas is about to get a visitor,' he said triumphantly. 'Pack your bags, Rachel. We're going to Carrickvaig Castle to make him an offer that will blow his kilt right up into his face.'

'Oh how exciting,' said Rachel. 'When do we leave?'

'Get us on the first flight in the morning, even if you have to buy the bloody airline to do it.' Hugh buttoned his shirt. 'And get my driver outside. I want to go home.'

Rachel saluted comically and remained naked while

performing her duties. Having a boss like Hugh was the most exciting thing in the world and she never wanted to leave her job. He pecked her on her cheek and slung his jacket over his shoulder.

'I want to be standing in front of Euan Douglas by lunchtime and shake his resolve so hard that his throat closes up around his haggis.' And he walked off wearing a half-smile that Rachel knew meant business.

After Hugh had left the building, having instructed her to let him know about flight details later, Rachel wondered if she would be even working for Vandenbrink Holdings beyond the weekend. Every airline that she called was fully booked or the flight had been rescheduled to the evening. No good to Hugh. She could see veins popping up on his reddened face and his mouth sucking air in and out like an indecisive vacuum cleaner when she told him. Once Hugh had set a plan, he insisted on following it through to the end.

Rachel called several charter companies. It was the same story but worse. What had happened to the aviation world? Was every plane grounded, every pilot ill and every commercial seat booked? Fearful for her job, Rachel dressed and hot-footed it down to London City Airport in order to beg for mercy – and a couple of seats to Dundee, the nearest airport to the castle. She would have sex with the operator – anything! – be they man or woman, in order to fulfil Hugh's wishes.

An hour later, she was sitting in the café, despondently flattening the froth on her lukewarm cappuccino. Nothing, nada, zilch, zip. Rachel had struck out and knew with confidence that Hugh would strike her off his payroll. What saddened her most about that was not the thought of leaving the Vandenbrink Holdings organisation, as impressive as it was, but rather the thought of never having Hugh forcing her over his desk or stripping her naked on the boardroom table. The minute-by-minute excitement and unpredictability her work provided, fuelled by Mr Vandenbrink's insatiable sexual appetite, ensured complete job satisfaction. She would never find another position like it. That was why she had to get them to Dundee in the morning if she had to steal a plane and fly it herself.

'Oh, sorry . . . !' some idiot said as he tripped on the leg of Rachel's chair and knocked her coffee cup-holding elbow. The remains of her drink sloshed down her blouse.

'Watch it, bozo,' Rachel snarled at the clumsy man while dabbing at her chest with a serviette. She glared up at him and was about to hurl more abuse, being in no mood to tolerate idiots, when she noticed that the tall and surprisingly good-looking man was wearing dark glasses, a black uniform consisting of a jacket with little gold bits at the cuffs and a matching cap. He was also carrying a square, box-like leather case. If she hadn't known better, Rachel would have thought her guardian angel had sent her her very own pilot. As it was, she knew it must be a mirage.

'Let me buy you another of those. What was it, cappuccino?' The pilot-ghost smiled a broad sunrise and placed his flight bag on the chair next to Rachel. 'No, really. I insist,' he continued, even though Rachel hadn't protested.

In a moment, he had returned with not one but two coffees and all Rachel could do was watch with her mouth hanging open as he sat and introduced himself.

'I'm Mark Maloney and feel awful for having ruined your nice blouse. If you leave me your address, I'll have it cleaned and sent to you.'

Rachel was speechless but when words did finally occur to her brain, it was like they had baked onto her tongue. 'You . . . want my . . . blouse?' She wouldn't have surprised herself if she'd slipped the garment right off and handed it over. It was what she was used to doing anyway. This man, *this pilot*, had thrown himself at her, joined her for a coffee and was now asking for her clothing. She was going to need a big pinch.

Instead, she said, 'Are you a pilot?' She sounded three years old.

'No, I'm a priest.'

Rachel laughed. 'And I'm an astronaut.' Animated by his sense of humour and charming confidence, she extended her hand. 'Rachel Harte. Pissed off PA, actually, not an astronaut. And sorry for stating the obvious. I can see you're a pilot. As well as clumsy,' she added with a wink over the top of her coffee cup.

'No really, I am a priest.' Mark removed his cap as if that would conjure a more holy image. It didn't. 'I'm in disguise.' He smiled and suddenly Rachel could see the link with God.

'So you're not a pilot?'

'No.'

'Then why –'

'Because I used to be.'

Rachel stopped. She wasn't dim. She'd got three A Levels and had done a secretarial course. 'You're a priest that used to be a pilot and now you hang around airports dressed like a pilot claiming to be a priest.'

'And I spill coffee and confuse beautiful PAs.' Mark slipped off his flight jacket and removed his aviation glasses. Now, he was just an attractive man in a white shirt and black trousers.

Rachel's heart began to pound with disappointment. Stupidly she had thought that her prayers had been answered and some random, left-over bit of good karma had been sent her way. Anyway, she didn't believe in the supernatural.

'So ...' Rachel tipped her head to the side and squinted. She didn't quite get it. 'You look like you've just been flying a plane, or are about to, but now you're . . .' she trailed off, pulling a face and wishing that her cup contained something stronger than coffee.

Mark Maloney, pilot or priest or whatever he was, was unbuttoning his own shirt – it seemed he had a fascination for the removal of shirts – and in an instant, a black garment with many buttons was revealed beneath.

'Lest I forget who I am.' He grinned at Rachel's bewilderment.

'Pfah,' she said in a silly voice. 'Happens to me all the time.' And she watched in wonder as the unusual stranger opened his leather bag, removed something white and fastened it around his neck.

'You really *are* a priest,' she said as if she'd just encountered an alien. 'Damn and bugger today to hell,' she cursed as it dawned on her that she still didn't have a flight to Dundee. She bumped her hand on the side of her head. 'Oh God, I'm so sorry.' Then, 'Oh no. Not God. Just, I'm sorry. Really.'

Next to her sat one bona-fide priest and he shone with all the gold and goodness of having just stepped out of the Bible. He had transformed from her saviour pilot into someone who could possibly save her soul when Hugh tore it apart.

'Be quiet, Rachel Harte,' Mark Maloney said gently. 'Listen to me very carefully while I explain.'

Rachel's insides turned to mashed potato as he trailed his finger beneath her chin, as if he was tipping her face to the light, so she could understand the meaning of life – or at least his strange career path.

'My name is Mark Maloney. It used to be Captain Mark Maloney when I was a pilot flying for British Airways and other airlines over the years. Five years ago, I wanted to become a priest. So I did. Now I am called Father Maloney. Are you with me so far?'

Rachel nodded. She was definitely with him. He still cupped her chin in his hand – a priestly, thoughtful gesture on his part but an ignition of shameful lust on Rachel's. The man, even in his godly get-up, was gorgeous.

'But from time to time, you see, I still fly. Sometimes for pleasure and sometimes to help out friends in the business. I keep my commercial licence up to date and once or twice a month I do some paid jobs for charter and cargo companies. But I'd never go back to full-time flying. God keeps me too busy.'

'He does?' Rachel was thinking fast.

'Hence the quick change of uniform that usually, I hasten to add, would occur in the men's toilets, not in front of bemused young women.'

Was he flirting? Rachel wondered. Was a priest flirting with her? Her breathing quickened, hurt even.

'So you're off to church now?' She wanted him to stay. So she could ask him.

'Confession in forty-five minutes.'

Rachel paused and tried not to fall into Mark Maloney's swimming pool eyes. 'Can I confess something?'

He laughed and looked at his watch. 'If you're quick.' He swigged a large mouthful of coffee.

Rachel nearly passed out at the way his eyes narrowed into almond shapes as he smiled. There was something about his face and his hair as it swept across his forehead; there was something about him generally. Mark Maloney had a special aura and despite her need to find a way to get to Dundee, Rachel was being sucked into it as surely as iron filings to a magnet.

'It's my boss, you see.' She swallowed although her mouth didn't feel like her own. When she looked down at her hands to fiddle with her nails, those didn't seem like hers either. In fact, nothing in the entire airport seemed real apart from the clear, defined image of Mark

Maloney – priest, pilot, whatever he was – sitting beside her. 'I've just had sex with him.' Rachel's hands weren't connected to her enough to clap over her mouth. What had she said?

'I see,' Mark said thoughtfully. 'And is this a good thing or something you needed to get off your chest.'

'Oh no, it's a good thing. We do it all the time.' Rachel reanimated slightly although her gaze was still transfixed on the priest's eyes. 'The problem is Dundee and if I don't organise that then there probably won't ever be any sex again because of the statue and Euan whatever-his-name-is at the castle and also, I think Hugh's a bit tetchy because his fiancée's gone AWOL and he says he doesn't trust her an inch. Even though he's at it with me three times a day and, if you ask me, other women too. He's got balls the size of –'

'Rachel, in my expert opinion, I would say it's a therapist you need, not a priest.'

'No!' Rachel blurted. It wasn't going well. 'Don't you understand? What I need is a *pilot*. We *have* to get to Dundee by lunchtime tomorrow.'

'Of course. Silly me,' Mark replied. 'So, why are you telling me?'

'Because I need a pilot! All the flights are booked up or at the wrong time and if I don't do exactly what Hugh wants, then he'll fire me and –'

'Whoa ... There's such a thing as unfair dismissal, you know.'

'Not when we're talking about Hugh Vandenbrink, there's not.'

Mark was silent for a second. '*The* Hugh Vandenbrink?'

Rachel nodded solemnly. 'He could destroy my life with one phone call and . . .'

'I'm not entirely sure that's true, Rachel, and the man certainly has no right to have such an emotional hold over you. I can see your dilemma though.' He drained his cup. 'So what were you hoping to achieve by sitting in this café?'

'I was praying that a priest-pilot would walk in and save me.' Rachel fluffed up her hair, wishing that she'd freshened up more after sex with Hugh. For all she knew, Mark could probably smell the scent of their lovemaking on her. She made her eyes go big and plumped her lips into a barely detectible pout. 'And God took pity on me and, hallelujah, he sent you.' She clasped her hands under her chin and wished she'd worn the little gold cross Hugh had given her last Christmas.

'Actually, tomorrow's my day off.' Mark stood and picked up his bag.

'That's ideal, then. You can fly us to Dundee. Hugh will pay you five times your normal rate.'

'What I meant was, *it's my day off*. As in, I'm relaxing. But I do hope you get to Dundee and that you keep your job. Goodbye, Miss Harte.' He smiled and walked off.

Rachel screamed.

She had never screamed in public before. In a flash of stupidity, she ripped open the front of her blouse, messed up her hair and began to wail and shriek and shout for all she was worth.

'Someone stop that priest! Look what he did to me!'

Rather than cause a flurry of help from passing passengers, she had merely created a temporary spectacle. No one, it seemed, wanted to assist a screaming woman who had just been molested by a priest.

Except the priest, that is. Mark Maloney stopped in his tracks, hunched his shoulders, turned and walked back to the hysterical Rachel.

'You win,' he said, trying to conceal the grin that pushed at his mouth. 'I have use of a six-seater but it's going to cost you. We will leave at ten a.m. sharp so meet me here with your boss at nine-thirty. You'll need your passports for ID. Be warned, I don't do in-flight service and there won't be any movies plus I expect payment in cash.'

'A tax-evading priest-pilot?' Rachel was pushing her luck.

'The money I earn from flying goes to the church fund. We are a registered charity and our books are open for inspection. Our roof leaks, you see.' Mark was solemn. He fished in his pocket and then handed Rachel a card. 'Any problems, call me.' Then he walked off.

Rachel's eyes widened and she drew in a deep breath. Had that really just happened? Had she secured a flight to Dundee with a priest-pilot? And more to the point, had she just screamed and exposed herself in a mega-tantrum to get it?

Slowly, she looked down her front. Aside from a coffee stain, she saw that her blouse was indeed wide open, exposing her breasts and confirming that it was all absolutely true.

5

All she'd wanted was a weekend away. The invitation to Carrickvaig Castle and time away from her philandering fiancé was just what she needed to get through the next week; to decide what to do with the rest of her life. But in the last few hours, her worries had doubled – no, quadrupled – and she was beginning to feel like the victim in a horror movie or, at the very least, the subject of a far-fetched elaborate practical joke.

Hugh, she decided, was the only person with enough contacts and money to pull off such a stunt and, if he was involved, then it wasn't doing anything to score him brownie points in Jenna's internal ledger. She would wrap his insides around her propeller when she got home.

'Do I really have to wear this?' Jenna asked. She still felt woozy and, while there was no sign of the barbarian at present, the company of the two unusual women made her twitchy. All she wanted was a telephone. 'Can't someone just take me to a village or a pub or a post office? There must be one around here somewhere.'

'Sshh,' said Iona. 'Your long journey from the other world has exhausted even a goddess. Save your energy for the festival. All our people will want to see you and touch you. No one knows of your arrival yet so when Brogan tells them that this is a double celebration – his hand-fasting to Cailla *and* your arrival – there will be much commotion.'

'What I'm saying is –'

'Laymar is making preparations!' The creaky willow door to Iona's roundhouse burst open and Brogan filled the gap.

Jenna gasped. The barbarian looked even more like a barbarian. Wearing nothing on his upper body and slack cloth pants below, the man's sun-darkened skin was drawn with terrible and frightening images in some kind of slate-blue paint. His forehead and cheeks were spiralled with demonic faces, making his dark eyes look like those of the devil. And his chest, back and shoulders were daubed with similar but larger primitive shapes, depicting fighting and murder and – Jenna whimpered – in the centre of his taut belly was a female form on her back being plundered by the biggest cock she had ever seen. Beside the woman was a crude image of her aircraft.

'Come in, Brogan, before our goddess is seen.' Iona pulled him inside.

'Cailla, our hand-fasting ceremony will be repeated in the presence of the Fire Goddess.' Brogan fell to his knees before his bride-to-be. 'Laymar says that the arrival of the goddess in a chariot of fire makes the magic of our union so strong it will last for all eternity. We are truly meant to be together, my love.'

'I hate to interrupt your games, everyone. But *please* can someone get me to a phone or lend me one with reception? My ankle's hurting and –' Jenna wanted out of this place and soon.

'You are in pain still? Then sit and I will apply a poultice of herbs to ease your discomfort.' Iona quickly prepared an infusion from dried bunches of flowers hanging from the thatch and then soaked a cloth before wrapping it around Jenna's swelling.

'What's that?' she asked. 'It feels nice.'

Iona smiled and suddenly Jenna was filled with comfort and ease and, strangely, a sense of place that suggested perhaps she wasn't too far from where she was supposed to be after all.

'It's a brew of meadowsweet, willow and sage. It will calm and soothe your pain.'

Iona ran her hand up Jenna's leg, lovingly and innocently, but with a power that Jenna felt throughout her body. Her eyes widened at the touch, which she wished could last a thousand years, and a sense of calm stitched itself through her mind.

'I'm a healer,' Iona added. 'Laymar sends anyone in the clan who is sick to see me and I make them well.'

'Clan? Druid?'

'Yes, we are the Dunlayth Clan. Brogan is our leader and Cailla will soon be his wife.' Iona smiled and pulled the cloth of the orange tunic that Jenna was wearing down over her legs. 'Laymar is our Druid priest.'

'Priest,' Jenna whispered and thought of Vic. If she had a telephone, he'd be the one she called. Vic would know what to do.

But Jenna's thoughts were allowed to go no further. Brogan was suddenly beside her and booming that it was time to show off his prize to the clan. Already Jenna could hear a gathering in whatever scene lay beyond the door of the hut. Then, for the second time that day, she found herself scooped up and draped over the barbarian's shoulder.

'Hey,' she squealed. 'Put me down, you brute. I'm gonna get Hugh to sue your sorry ass for ... for ... something.' As the ground passed beneath Jenna's view, she suddenly realised how she always threatened with Hugh's power and riches whenever anything bad happened. What about her calling upon her own inner strength?

With this in mind, Jenna beat and bashed on Brogan's painted chest and finally, when the man didn't flinch, she took to pulling his hair and biting his back.

'I said *put me down*, you great big bully . . .' But Jenna's words were suddenly lost in a storm of cries and chants and wailings all against a backdrop of beating drums and blaring horns. Jenna stood no chance of being heard.

She was carried upside-down through the noisy crowd and all she could see were the many feet wearing crude sandals or basic moccasins standing on rough earth. She knew, though, from the slim ankles and slender toes that Iona and Cailla were right behind her. This offered some kind of comfort, especially as Jenna was now somewhat fearful for her safety.

What if she had stumbled upon some undiscovered tribe that had failed to progress with civilisation? There might well be a major city within ten miles but this pocket of primitiveness had ignored modern ways.

You're just being stupid, she convinced herself, believing that she would have seen a TV documentary about something as weird as that. She concluded it was just a crazy re-enactment and she'd been caught up in their silly role-playing.

Jenna felt a gentle hand run the length of her spine and instantly knew it was Iona's by the sudden warmth and calmness that pervaded her being. 'That, or I banged my head real hard in the crash and I'm in hospital having crazy dreams.'

Suddenly, Jenna found herself being dumped on a platform and, once her skidding vision had slowed and focused and her hair had fallen off her face, her eyes widened at what she saw.

Jenna Bright, pilot and soon-to-be-married woman who honestly just wanted a quiet life, was face to face with at least two hundred other savages, barbarians, whatever they were meant to be, all painted up like Brogan and chanting and stamping and clapping and blowing horns and . . .

'Peace!' Brogan cried in a voice that instantly dampened the chaos like water on fire. The crowd simmered and hissed and finally silenced. 'Today is a sacred day. Not only do we celebrate the fire festival of Beltane but the union between Cailla and me.'

More cheering, hushed by the rise of Brogan's arm. His face glowed orange in the burnt-out sun as it cut behind the trees of the surrounding forest. 'And today we have received an offering from the skies. The gods have sent us their Fire Goddess as a sign of strength and power and continuing fertility for our clan.'

There was more cheering which Brogan allowed to continue. He turned and spoke privately to Iona.

'Fertility,' Jenna mumbled through tense lips. 'You can count me out of that, for a start. Fire Goddess? What has got into these people?'

Then she tried to scream but nothing came out. Several pairs of hands were immediately upon her, deftly unwrapping the itchy wool cloth from her body. She couldn't even recall how she had come to be wearing it. The chanting and horn blowing grew more and more frenzied and the crowd drew in around the shaky platform.

In seconds, Jenna found herself standing completely naked in front of all these crazy strangers and Brogan, as pleased as a magician who'd just pulled a dove from up his sleeve, presented his find to the clan. Her entire body shook.

'Our Fire Goddess,' he yelled, arms outstretched towards Jenna, and again there was more stamping and clapping and drumming in the darkening forest.

Jenna's heart, wrestling to stay contained within her chest, suddenly wrung itself out as Brogan approached and took hold of each of her breasts. She was about to reach for her tunic, dropped on the floor, but was halted by his grip.

'What are you doing, you crazy fuck? Get off me!' This

time she allowed the thought of Hugh's lawyers slamming the organisers of this farce into prison. 'You are so going to find yourself in a cell tonight if you don't –'

But Jenna could speak no more as her mouth was suddenly gagged from behind. She fought as best she could, wondering why they were treating their new goddess so badly, but her flailing arms and legs only led to the binding of her wrists behind her back. Her whimpering stood no chance of being heard through the demonic noise of the crowd. It appeared that they treated revered guests with hostility.

'To seal the fertility of my union with Cailla, I will anoint myself with our goddess and take what she has brought us.' Brogan was half yelling at the eager crowd and half telling Jenna what his plan for her immobile body contained.

She delivered a sharp kick at no one in particular, wishing she'd carried on with karate lessons. It was a warning, she hoped, for Brogan to stay away. Her voice squealed weakly through the gag, which she tried to chew and bite out of her mouth.

Iona came to her side. 'She seems scared of her new home,' she crooned. 'Be gentle with her, Brogan. Would we want her to leave because you treated her too roughly?' Then, to Jenna. 'Peace with you, Fire Goddess. You have been sent to us for a reason this Beltane and must fulfil your duty. We are grateful of your presence and will honour your power.'

Jenna thrashed her head from side to side and couldn't even move her legs now because two of the male clan members had taken hold of her ankles to keep her in place. Her feet were stretched apart and she felt the cool air of night threading between her thighs, similar to the way Hugh sometimes liked to trail a silk scarf across her skin. In her head she screamed for him; in her heart she pushed him away.

Suddenly, Jenna felt warm breath between her legs. She noticed the irritation of hair on her legs first, added to the tight grip on each ankle. With sweat beading on her face and a deep growl brewing in her throat, Jenna brought her head forwards from its defiant back-thrust and saw to her horror that Brogan had dropped to his knees and had his face only inches away from her exposed sex.

She thrashed crazily, making her breasts bounce angrily at her chest and her hair to fly across her face. She hated what was happening to her! She hated the grizzly man that had held her captive for hours; she hated this blasted village experiment, whatever it was, and she hated the stupid, primitive people in it.

Most of all, and her thoughts churned and tossed the way her Saratoga had been sucked into the curdled grey vortex, most of all she hated the warm, soft, breathy sensation of Brogan's tongue ... gently lapping ... slowly prising, invading ... she hated ... no, not quite hated anymore ... Brogan's tongue dizzied her thoughts as it swept the length of her lips ... back and forth ... devouring ... and she only rocked her hips the once, just a little involuntary twitch that caused him to plunge his tongue deep inside her ...

'Oh,' she choked, her voice bound up by the gag. Jenna couldn't help it that her hips rose and fell like the valleys and hillocks surrounding the village.

To Brogan, her moan signalled appreciation and, twinned with the reflex action of her hips, he knew that he was finally pleasing the beautiful Fire Goddess.

In another second it was all over and Jenna was left with the memory on her skin and the cool breeze again soothing her confused body. She was more convinced than ever that she would wake up in hospital on a drip with a head injury to account for her situation.

Brogan stood and dragged the back of his forearm across his mouth, leaving a broad grin in its wake. 'Come!' he yelled to the enthralled crowd. 'Take your turn and sample the delight we have been sent.'

Jenna thought her eyes might pop from her head as she realised what Brogan was suggesting. A couple of moments' thrill, like a cherry sitting on top of layers and layers of fear, were nothing compared to what she was now expected to endure. Was he really suggesting that the crowd line up and . . .

She shuddered – or was it tingled? – at the thought of each of the painted clan members advancing upon her and tasting her.

'Iona, make her be still.' Brogan waved his hands as the gathering swelled and advanced and moved in on the wooden platform upon which Jenna was bound, gagged and held in place by two men almost as fearsome as Brogan. It wasn't a queue or a line as such but strangely, respectfully and with more awe than Jenna had ever seen, the mesmerised clan members made their way up to view what had fallen from the skies.

Fleetingly, Jenna considered that they really *did* believe she was a goddess. That they really *were* a primitive clan from several thousand years ago. If she'd not been strapped and helpless and drugged from adrenalin, she would have fallen over laughing at the thought.

Prehistoric warriors? Goddess from the sky? More like a premarital joke from Hugh. And the stab of guilt that should have been present as she thought of her future husband simply wasn't there – most likely demolished by Hugh's recent antics with Mel.

As the demand on her body approached in the form of hundreds of eager, hungry eyes, Jenna stiffened. Every muscle in her body contracted with fear and drew a hard landscape on her sweat-soaked skin. Between her breasts, her ribs barricaded her heart and running the length of her slim legs, the larger muscles fought in vain to shield what Brogan had already taken.

'Aahh, grhh!' she moaned through the gag. Briefly, she locked eyes with Brogan as one by one he guided his fellow clansmen onto the platform. If she hadn't known better, if she'd been able to cut and paste his look onto a blank canvas, she'd have sworn it was Hugh flashing his dark, intense pupils her way.

The look flicked a switch inside Jenna; turned her mind to what she knew her fiancé had been up to with Mel. Suddenly revenge seemed sweet; suddenly her body shuddered with anticipation as she knew she would enjoy what was about to happen.

'One at a time and everyone will receive their blessing.' Brogan ushered the first towards Jenna. A skinny young man with wild hair and a plaid tunic approached and knelt in front of Jenna. His eyes were saucers of water and his thin lips twitched as he looked up at the sacred body of the Fire Goddess.

Jenna thrashed and bucked again as the young man drew his blessing from between her legs. The men at her ankles fought tirelessly to keep her in position and Iona and Cailla soothed her reddening face with gentle strokes.

'This must be her first time to our mortal land,' Cailla marvelled. She thought the goddess was beautiful and selfless to offer her body in this way.

'Don't be scared,' Iona coaxed.

Jenna cried and moaned as the young man had to be pulled from her. Iona stroked her breasts. 'This really is your honour as much as it is ours.' She smiled and drew a cloth across the goddess's forehead. 'Later I will bathe you and feed you and the men can decide where you will be kept.'

Kept? Jenna thought, wondering whether to panic

about that news or the sight of the next approaching male, who already had his tongue sticking out. A second later and it was jabbed against her clitoris in a way that told her he'd never been down on a woman before. She felt his hot breath on her pubic mound as he awkwardly poked her increasingly wet sex, glancing up for a second to catch Jenna's eye.

'Aargh mwrah,' she screamed at him, which meant *get off me you beast* but when the clan member was hauled away, Jenna felt her sex pulse with an annoying tingle of pleasure and she found herself pushing forwards her hips in readiness for the next in line.

Her mind was cut cleanly in two: she was being held against her will and one by one, several hundred strangers were taking a taste of her and causing her to – how could she admit this? – feel pleasure from this barbaric scene. Her common sense screamed *get out* while her body was hungry for more. Where in the world she actually was and how she planned to get home wasn't even a consideration anymore. She'd get home eventually and . . .

'Aaaah,' she wailed as yet another mouth latched onto her. Jenna could feel her body melting under the weight of its own pleasure as mouth after mouth came to kiss her and lick her and nibble her or just be content to press a wet tongue against the now dripping place between their goddess's thighs. The clansmen showed their adoration of her body and now, despite her earlier fear, if pressed for an explanation, she would say she had died and gone to heaven.

Jenna's thoughts boiled over like a pan of hot syrup. All she could hear, with her eyes closed, was Brogan ordering the hungry crowd, the pulse of drums and horns around the giant fire that had been lit to herald the approaching night and the appreciative moans of the clansmen as they worshipped their goddess. Down her left side, she could feel the heat of the fire, while the flesh on right side prickled cold from the dark forest that bound the encampment together.

'You truly are a gift from the gods,' said one as he hurried away, his lips glistening from Jenna's juices.

'We will cherish you forever,' said another as he gazed adoringly at Jenna's body, which was now in a trance-like state, sweating and moving in time with the drumming.

Everything tumbled through Jenna's soul during the time it took for the adult males of the clan to worship her. Her entire life whipped through her mind, bringing a heady mix of frenetic brainwaves and clarity as her body was gradually possessed. She was steered closer and closer to orgasm with each visit and opening her eyes to take a tentative look, she could just make out that the camp was now dark and bathed in the flickering orange glow from a large central fire. The villagers that had already tasted her danced and celebrated around the fire.

Jenna saw that only a couple of dozen now waited in line. Had it really been that long? Had so many mouths pushed up into her sex? Her first orgasm came when an older man peeled apart her lips and exposed the nub of her clitoris to the night air. Skilfully he sent her over the edge in a griping series of spasms that made her never want to go back home. Wherever she was, she was staying put.

'Hurry,' Brogan called to the next in the queue. A shy young warrior crept up to Jenna and knelt before her. Tentatively, he eased his lips against Jenna's so that it may have been two mouths lightly kissing. If Jenna's hands had been free, she would have pushed his face harder against her sex and bucked until she came again. As it was, the feather touch prepared her for the next man, who drove his long, hard tongue deep up inside

Jenna and once again ripped her through a powerful climax.

'Aarrrh,' Jenna screamed and still she got more, wanting this forever as the last few clan members brought her four more delicious orgasms. Never, ever before had she experienced such exhausting, intense pleasure. Her body didn't belong to her anymore and she wasn't sure if she wanted it back. Wherever she was, she wanted to stay there . . .

What was this? Jenna felt the strap around her head loosen and her aching hands being released. Iona and Cailla were beside her adorning her with strips of colourful cloth and ornate metal jewellery. Nowhere was there any sign of clothing to cover her naked breasts and soaking thighs.

'This has come especially from our craftsman's fire.' Iona fitted the heavy torc around Jenna's neck and stood back to admire it. 'It is almost as beautiful as you.'

Cailla fastened a wreath of leaves in her hair followed by a spray of spring flowers. 'You truly are our Beltane Goddess.' She clasped her hands under her chin and watched as Jenna was carried away by the two men who had been holding onto her ankles. High above the crowd, Jenna was taken into the central area of the village.

'OK, guys,' she called out. Her jaw was stiff from the gag. 'You'd better tell me what's going on now. Was it Hugh? Tell me, did Hugh put you all up to this?' Her mind whizzed through the possibilities. He could have arranged for the Saratoga to be tampered with – just enough to cause a minor crash landing. But how would he have known exactly where she'd ditch or that she wouldn't be killed? None of it added up. Who *were* these people?

'This is our Druid priest, Laymar,' Brogan said to Jenna and gestured to a tall, slim man glowing orange in the firelight. He wore a grey cloak with a hood, making his face appear as a series of ghostly shadows.

Jenna shuddered. Druid priest?

'Cailla, Brogan, stand before me so that your union may be completed.' Laymar pulled his hand from within his cloak and raised a long, twisted piece of willow with metal ornaments attached.

The pair did as they were told and Brogan placed Jenna between them. Then Laymar, the only one not to have taken a taste of Jenna, fell to his knees and chanted what sounded like a prayer at her feet.

'Look, really,' Jenna started. She was running out of things to say and was so fearful of the power of these people that she didn't dare kick up too much of a fuss. The number of swords glinting in the firelight kept her in check and her ankle was still too weak to allow her to run. 'I'm very tired and would just like to go home. Is there any chance at all that I could make a phone call? Hell, even prisoners are allowed one of those.'

Tears drew across her lower eyelids but no one noticed or even heard what she was saying. The crowd was transfixed by the unusual ritual that Laymar was reciting. He was chanting in what seemed to be another language and occasionally the crowd joined in.

'Brogan and Cailla, link hands.' They did and encircled Jenna between them. Her eyes widened and her skin prickled as she felt their proximity against her naked body. The decorative strips of cloth and jewellery did nothing to cover her flesh.

Laymar continued. 'As the fire burns through Beltane, so shall it burn through the days of your union . . .' At this point, Jenna saw Iona light another smaller fire around which the herd of farm animals was led. 'For four seasons your union will be sacred and forever will your bond be secured. With the blessing of our Fire

Goddess and the power of earth, air, fire and water, I bind you as one.'

Laymar tied a strip of coloured cloth around the couple's wrists and then three women dressed in magical costumes did the same. The first was dressed in a brown cloth slung low over her hips and the remainder of her naked body was smeared in mud. Her brown hair hung with leaves and twigs and around her neck was a garland of spring flowers.

The second woman, blonde and much taller than the first, approached Cailla and Brogan wearing nothing but the slate-blue paint similar to that adorning Brogan's body. It flowed across her skin and around her breasts like the current of a whirlpool. In her hair she wore blue flowers and her eyes were skimmed with tears. She tied the cloth and then bent double in a flexible bow to Jenna, backing away in a dance to the rhythm of the horns and drums.

Lastly a young woman wearing a shroud of white approached and sealed the wrists of Brogan and Cailla. Through the sheer, air-like fabric Jenna could see the faint outline of her mobile breasts. Everything about this woman was pure and clean, like the unusually clear air that Jenna sucked quickly through her nostrils.

'Earth and water and air and now fire will seal your union.' Laymar's voice was rich and carried through the night. He handed Jenna a piece of orange cloth to tie around the couple's wrists.'

'Like the others did?' she asked and received a nod from the priest. *Just do it*, she thought, convinced that she would soon wake in hospital or Hugh would peek from behind one of the forest oaks. *Just tie the scarf and then maybe they'll get you a phone.*

Jenna's fingers trembled as she knotted the fabric in place. So much had happened since her plane had come down – *her plane had come down* – that her mind was operating in safe mode. She could see the unusual, tribal scene around her. She could hear the beat of the drums and feel the heat of the flames on her bare back. She could taste her own fear and shook from disbelief but her brain simply couldn't piece all the information together into any kind of explanation.

'Where am I?' she wailed and brought everything to a halt. The drums, the dancing, the animals, even the night itself stood still as Jenna's words echoed throughout the trees.

'Please, tell me where I am.' Her voice was quieter now, everyone listening, and Laymar nodded to the crowd to continue. He took Jenna's shaking hand and led her aside.

'We are the Dunlayth people. The most feared clan in the land. We are peaceful unless challenged. Rest assured, you will be safe with us.'

'But am I in Scotland or didn't I make it that far? Don't you understand that my plane crashed and I need to alert the authorities? What's wrong with everyone here that they don't understand me?' Jenna fought the tears in her eyes and Laymar wrapped her in his woollen cloak.

'Our land is in the north. Travel a little further over the hills and you'll encounter Cathan and his clan. Count yourself fortunate that you were sent to us and not his people.' Laymar softened his words with an embrace. Jenna could smell smoke and herbs on his skin.

'Really?' she asked earnestly, being drawn into their pre-historic world. 'There's another clan near here?' She wondered if the man meant another village, perhaps one with people that weren't stuck in the Iron Age. 'Can I go there?'

'It is unwise to travel across the hills. The clan is not far but there are dangers along the way, not to mention what Cathan and his people would do to you.' Laymar frowned.

Jenna recalled what Brogan's people had just done to her. Her back arched involuntarily. The possibility of another ritual tasting of her body certainly had latent appeal, even if she couldn't admit it to herself.

'Besides,' Laymar continued. 'You were sent to us. A goddess in mortal form will be revered in our clan and Brogan is a good and strong leader. He will look after you.'

Jenna glanced around the village. It just didn't add up. Surely, if it was some prehistoric society acting out a primitive lifestyle then there would be paying tourists watching. What was the point of such a spectacle otherwise? And if these people really were fanatics living an ancient life, they'd surely have enough sense to get her checked out at a hospital after her plane crash. They didn't even seem to know what a plane was.

Jenna could hardly speak. 'You ... really are ... an Iron Age man, aren't you?' Her words were a slow string of disbelief. But there was no other explanation.

She recalled the unforgettable approach of the tornado from the cockpit window before the plane was sucked up and spewed out and thrown to the ground in a crumpled wreck, in spite of the clear weather report. The way the cargo in the wooden crate had been whispering to her and the strange smoke that filled the cabin before disappearing. Something bizarre had happened. Something supernatural. Something she wasn't able to understand.

Jenna looked around the scene – the fire, the night, the half-naked clansmen, the silhouettes of Brogan and Cailla leaping through the flames – and she whispered to herself, 'I'm about two and a half thousand years away from home.'

6

Hugh had his mind set on Mel and Rachel together; the two of them eating each other out while he watched. As long as he was able to go from one to the other with his cock the size of a marrow, then he'd be a happy man. Something to look forward to in Scotland, he pondered, as the aircraft sped down the runway.

'What are you smiling at?' Mel asked. She stared down as the Docklands dropped away beneath them.

'Private,' Hugh said, winking and still thinking. Maybe a bit of wine, some dirty talk later. Women were stupid creatures, too intent on their own security. Fucking a man like him, winning him over, would mean they were set for life.

'Don't expect Euan Douglas to just take your money and hand over the statue,' Rachel commented. 'To pay a sum like that at auction, he's going to be as shrewd as you, Hugh.'

'Maybe I'll get you two girls to offer him sexual favours as well.' Hugh licked his lips. 'I can just see it. Mel crouched over your face, Rachel, and the Douglas man taking you up the –'

'Do you ever think of anything else?' Mel interrupted, shocked that he was actually voicing what was always on his mind within earshot of the pilot.

'No,' Hugh admitted. 'Sex and money. What else is there?'

Mel and Rachel eyed one another, still sizing each other up. He had a point.

Rachel giggled. 'If it helps you get what you want,

Hugh, then I'm game.' She adjusted her harness, making sure that her fingers brushed against her nipples. A tingle threaded its way to her knickers. Just to get in the mood for the plans that she knew her boss would have mentally planned for later. He'd not had it since yesterday, unless he'd taken Mel early that morning before they'd gone to the airport, and she knew that Hugh was a three times a day man. His tetchiness rivalled the noise of the straining aircraft engines if he had to go without for very long.

'So we're staying at the actual castle?' Mel asked.

'Yes, thanks to Rachel and her superb investigative skills.' Hugh shot his PA an adoring glance and overlaid an image of her naked body over her business-like day attire. 'Aside from being the home of Euan Douglas, Carrickvaig Castle is a five-star hotel and this weekend it happens to be hosting a shooting party. And guess what? There was a suite left.' Hugh loosened the large knot in his tie. 'Time enough for me to work out the mind of Mr Douglas as well as . . .' He eyed the two women again. 'As well as being able to enjoy the company of two beautiful females.'

'One room?' Mel queried. 'For the three of us?'

'It's their largest suite so I wouldn't be worried. There'll be plenty of space for us all. On the other hand, if you both want to snuggle up with me at night, there's a four poster bed –'

'Just to let you know that the weather's clear all the way and we're due in at Dundee airport right on schedule.' Captain Mark Maloney, sequestered pilot for the weekend, addressed his three passengers on the intercom.

'Thanks, Mark,' Rachel called up to the front of the small plane they had chartered. 'What about him?' she asked Hugh quietly. 'We can't expect him to stay in a cheap bed and breakfast down the road.'

Hugh studied the square shoulders and lean lines of the pilot's face as he turned to acknowledge Rachel's remark. Wearing dark aviation glasses and a black uniform, he looked mysterious, handsome and totally in control of all their lives. He considered what it would be like watching another man fucking Mel and Rachel. The pilot would do.

'The suite's massive,' Hugh stated. 'By the sound of it, this chap's bent over backwards to get us to Dundee so the least we can do is show him a good time.' A lopsided smile spread across his face as he concocted various ways that Mel and Rachel could ensure the pilot had the best weekend ever.

The flight passed uneventfully and before lunchtime, Hugh, Rachel, Mel and Mark were riding in a pre-ordered limousine to Carrickvaig Castle. When they arrived, Rachel and Mel hardly dared to breathe at the sight of their weekend residence as they circled around the drive.

'It's fantastic!' Rachel squealed.

Mel, even though the two women hardly knew each other, gripped Rachel's hand.

'We're going to have a ball,' she answered, peering up at the imposing turreted roof. A series of flags snapped in the wind as the party were escorted across the drive and into the reception hall.

'Seems like Douglas has things pretty well sewn up.' Hugh stalked about the massive hall that would have easily swallowed up his Kensington apartment. Even though the rest of his property portfolio would outstrip Euan Douglas's pad in terms of value, Hugh had to remind himself that size wasn't everything, as he dragged his hand along an antique oak sideboard that was carved with what appeared to be the Douglas coat of arms.

'All done?' he asked Rachel, who had been checking them in to their suite.

Lying on the four-poster bed, staring up at yet another heavily carved and polished piece of furniture, Hugh wondered where in the castle his precious statue was kept. That was if it had even been transported from the auction house's safekeeping yet. God, if *he'd* just bought the beautiful thing, he'd want it teleporting to him immediately.

Then he got an erection and Mel noticed. She was splitting drawer space with Rachel, each laying out their weekend lingerie and both women, it appeared, had had similar thoughts as to what would be required of them. Their cases abounded with flimsy triangles of lace and silk.

'Fuck me, someone,' Hugh demanded. He glanced at his watch. This wouldn't be the big one, he thought. No, that would be done properly after food and wine and all of them piled on together and that pilot chap doing just as Hugh ordered. He was paying him a fortune, after all. 'Where is he anyway?' he asked.

'Who?' Rachel turned.

'Mark what's-his-name, the pilot.'

She smiled. 'He wanted his own room and there was a single available down the hall so I booked it for him. He's gone above and beyond to get us here so I thought the least I could do was –'

'Yes, yes, whatever. Now, bugger off and find out when I can meet with Euan Douglas while Mel sorts me out.' He sat up, pulled off his jacket and shirt and was nearly out of his trousers by the time Rachel's mouth had finally closed. She clicked the heavy panelled door shut as quietly as she could and went in search of the castle's owner.

'Now,' Hugh said. 'Come here and make me better.'

'Are you ill?' Mel, now alone with Hugh, instinctively peeled off her clothing. Her jeans and floaty top fell to the floor and she paused while Hugh admired her in her pretty underwear but, as usual, his impatience grew too large to contain in his shorts and Mel adopted complete nakedness, her lover's preferred state. No, her lover's *insisted* state. When they were alone together, she was under strict orders never to wear clothes.

'Have you heard from Jenna?' She knew she shouldn't have said it.

Hugh flopped back onto the bed and sighed. 'I'm naked with a dick the size of this castle. You're naked with your arse inches from my face. Now you're asking about my fiancée?'

'I just –' But Hugh silenced her by pulling the heart shape of her rear down beside his head and streaking his tongue along the cleanly shaven seam. In a moment, he'd forgotten all mention of his future wife although there was a vague nagging thread still caught in his mind that no, he hadn't heard from her and yes, maybe he should start to worry.

But the taste of Mel, the velvet of her sex and the sweet and sour tingle that latched to his tongue with every stroke soon made him stop worrying. By nature, he believed that things always had a way of working out or in the worst cases, could be bought.

'God, I could eat you all night,' he said as he rotated Mel to face his neglected cock. It had been hours since anyone had nursed it. 'Get your tits or your mouth or something around it, for heaven's sake. I need something to . . .' And that was when Hugh experienced the first flash of unease. 'I need something to take my mind off . . .'

Something was wrong although he didn't know what.

But the feeling didn't last long – not consciously, anyway – as the warmth of Mel's mouth encased his impatient, already fit to explode erection. And when Mel took it upon herself to put her sex back over his face – without even being told! – Hugh virtually blasted off through the ornate plaster ceiling with pleasure.

Suddenly, he couldn't breathe. And he couldn't feel the warm and gentle chewing on his cock, either. Mel, it appeared, was now sitting upright and facing the end of the bed, and grinding herself onto his mouth so hard that with her buttocks sealing off his nose and her sex intent on being devoured alive, air was in short supply.

Hugh didn't care. For the first time ever – *ever* – a woman was using him and to his disgust, to his utter fascination and delight, he found that he loved it.

'Oh!' Mel cried out, perhaps even forgetting that there was a man beneath her. 'Oh God,' she moaned and reached out for something to grip. One hand found Hugh's hair and the other found his chin and she steered the lapping, hungry creature below into giving her a series of selfish climaxes.

'Hugh, that was fantastic,' she said, flopping down beside him on the luxurious antique bedspread. She wondered how many layers of lovemaking the rich tapestry stitches had seen over the years.

'Was?' Hugh asked while running his palm along the length of his forgotten cock.

'I'm still here, aren't I? Climb on.' Mel's arms dragged up behind her head and she opened her legs so that the space between them offered an obvious, if not a little half-hearted invitation to Hugh.

'Climb on?'

'If you want me, you'll have to take me for yourself.' Mel closed her eyes and besides leaving Hugh wondering where his usually compliant lover had gone, Mel herself was wondering the same thing. As Hugh wrangled his hot body over hers, she decided that the ancient castle must be having a mystical effect on her. That, or she just wanted more than Hugh was offering.

7

Jenna woke and reluctantly allowed the sunlight and the previous day's memories to bleed into her consciousness. She wasn't sure what was most painful – the brilliant rays as they shot through her sore head or the realisation that something supernatural and beyond comprehension had happened to her.

Being transported back in time over two thousand years soon won hands down and, in comparison, made the headache seem like a feather tickling her skull.

Jenna sat upright in what appeared to be a bed, although was no more than a pile of straw with a heap of animal furs thrown on top. She looked around the mud house. Chinks of daylight filtered through the chimney hole and willow door, slicing up the interior and revealing two other bodies still sleeping. The rippling embers of a central fire reminded Jenna of the strange brew she had taken before sleeping and the crack of orange dawn between the trees when she retired reminded her that she couldn't have rested for more than two or three hours.

'Whoever they are, they sure know how to party,' she whispered holding her sore head, convinced that the foreign drinks she'd had were drugs of some kind. 'Or it could still be shock from the crash,' she said louder as the memory of her beloved Saratoga abandoned with crumpled landing gear became yet another sickening reality. Then, 'Oh hell, I am in *big* trouble if I don't deliver the cargo on time.'

Ignoring her headache, Jenna leapt from the fur bed

and scouted about for clothing – hers or otherwise. The two sleeping bodies stirred simultaneously and sat up, swiftly reaching for iron daggers that were drawn from beneath the straw.

'Who is it?' one of them cried and Jenna hazily recalled that the female voice belonged to Iona, the owner of the roundhouse.

'It's me. Jenna,' she whispered, hoping they would go back to sleep after the exhaustion of all their festivities. In the early morning light, Jenna noticed a smile spread across her unusual host's face.

'Our Fire Goddess,' she said dreamily, giving hope to Jenna that indeed she might curl into the fur again and sleep.

'Our guest needs food and water and comfort,' the other woman said much more alert than her friend.

'Cailla, you are right,' said Iona, crawling from her nest like a newborn fawn, shaky on her legs. 'We must get her some food.'

'Really, I'm not hungry.' Jenna saw that Iona was completely naked and that her skin was as velvet as the fur from which she had emerged. The woman's large breasts hung down almost to the mound of her large belly while her long dark hair filtered around them like a flimsy curtain.

'Then you must take a drink,' Iona ordered, squatting now and revealing to Jenna the place between her legs that, judging by the protrusion of her inner lips, had recently received some attention from one of the male villagers. What had happened last night was mostly a fuzzy blur.

Jenna looked away quickly, fighting the urge to allow her gaze to linger on the dark creases between Iona's thighs. 'I'm not hungry or thirsty,' she replied and before her words were out, she found her eyes tracking a path back to Iona. Sitting like that, the woman was surely inviting her to take a look. And it was only when her eyes finally settled on the pretty shape of the other woman's sex that she remembered she was without clothes herself.

'Do you know what happened to my stuff?' However much she tried, her eyes would not steer away from Iona. 'I ... er ... think I ought to get back to my aircraft and assess the dam ...'

Jenna staggered backwards and sat down heavily on the fur bed. Talking sensibly while Iona was doing *that* seemed inappropriate and standing above the woman, quite naked herself, seemed as if she wanted to be involved in some way and truly, that wasn't the case. Was it?

'Oh, Brogan ...' Iona murmured, while flicking her finger swiftly over the ripe nub that protruded like a little sweet. 'Why do you do this to me?'

Jenna swapped looks with Cailla, who was now stroking her friend's hair away from her face as she worked on herself. From offering breakfast to masturbating on a whim, nothing appeared out of the ordinary to them. For Jenna, simply breathing the unusually clean air and not being able to light a cigarette – she had completely run out – was a million miles from normal.

When she looked again, they were kissing. Cailla, from behind Iona's head, had dropped her mouth onto the other woman's so that her lips brushed against the parted mouth beneath. There was a sliver of air between them, so fine it took Jenna's breath away as she witnessed the lightest of kisses, the tiniest of licks, the briefest moment of female intimacy. Jenna wasn't sure if the pulse that she heard hissing in her ears and tingling between her legs was one of desire or jealousy. Never before had she seen anything so beautiful.

Cailla glanced up. 'Iona has needs and when a man is not present ...' She trailed off as her friend began to moan louder. Iona grabbed Cailla's small hand and pulled it to her breast. Cailla instinctively knew what to do and began to gently tease the pregnant spread of Iona's nipple. 'She is usually with child and often desires to pleasure herself. It is quite normal.' Cailla smiled. 'When she is finished, we will prepare some food.'

Jenna stared in disbelief. Normal? Usually with child? A man not present? Her mind spun with possibilities. Where she came from, it wasn't normal at all for naked strangers to pleasure themselves in front of house-guests, pregnant or not. And it certainly wasn't normal to put on a lesbian show, either.

'I just think I'll take a walk while, er, you two get it on. And please, don't worry about food.' Jenna stood up again and retrieved the itchy tunic she had borrowed yesterday. 'I'll pick a berry or something on the way back to my plane.'

'No, don't go!' Cailla's voice was urgent. 'This is the place of fertility and Iona's role is to bring happiness to couples in our clan. Her body will bring great pleasure to Brogan and me. And with your great power added to the mix . . .' Cailla's expectant face finished her sentence and she reached forwards and pulled on Jenna's wrist. 'At last night's celebrations, you were so generous with your own body so now is the time for you to take something back.'

Jenna's eyes widened at the suggestion and also at the recollection of what had occurred last night. Had she been drugged? Never in her wildest dreams – especially after the trauma of her plane ditching – had Jenna ever contemplated such a ritual tasting of her body. Never before, if she was honest, had she experienced such pleasure. Not even with Hugh.

'Come,' Cailla urged. She beckoned Jenna over to Iona's writhing form. It was almost as if the woman was in labour, she squirmed and moaned so much. 'Touch her breast. It will bring you luck in love and you will be doing Iona a great service by honouring her body with yours.'

Cailla's words wrapped a tight sheath of interest around Jenna's mind. Again, her predicament and the puzzle of the strange land that she found herself in took second place as her body urged her to sample the woman lying in the fur. Jenna had never seen anyone so bursting with sexuality.

'What do I have to do?' she asked, hearing her voice but not believing it to be her own.

'Just stroke her. Touch here.' Cailla guided Jenna's fingers to the dark mound of Iona's nipple. 'Anything you do will be deemed a great honour by her and ensure her future fertility and pleasure. Iona is visited by all the men in our clan. She is seldom alone.'

Cailla offered a giggle, such an innocent yet loaded laugh that Jenna was even more convinced that these women were not from twenty-first century Britain. The thought of anyone behaving in such a subservient and on-call way made her shudder.

If she hadn't now been convinced by the prehistoric setting, she would have labelled Iona nothing more than a cheap whore. If she hadn't been tempted by the succulent curves of Iona's breasts, she would have headed back to her aircraft and prevented the looting that was taking place. As it was, she remained entranced by the sexual naivety of the women that, although primitive in lifestyle, were more erotic than anything she had ever encountered.

'Oh!' Jenna said and felt immediately silly. The warmth and almost edible quality that her fingers felt upon her first touch ever of another woman made her quickly withdraw her hand. Iona's breast was truly exquisite.

'Don't be shy,' Cailla urged. 'Touch her again. She likes it.'

Jenna, fighting against every cell in her body, reached out and draped her hand over the full breast. She liked the warmth, the spread of flesh and the way Iona's waist tucked in just beneath her ribs before flaring out in a firm mound. She was conscious of her own breathing and felt the tick of her pulse in her neck. Truly, the distraction of these women was the only thing preventing her from losing her mind.

She just wanted to go home.

'She has the touch of a goddess,' Iona murmured to Cailla. 'We are the luckiest women in the village.'

'It won't be long before the men begin their visits to worship her. It will be our mission to ensure she is kept healthy to please our warriors.'

Jenna's thoughts tumbled in her head. The possibility that this was some kind of mega-prank or reality television show had finally shrunk and even the likelihood of Hugh stepping into the roundhouse and laughing at his amazing joke was not going to happen. Her fingers toyed with the gem of Iona's nipple – the colour of hazelnut and the size of one, too.

'Kiss me,' Iona called out as she continued to pleasure herself.

Even though she was touching her breast, Jenna still felt disconnected from the scene, as if she was watching a play at close range, and didn't dare bring her face to Iona's for the requested kiss. She'd never considered another woman before; never even messed with any of her girlfriends even though she reckoned that Mel would have given it a go should she have suggested it.

But she didn't want to think about her best friend. Mel's sexual habits had already caused her enough angst and stuck here, there was little she could do about it.

'Aye ...' Iona wailed as her muscles tightened around her bones. Her back arched, thrusting forwards the tight mound of her belly, beneath which the centre of all her bliss nestled. She reached out and gripped Jenna's thigh as her body vaulted through climax.

Jenna had never seen another woman come before and wondered if this is what she looked like when Hugh worked her to orgasm – all strawberry-cheeked and eyes awash with a milky glaze.

Then, without knowing why, Jenna leant forwards and brushed her mouth over Iona's parted lips. Ever so lightly, she stamped her goddess-kiss imprint before reaching for the woollen tunic and fleeing the round-house as quickly as her shaking body would allow.

As she ran through the village, pulling on the garment and fastening the string belt, Jenna felt the buzz on her lips. The last person she kissed had been Hugh. The last person she loved had been ...

The fact that she couldn't answer this question sent Jenna fleeing for her aircraft. She had to find a way to get home.

From behind the rock, Jenna watched breathlessly as four village warriors – one of them Brogan – paced around the Saratoga, swords drawn, shoulders tensed and their eyes darkened by fear of the unknown. This, more than anything, convinced Jenna that she had been hurled back in time. If she recalled her history lessons correctly, she had fallen through two and a half thousand years and smashed her way into Iron Age Britain. Judging by the scenery and her brief memory of viewing it from several thousand feet above, she would guess that she was in northern England or, even more likely, South East Scotland.

But it was the trees that threw her. As far as the eye could see, the rolling land and hills as curvaceous as the lingering image of Iona's body, were littered with forest. A glistening snake of river, its edges seemingly stitched to the land by the sparks thrown off by the sun, wound through the valley beneath the hill upon which Jenna had crashed. The same hill where she was now crouched, peeking from behind a large rocky outcrop as the men dared to touch the metal of her aircraft.

'It's surely dead,' one said as he swiped a hand along the engine cowl. 'Its body is as cold as the water in the river.' He knocked the edge of the propeller with the black iron of his sword, causing Jenna to screw up her face, as if he had actually hurt *her* with his weapon.

'Be careful of the damned prop,' she whispered. 'I don't need that damaged too.' Silently, she assessed the damage and realised that it wasn't as terminal as she'd first thought. The landing gear was crumpled badly and it was unlikely that she'd even be able to taxi, let alone take off with the wheels aligned like that. And the side of the engine housing was dented from impact but again, not as serious as she had thought yesterday when the engine was smouldering. Above all, the wings appeared undamaged and from what she could see, the same could be said of the rudder and elevators. Electrically, mechanically – she had no idea.

There was a small hope that she may take to the skies again. And an even smaller one that she would encounter the same unusual storm that she believed was responsible for her time shift. Why it had chosen *her* to swallow up was still a complete mystery.

'There are treasures inside the beast!' Brogan had his face pressed to the side cockpit window and was obviously referring to the few possessions that Jenna had left on the pilot's seat. Foolishly, she had left her other belongings at Iona's roundhouse.

'Just keep your dirty hands off my cargo,' she prayed quietly. The only brief she'd received, apart from delivering the crated goods on time, was that she was carrying an extremely valuable artefact which would be irreplaceable if lost. 'No pressure, then,' she muttered as the other men gathered around Brogan. She recognised one of them from last night as particularly hungry when it came to tasting between her legs. She shuddered at the thought, hardly able to believe she had actually been through such a thing.

'No!' Jenna screamed involuntarily and leapt from behind the rock. 'Don't smash it!' Her cries prevented the drawn up arm of Brogan, his veined hand gripping the sword, from crashing down on the glass. With a smashed window she'd never be able to get home. 'You'll hurt it,' she finished more calmly as the warriors suddenly turned her way, swords at the ready. They slackened their defence when they saw who it was.

'It is dead. Your beast is dead,' Brogan said, obviously trying to be compassionate but still transfixed on the treasures within.

'That's where you're wrong,' Jenna said, not knowing where this was going except she had to stop them damaging the Saratoga any more than it already was. She didn't know much about these people but, armed with the information she had already gathered, she would charm them into helping her. If they wanted to believe she was a goddess, then that was fine by her. Goddess she would be.

'If you hurt my beast then it will rear up and kill you in one swift move.' Jenna spoke calmly, not wanting to anger the men. She had witnessed how determined they were when amiable at the festival, and could only assume that their exuberance turned to power and strength if antagonised.

The men looked at each other and laughed. The others put their swords away but Brogan still gripped his, unsure whether to believe Jenna.

'Prove to us that the beast is alive,' he demanded. 'Prove to us that the goddess from the sky still has her power.'

The mocking expression, the doubt in his voice – Jenna knew it was the erosion of Brogan's belief in her origins. 'Stand aside,' she said defiantly, 'and prepare for the beast to wake. But, if he thinks you were trying to hurt him . . .' Jenna trailed off. She didn't want to push it too far.

As she strode up to the aircraft, she noticed that although less swollen, her ankle was still painful. Last night . . . this morning . . . the distractions to other parts of her body had dulled the discomfort but now, having run away from the village and up the hill, her injury was niggling away again. Jenna unhooked the engine cowl and retrieved the spare key that she kept hidden in a magnetic box clinging to the metalwork. She had never had to use it before.

'She is waking the beast,' she overheard one of the men say as she unlocked the cabin door and climbed inside. The interior smelled of burning rubber, fuel and something else – something like incense or perfume or the smell of the earth after rain. Jenna wasn't sure where it was coming from but it stuck in her throat and even made her a little dizzy.

'Don't let me down, now,' she said, preparing the instruments for ignition. She rattled through a few usually essential checks, feeling strange that she wasn't contacting air traffic control and offering up her flight plan. Then she crossed her fingers and turned over the engine, half expecting to hear nothing. 'Go, baby!' she squealed, as the propeller coughed and wheeled into semi-life.

Jenna glanced out of the window in time to see the four warriors leap back in fear. All but Brogan fell to the ground in honour of the beast's resurrection. She smiled to herself, keen to maintain the power she obviously held over these people. After all, she couldn't be sure there was anyone else around to help her. Keeping her goddess status was imperative.

'Stand clear,' she called out of the window. 'I can't be sure that my beast won't attack.'

At mention of this, Brogan raised his sword in front of his naked chest. His skin still bore the traces of the indigo paint from the night before and the complicated patterns distorted as the muscles beneath tensed for action.

Jenna ensured the brakes were fixed and levered the throttle as much as she dare. The engine, obviously not running at all well from the recent fire, spluttered and choked and coughed life into the single propeller. Gradually, the engine noise increased and thick black smoke billowed around the aircraft. Surprisingly, the propeller's speed increased and she felt the strain as the brakes fought to hold the aircraft steady.

'You see,' she yelled through the smoke and noise. 'Plenty of life in the old beast yet.' Then, to confound the bemused and scared warriors further, Jenna flicked all the external lights on and off and watched as their eyes widened and their jaws dropped.

Only Brogan displayed a wedge of disbelief. He wiped the back of his hand across his forehead and dared to lower the heavy iron sword. He stepped up to the aircraft, sensibly keeping away from the spinning blades of the propeller, and leant in through the small open door.

'You are a mysterious one, Fire Goddess, but I don't believe your beast is alive.' His eyes were black and mistrusting. 'My people believe in your powers and worship your body –'

'And you don't?' Jenna had to stop the fraying of his belief. She forced the throttle further, causing a sudden burst of engine noise and smoke. Brogan nearly burst from his skin.

'Doubting you doesn't seem wise and, being leader of our clan, I am a shrewd man. You have come to us for a reason and it is my duty to discover what.' Brogan's gaze slid down Jenna's open-necked tunic and hesitated on her cleavage. The itchy garment was a bad fit.

'Well, if you happen to find out, then please do let me know. I'm kind of intrigued myself.' Jenna noticed the fuel gauges and decided to cut the engine. There was no way she was sticking with this crazy bunch much longer and if mending her plane and flying out was her only chance of escape, then she would need to conserve fuel.

Brogan eyed the propeller as it slowed and eventually came to rest. Once the Saratoga was quiet, they could hear the wind in the trees again and the birds settled back on the hillside, thankful the disturbance was over. But the bitter smell of exhaust still hung in the air as Jenna climbed out of the cockpit and she was reminded of London and the airport. Brogan and his men coughed, not used to the pollution.

'Your beast contains many treasures that we have not seen before. Will you be sharing them with the village?' Again, Brogan's gaze darted over the contents of the cabin and Jenna decided to appease him with a simple offering. It would seem like she cared.

'I come bearing gifts, yes,' she replied. She opened the rear stowage compartment and sifted through items that had been left in there from previous trips. She half smiled at the unopened bottle of expensive French wine that was strapped in the compartment because it reminded her of Hugh, of home. But she also felt pain in her heart when she recalled the aborted surprise picnic that she had planned for him, even though she was flying them to the beauty spot and wouldn't have been able to enjoy any of the wine. She had made the gesture for her fiancé and it had cost her nearly eighty pounds for the bottle. Nothing to him but it had made a hefty dent in her budget. Jenna sighed at the memory. She had left the wine in the locker because she was upset that Hugh had cancelled at the last minute, citing urgent business at the office as an excuse. At least he called, she thought, wondering why she hadn't drowned her sorrows alone.

'Here, you can have this.' She handed over the wine and Brogan immediately sheathed his sword and held out large hands to receive the gift.

'It is truly beautiful,' he said, taking the bottle carefully. He smoothed his palms over the green glass, carefully avoiding the lightly foxed vintage label confirming to any wine lover that this was an expensive sample. 'What is it?'

'It's a bottle of wine,' she said, rummaging through the other stuff in the locker. She found a half-used bottle of perfume that she thought she'd lost and a mobile phone charger, eighty three pence in coins and an atlas of Britain. She tucked the map back in place but handed the other items to Brogan. Unless he was a trained actor, his reaction was not that of twenty-first century man.

'Your gifts are truly unique and unlike any I have ever seen.' He turned the bottle around, admiring the shiny glass. 'Some of our men fashion iron objects for celebrations and Iona offers bags of herbs to the gods but to receive such items from a goddess of the fire can never be equalled. We will forever be in your debt.'

Jenna smiled. Even cautious Brogan was impressed by the items. She needed to keep the clan leader on side. 'Nonsense,' she insisted. 'Cailla will adore the perfume. It's Yves St Laurent. Hugh gave it to me.' Again, that tug in her heart. 'And the coins can go on your mantelpiece or something.' She knew that Brogan hadn't got a clue what she was talking about. Exactly what she wanted.

'Let me see,' one of the other villagers said. The four men stood together in a knot of curiosity, each fondling Jenna's gifts, each convinced they were in the presence of someone very special.

It was only when Brogan ordered his men to remove the wooden crate from between the rear seats that Jenna realised that, goddess or not, she stood no chance of overcoming four warriors.

'No!' she cried as the men levered the packing crate from the cabin. 'You must leave that in the beast.'

'Is our goddess refusing us gifts? You have been sent to us with many treasures and it is right for you to share.' Brogan, it seemed, was wise and suspicious beyond his times. Jenna thought quickly.

'OK, you can have a quick look but then it goes back in the plane, I mean beast.' She allowed them to drag the casket onto the hillside and, after trying to fool them that the plain wooden box was all it was, that the cube of pine was the thing to be looking at, she suddenly screamed and was forced to lever it open with Brogan's sword.

'It's on fire!' she yelled, as the demise of her business flashed through her mind. Whoever owned this property obviously cherished it and to have it go up in smoke before she could deliver it would wreck her reputation. Much of her business came from word of mouth recommendations.

With the lid prised open, Jenna coughed and stepped back as a cloud of grey swirling smoke plumed from the container. The same mist that had filled the cabin early on in the flight. Just what *was* she transporting?

'Eugh, it's as ugly as hell,' said Jenna laughing when she was satisfied that the fire was out. Beating it with the plane's fire blanket had dissipated the smoke, which certainly explained the strange smell in the cabin. The air was now filled with a not unpleasant aroma of herbs or incense or some other earthy scent. 'What on earth is it?'

It was only when she had rolled up the blanket and taken a proper look at the crate's contents that she realised something was up. And it wasn't the primitive stone carving that made her heart burst through her chest or sent her pulse so wild that she heard it fizzing in her ears. It wasn't even the size of the statue's breasts or the way its crude legs were parted without shame that sent her body into spasms of fear and excitement.

No, it was because the four warriors had each released their own cocks and were massaging their growing lengths while chanting and bowing their heads to the carving.

Jenna stood motionless. She'd never seen anything like it. The men were openly masturbating and she thought that she might slip away unnoticed until Brogan approached her with his very own offering. The last thing she remembered was her head hitting the grass.

8

For the second time in two days, Jenna was hauled back to the village like a wild animal being tamed. With her long auburn hair trailing in the wind, Brogan hoisted her over his shoulder and in a few panting minutes he had her back in the village.

What happened to the other warriors, she wasn't sure. And neither was she certain what would become of the stone artefact left out on the hillside. She prayed that the men had the sense to pack it away carefully. As ugly as it was, she had a duty to look after it until delivered. And deliver it she would.

'Hey!' she protested as Brogan barged through the door of a dwelling in the village. It wasn't Iona's home although similar in its primitive build but missing the sweet scent of herbs. Instead, Jenna smelt straw and mud and . . . something manly. 'Where are you taking me?'

'It seems,' Brogan boomed, 'that you are not who we first thought.'

Christ, Jenna thought. Now I'm in for it. She held her breath as she was dropped onto a pile of furs. Brogan's bed, she assumed, and couldn't help notice the musk that wafted from the skins as she sank deep into their softness. Animal or Brogan, she couldn't be sure, but the smell was as evocative as the aroma that had seeped from the stone carving and both suggested one thing: sex.

'I am whoever you want me to be.' She decided to be cryptic. Surely she would be able to out-smart Iron Age man.

'Fire goddess or fertility goddess?' Brogan demanded. 'Or both?'

Jenna was relieved to see that his tawny shaft had been tucked back inside his clothing. She hadn't a clue what to make of the sudden display of masturbation on the hilltop although she supposed it was brought about by the rather rude statue. She imagined that its new owner in Scotland would display it on a shelf to cause hot discussion and titillation at dinner parties. Only those as rich as Hugh would pay mega-bucks for such a folly.

'What would you like me to be?' she continued. Her identity was obviously important to the clan leader and, she suspected, vital to getting him on side. 'Although I thought that Iona was in charge of fertility around here.'

'Iona is a mortal. She uses herbs and her body to satisfy the needs of our men and betrothed couples. She rarely fails in her work. You, however, have come from another place.'

He's intuitive, Jenna thought, and couldn't help picturing Iona's full body, her desire for pleasure on a whim. She lifted her fingers to her nose, hoping to catch a whiff of Iona's skin because suddenly her own body was needled with something inexplicable. Something inappropriate and she was completely unable to ignore it.

Brogan continued. 'My men will defend our village ten-fold now that you are among us. Word will soon spread to neighbouring clans and we cannot allow anyone to steal our goddess. Cathan will no doubt discover your whereabouts and demand you and the stone statue for himself.'

The mention of Cathan again caused Jenna to delve further. She recalled the Druid, Laymar, warning of him. 'And what would happen if Cathan got wind of my presence?'

'He would steal you for his own, of course.' Brogan's hand twitched at his sword at the mere mention of his rival. 'He has already helped himself to a number of our clan's most beautiful women.'

Jenna sensed the crackle of rivalry between the two men. But the mention of another clan intrigued her and offered some hope that she may not be totally stranded in prehistoric Britain. Perhaps Cathan could help where Brogan couldn't.

'Now tell me –' Brogan paced the roundhouse, his feet scuffing the dirt around the fire '– why have you been sent to our clan? What have you come to show us?'

Before she could answer, Brogan was on his knees beside her. The sweet and sour tang of sweat stopped her answering immediately and the pull of his hand on her hair, gently arcing her head backwards so that she was staring at the sky through the chimney hole in the roof, caused the words to catch in her neck. Even more so when Brogan pushed his lips onto the marble-white skin below her ear.

'I . . . can't . . .' Jenna began, but her body was already telling her to shut up. That however much she felt she should protest, that having been mass-tasted by an entire village at the core of a frenzied festival, that having touched Iona's sweet body and witnessed four warriors handling themselves in front of an erotic lump of stone – that after all that, Jenna really thought she should stop Brogan pushing his tongue between the sinews on her neck and protest that soon, very soon, she would be a married woman.

If she ever got back home.

'Why are you here and what of your iron beast?' Brogan pushed his hands against Jenna's breasts, melding his palms over their fullness. 'You are made a similar way to my Cailla,' he breathed, squatting in front of Jenna. She hardly dare look between his spread legs. As it was, the proximity of his naked chest was causing her heart to bang behind her ribs.

'I came here by accident,' she admitted. She wanted him to help but also wanted to maintain her goddess status. 'My aircraft – the beast – hit a freak storm and we got chucked out of the sky onto your hillside. I was lucky not to ... have ... been killed.'

Brogan pressed his face into Jenna's cleavage and even through the thick fabric, she could feel the humidity and warmth of his breath increasing with each rise and fall of her chest. 'Then you have been sent to us by the gods of the sky in your chariot beast but...' Brogan trailed off and looked up at Jenna, frowning. 'But I don't understand how you came by the likeness of Druantia. How did the cold Fire Goddess come to own the stone goddess?'

Brogan let out a gravelled laugh at his attempt at humour before stripping Jenna's breasts bare with one swift tug of cloth. 'But no matter. You are both mine now, both goddesses and...' He sank his open mouth around the end of Jenna's breast, sucking in and pressing his tongue over the soft flesh. Then, '... either way, Cathan can't have you *or* the stone carving.' And that laugh again before he pushed Jenna back into the pile of animal skins.

'What are you doing?' Her voice had as much impact as a mouse's. 'I'm getting married soon. If Hugh finds out that you've...' She didn't carry on. Not when the image of what she knew Hugh had been doing to Mel clicked back into her mind. Really, she should be entitled to fuck anyone she liked. And, although it was guilt after the fact, she realised that she virtually had. Here she was, in another place, another time, with a warrior of god-like stature virtually forcing himself upon her. Under the circumstances, she really shouldn't be feeling guilty and besides, it didn't seem like she had a choice.

Jenna tried to relax as Brogan climbed on top of her. He straddled the thin line of her body and stripped off his own loose clothing. Every muscle was ridged and highlighted by the rays of sunlight beaming through the roof.

She studied him thoroughly as if sizing up a stallion for purchase. True, his body was lean and honed and his mane was wild and hung loose around his shoulders. And true, too, that his eyes bore the slightly demented look of a crazed animal, as if he'd been frightened by a flapping flag or brightly coloured sign. But there was something else about Brogan, something other-worldly and enigmatic or perhaps even something *recognisable*.

Was it because she was becoming used to prehistoric Britain that the twenty-first century now seemed foreign? Surely not, Jenna decided, but there was something disconcertingly familiar about the way Brogan held his head while studying her and the way his throat began the resonance deep within. Something all too familiar about the structured lines of his body, that if only he wasn't so ruddy and hadn't eaten lean meat and berries all his life, that if he'd indulged in a few pints of beer and the finest wines and rich food as often as he liked ... If his skin was paled by a life of wearing suits and working beneath artificial lighting and he'd been for a regular manicure and massage and ...

But more than anything, it was the way Brogan demanded her body, as if she was without doubt his possession that caused Jenna to wonder.

'Hugh?' she tried, gently, while Brogan flung his woven check pants aside. His long erection sprang free, seemingly a separate entity to its master.

Barely acknowledging her, Brogan lowered himself towards Jenna's hips. He grunted – or was it a growl? – and nudged his goddess's legs apart by inserting a knee between her thighs.

'Is that you?' she asked again, desperately trying to sort out the puzzle in her mind. Had characters from the past become players of the future? Was there a link, however vague, to the twenty-first century? If so, and this caused her face to widen with hope, then perhaps somewhere there was a bridge home to be crossed.

Brogan took her expression of pleasure as an invitation and without warning, he plunged himself home, filling the small channel of Jenna's sex in several forwards strikes.

Then the growl again. Low and deep at first but becoming as recognisable as Hugh's trademark noise and when Jenna closed her eyes, she might as well have been lying at home after an evening with her fiancé, allowing him to penetrate her as he usually had to do several times a day if they spent time together.

The only difference now was that she felt the large warm lips of a warrior bearing down on hers. With his hand cupped around the back of her head, she was pulled onto his face for the deepest kiss she had ever had. The heat from his pumping cock – having worked up her natural juices – sparked a line of electricity to the sensations on her lips. Brogan's mouth was controlling her every last thought.

Just like Hugh, she managed to comprehend before her mind went blank and all she could do was drown in the shots of pleasure, and sometimes pain that took over her body.

'If Cathan sent you,' Brogan grunted, each syllable in time with a powerful thrust that took him up to the hilt, 'then he will never get you back. Evil is what he is, with powers beyond his control...'

He suddenly withdrew from Jenna, as if the image of his rival was too much to bear while inside Jenna. He stood and strode around the dim hut, pacing around the fire pit like an animal, his body glowing red with heat, desire and anger.

'What is it?' Jenna asked, bereft that he had left her body although determined not to show it. However much she'd been enjoying the deviant attention of an Iron Age warrior, keeping her senses, keeping Brogan on side and gaining information was essential. Seeing Hugh in Brogan, however thin the thread, had lit her mind like an exploding firework. Then she had an idea. 'Come here,' she begged, crawling on all fours across the dusty floor to the man she suspected adored to be treated like a man. 'Let me taste you.'

Powered by the residue of feelings settling inside her sex, Jenna edged to Brogan so that her face was level with his groin. She tentatively drew her tongue along the underside of his erection, skirting the tightened skin of his scrotum and beyond.

Brogan remained perfectly still, a man caught in the glare of headlights. His breathing quickened and Jenna noticed his fists ball up by his thighs, while she licked her way to the place that would confirm her suspicions – that somehow, in a timeless genetic mystery, Brogan was in fact her fiancé.

Desperate hope or supernatural fact? Jenna took a deep breath.

She ducked between his legs, her head upturned to inspect the space behind the globe of his balls. It was dark in the roundhouse but by the irregular flicker of firelight, Jenna could just make out what she was looking for. In fact, as her senses adjusted to the proximity of the warrior's most private place, the mole might as well have reached out and slapped her in the face.

Hugh had one in exactly the same place.

She stuck out her tongue and swiped a firm wet streak and stopped just short of the tight knot of his anus. That did it. Brogan let out an animal moan and drew in a breath so that even the flames gasped for air.

'What are you doing to me?' he rasped. Needy for something to grip, Brogan latched his fingers into Jenna's hair, forcing her face harder against the parts of his body that didn't feel like his anymore. He had never been ignited like this before.

'Just checking,' Jenna whispered when she finally surfaced for air. She drooled a line up Brogan's lengthy cock, skipped onto the flat landscape of his stomach and up through the valley of his chest. She breathed into the curve of his neck, allowing her lips to settle on the apple of his throat. 'Just checking who *you* are, since you've been asking all about me. Although, where I come from, it's more socially acceptable to discover this *before* the fucking stage.'

Brogan's heavy brow drew together and his eyes narrowed. He didn't understand what the goddess was talking about but then, this was to be expected. However mortal she appeared, he knew she was a deity to be worshipped. By making his mark on her body and securing her for his own, he was ensuring that no other – Cathan, especially – would come sniffing about to steal her.

'And did you find out?' he asked, drawing her upright. He pulled her close so that the end of his erection was able to nestle in the crook of her legs. His hands followed the curve of her breasts, slipping down onto the gentle shelf of her hips and buttocks. She was better than anything he'd ever had; better than Cailla and the constant comfort of Iona. As the young women in the village ripened, Brogan took it upon himself to initiate them. There simply weren't enough women in the clan to satisfy his needs.

'Oh yes,' Jenna revealed. 'I certainly did.' She pulled away from Brogan's grip, something at the edge of the hut having caught her eye. It was nothing more than a ball of crude twine wrapped around a hazel twig. She picked it up and waved it at Brogan. 'Wanna play?'

The growl again and Brogan stalked towards her; a hunter sizing up his prey.

Jenna darted aside and drew up against one of the internal poles that supported the roof of the roundhouse. She dragged her hands up and down its knotty length as if it had human form. Then she tossed the twine to Brogan and pressed her back against the pole, not caring that the bark abraded the skin between her shoulders.

'Play?' he asked. His large hands deftly unravelled the twine and he cut off several lengths with a small dagger that he withdrew from the leather belt slung around his hips – the only thing on his otherwise naked body. He seemed to know what he was doing, despite his apparent ignorance.

'Sure,' she giggled, not knowing where or how or why this behaviour had surfaced. Gone was the usually sensible, reliable, trustworthy pilot and fiancée and loyal friend, Jenna Bright. The heat of the fire lashed at her left side, igniting something close to fever in her body as well as mind. 'Tie me up to the pole,' she demanded rather than asked. An unusual display of authority.

Again, that knitting of brow before Brogan forced Jenna's hands behind the pole. In seconds, he had them lashed together as if stringing up a wild animal, the only difference was that his catch wasn't protesting. That alone made him grow harder.

'Now ... fuck ... me,' she whispered, the words winding upwards with the fire smoke and curling their way out of the hole in the thatch.

But Brogan heard and a grin slashed across his face. He swiftly sheathed the crude iron knife and appraised his catch. The globes of her even breasts sported upturned nipples that made his mouth water. With her hands pinned behind her and her shoulders wrenched back, each breast presented itself proudly.

Brogan stuck his tongue onto a nipple and circled the pale island with delight. At close range, he eyed the darker skin as it bled into the almost white flesh surrounding it. He couldn't stand it any longer and dipped a finger into Jenna's already worked-up sex. He felt her arch against the pole; moan as her head fell back against the wood. Knowing what was coming.

The breath was forced out of her as she took Brogan's impressive length of cock deep inside. At first, he had to hold her open and guide himself into the small passage between her thighs. But she didn't mind. It made it all the more real. All the more Hugh. And this could only mean one thing. All the closer to being in touch with home. With reality.

'Oh Hugh,' she mumbled, not quite clearly enough for Brogan to comprehend or even care. If she'd been able, she would have clawed tracks down his back, just as he loved. Her wrists strained within the ties, grateful – no, delighted! – that they had been bound up. One of Hugh's favourite games to play with her.

The pagan ... the warrior ... the Iron Age man ... whatever he was, had his face firmly embedded in Jenna's neck. It remained there while his back arched and his hips ground and his hands pulled and kneaded the soft flesh of her breasts. And gradually, like a disturbed bottle of the finest champagne – most likely the kind that Hugh would order – Jenna began to bubble and fizz and push the limits of containment.

The deep rod of climax had begun the climb through her body.

Beginning at the core of her sex, almost unbearable pulses of heat drove outwards to reach every extremity. Urged by the staccato rhythm of Brogan, Jenna allowed the pleasure to build. Radiating down her legs, touching her toes, her fingers and speeding through her shoulders, neck and face, the first phase of orgasm painted her cheeks crimson and her lips cherry red.

She closed her eyes as Brogan pushed his tongue down her throat and again she was reminded of Hugh. A worlds-apart comparison, she knew, and it was quite possibly distorted by the drenching of bliss that drew back down into her sex like a tornado sucking up a forest as she came and came again. But nonetheless, Brogan – with a little less muscle, with a little less hair, with a little less raw anger and buckets more refinement although the same, familiar feral need – was, in Jenna's mind, her very own Hugh.

'Untie me,' she finally gasped as Brogan collapsed, spent at her feet. A warm trickle of semen wound its way down her thigh.

And as soon as her hands were freed, as soon as she had rubbed feeling back into her fingertips, she cracked a slap across the side of Brogan's face.

'That's for fucking my best friend,' she spat and went to retrieve her tunic.

Only when she was pacing furiously through the cluster of other roundhouses, passing by fenced-off goats, several fires and a group of villagers – some of which dropped to the ground at her passing – only then did she consider that it was likely she was going mad.

9

Euan Douglas was on the telephone. He sat on a mahogany chair behind an antique desk and beneath a gallery of ancestral oil paintings framed in heavy gilt.

The man, dressed in jeans, sturdy boots and army-style sweater couldn't have looked more out of place if he'd tried.

Rachel cleared her throat.

Euan Douglas glanced up from the papers on his desk with the phone still pressed against his ear and beckoned her in. His eyes were as green as the loch that Rachel could see through the tall window. He held up two fingers.

Two minutes? Two hours? Peace? A secret Scottish greeting?

Rachel nodded slowly.

'If the usual vet's busy then get another one out. The animal needs medical attention and if it doesn't get it, then you'll need medical attention too.' Douglas's voice remained level, asserting its command.

He has all this, Rachel marvelled, gazing around what she guessed would be called The Library or The Trophy Room or The Hunting Gallery. At around fifty feet long and panelled in polished oak on either side, the long room was studded with trophy stag heads, each peering at her through forlorn glassy eyes. And in large display cabinets were cups and shields and cut crystal most likely all showing off Euan Douglas's keen eye for a kill. She had a quick scan for the desirable, priceless statue but could see nothing.

Locating the prize and getting back in Hugh's good books would be a bonus, especially as she'd been excluded from shenanigans in favour of Mel. Still, Mr Douglas was a mighty fine looking man, she thought, and she could do worse than flirt with him to rile Hugh's jealousy.

'All my father's and grandfather's and his father's et cetera ad infinitum.'

Sorry? Rachel hadn't realised that Euan Douglas was off the phone and was watching her prowling amongst the stags' heads.

'Impressive,' she lied. She didn't much care for hunting.

'How can I help you?'

Rachel felt the warm appraisal of the castle's owner and for a beat, she didn't speak but soaked up his gaze. He was definitely checking her out. Now she wished she'd put on her really sheer blouse. The one that even if she wore a bra, still showed off her nipples. She loved it when men stared at her tits.

'My name is Rachel Harte and I'm PA to Mr Vandenbrink of Vandenbrink Holdings.' Rachel paused, quite used to the following gasp or breathless moment of shock as it dawned upon whoever she was speaking to that they were dealing with a powerful man.

Nothing.

'Mr Hugh Vandenbrink,' she repeated, wondering if Mr Douglas was slightly deaf.

Euan Douglas shook his head. 'Sorry. Never heard of him. But please go on.' The green eyes were fixed firmly on hers. No quick dash to her breast. No lick of the lips or surreptitious brush of hand against groin.

'Well, he's very important. And he wants to meet with you. To discuss business.' Rachel noticed the quiver in her voice and hoped Euan Douglas hadn't. 'Is there a time that would suit you? Mr Vandenbrink is a guest in the hotel for the weekend. We have the Cameron Suite.'

'Ah,' Euan replied thoughtfully.

Finally, Rachel thought, he knows who we are.

'Well I hope you have a lovely stay. I believe there's some Scottish dancing in the lounge after dinner tonight. You might want to tell your Mr Vandenbroke what excellent entertainment it is. Plus, there's complementary whisky for all our guests.' Euan smiled a smile as intricate as the hills surrounding the castle, pulling his narrowed eyes into a map of friendly lines. Making him even more attractive.

'Vanden*brink*,' Rachel corrected. 'And he insists on seeing you. Perhaps you will be in the lounge this evening?'

Euan sighed and scratched his head, mussing his already unkempt hair. 'Of course.' He smiled politely, glancing at his watch. 'My guests are priority and I will be happy to meet with Mr –'

'Vandenbrink,' Rachel finished for him. 'Shall we say nine o'clock?' She held out her hand because she couldn't think of any other way to get to touch him. Not yet, anyway.

The loch was mostly surrounded by forest and flanked to the north and west by the steep climb of ridged hills. Rachel stood on the jetty and stared out at the deeply green water and wondered what lay beneath. She squinted as the sun dipped behind the trees in the west and held back her hair against the wind as the last rays from a pleasant May afternoon filtered through the trees. She couldn't help but wonder what the stunning landscape had witnessed in its time.

'Everything from dinosaurs to cave men to medieval feuds to kings and queens and fairies and –'

'Just an old romantic, you, eh?' Familiar hands were suddenly around her waist and then pinning her wrists together behind her back. 'I just fucked Mel into unconsciousness,' Hugh lied. 'Now I want to do the same to you.'

Rachel felt her insides melting; felt the magic of the Scottish loch bleeding into her veins as if she was hooked up to a drip. What she really wanted was to be loved by a man, which was probably why she was thinking about Euan Douglas even as Hugh's mouth came down on her neck.

'You are insatiable,' she giggled. She was feeling sexy. More mischievous than usual. 'I spoke to our Mr Douglas, by the way.'

'And?' Hugh pulled away. Spun his secretary around. Business was business. He wanted that statue.

'He'll see you in the lounge at nine o'clock this evening.' Rachel beamed. She had done well. 'Apparently there's Scottish dancing and whisky and –'

'Better get my kilt ironed then.' Hugh grinned, planting a kiss on Rachel's forehead. It would all work out perfectly. A meal for them all, at his expense of course, followed by plenty of whisky in the bar while wrapping up the statue business with Douglas – he would make him an offer he couldn't refuse – then all back to the suite for a night of so much sex that even *he* would be satisfied for at least twenty-four hours.

'And you know what they say about men in kilts,' Rachel said winking, reaching down and cupping the growing package within Hugh's trousers.

The kilt came boxed complete with a fur sporran and Argyle jacket and was personally delivered to the castle by the shop owner from Dundee. As an added bonus and for paying twice the retail price as a tip, the shop owner threw in a *Sgian Dubh* – a traditional Scottish dagger – for good measure.

What Hugh wanted, he got, with the price being

inconsequential. That's why he knew he'd be travelling home with the stone statue.

'I was only joking,' Rachel laughed. Hugh paraded up and down the bedroom in full Scottish dress. 'Go on then, show us your Trossachs.'

'Later, darling,' Hugh said, admiring himself in the mirror. He truly did look magnificent. Appearing out of place tonight would be a disaster. He wanted Euan Douglas to respect him as a fellow Scot, cultivate some mutual respect, indulge in some whisky appreciation followed by some cheque writing and statue crating.

It would be a good evening, filled with cheer, new friendships and maybe even the promise of a return visit to the castle in the future. It was the perfect place to get away for a long weekend of uninterrupted sex.

'Wow,' Mel said as she emerged from the bathroom. She had been languishing in the biggest Jacuzzi tub she had ever seen. Her cheekbones were highlighted strawberry and her skin fizzed from the luxurious salts she had sprinkled into the water courtesy of Carrickvaig Castle. 'You look ...' she let her towel drop to the floor.

'Sexy?' Hugh finished for her.

'Different,' Mel added. 'But sexy, yes, in a kind of I-want-to-lift-up-your-kilt kind of way.'

'Well you'll have to wait.' Hugh reached out and spanked the ripe moon of Mel's bottom. He loved it. Wanted to sink his cock up there right now in front of Rachel.

'What are you wearing tonight?' Mel asked Rachel. The two women locked eyes for a second, Hugh standing between them.

'This,' Rachel snapped and turned to the mirror to put on her earrings. She thought she looked perfect in the loose white pants that showed off the curve of her tight ass, which was as good as Mel's any day. She also rather liked the black tube top that had a habit of slipping too low and exposing a crescent of nipple. If it happened tonight, she would leave it showing. Hell, she might even pull it down herself.

'I think I'm going to wear a dress. Something nice and feminine.' She breezed over to the wardrobe and retrieved a scarlet garment off a hanger. 'This will do perfectly.'

Hugh sat on the four-poster bed watching as Mel shimmied her body into the gossamer fabric. It took a bit of arranging but when finally in position, the dress barely reached below the fullness of her bottom and left little to the imagination at her chest. Two thin bands of fabric ran vertically down from the neck tie, skimming the tips of her breasts and finally joining the dropped waist below her navel. The effect was a neckline that wasn't so much plunged as not there at all.

'You have a belly button piercing,' Rachel commented, thinking that Hugh's friend looked far too sexy to accompany downstairs. She would have changed except that she hadn't brought any other evening wear with her. Rachel would just have to be outshone. 'The dress is lovely,' she finished, believing that politeness won over envy any day.

'Thanks. Hugh bought it for me.' Mel swung around and planted a warm kiss on Hugh's head. His face lingered in the valley between her braless breasts. 'It came from a little place on King's Road. Cost a fortune.' She giggled and returned to the bathroom to apply her make-up.

'You look ravishing, too,' Hugh said, sinking his fingers into the firm mass of Rachel's buttock. 'I'm a lucky man with two gorgeous women. Are you up for a bit of fun with Mel later?'

Rachel glared at her boss. It came with the job, she knew, and maybe her reaction to Mel's appearance had been genuine. She really did think she looked lovely. *Too* lovely. 'I'll give it my best shot,' she winked, aware that the thin strap of her knickers was rubbing against her clitoris. Besides, she couldn't risk losing her job.

'Excellent,' Hugh said, grinning. 'I'm going down to the bar. I'll meet you two ladies shortly. Don't be long now.'

'Getting up to no good in that four-poster, you two?' Hugh was on his second drink and had loosened the scarlet knot of his new tie when Mel and Rachel finally arrived.

He'd been waiting at least half an hour for the women to come down and the jacket, the stiff shirt and tie, the itchy kilt and long white socks made him feel like stripping naked more than ever. But to build a rapport with Euan Douglas, Hugh had decided to give up the comfort of an open-necked shirt and loose pants.

All to get the statue, he reminded himself. All for Jenna on her wedding day.

He surreptitiously levered a hand in Rachel's crotch as she stood next to him, wondering what to order from the bar. 'Been eating a bit of Mel's pussy?'

'Hugh!' Rachel said. 'Keep it down. You're embarrassing me.'

'It's what he does best,' Mel chipped in. 'You sit, Rache. I'll go to the bar.' Mel pulled Hugh's hand from between Rachel's thighs and wound her own arm around the PA's waist. 'I'll get advice from the barman on what we should have. Leave it to Hugh and he'll have us on our backs before dinner.'

'That's the general idea,' Hugh said although no one heard. He eyed Mel's arm as it levered Rachel into a chair.

'Thanks,' Rachel said, letting her own hand trail along Mel's arm as she headed for the bar.

'You two make up?' Hugh took a large mouthful of whisky. 'She called you *Rache*.'

'I wasn't aware that we'd fallen out.'

'Let's just say I sensed a bit of female rivalry back in the room. A quality I admire in women as long as I can watch them make friends.' He laughed and necked the last of his drink.

'Well Mel and I get along just fine, thank you and –'

'Come here,' Hugh ordered in a voice that Rachel knew not to ignore. 'Put your face near mine.'

She did as she was told and Hugh sniffed around her mouth like a dog sizing her up.

'You have, haven't you? You dirty bitch!' Hugh leant back in the chair and felt the familiar stirrings of yet another erection. It would surely show through his kilt. 'Your face smells of pussy.'

'For God's sake, Hugh, shut up.' Rachel blushed the colour of the red velvet chairs although she admired Hugh's instincts. Anything to do with sex and he would sniff it out.

It was true. For the last half an hour, she and Mel had been all over each other. Tongues poking in and out of every hole so that they soon forgot what belonged to whom.

It was Mel's fault entirely, and partly Hugh's for sowing the seed that he'd like to see them together. Mel had been in the bathroom and Rachel had needed to pee. Mel watched in the mirror as Rachel slipped her pants down, slowly wiping herself afterwards.

'Let's see,' Mel had said. She'd even clapped her hand to her mouth when she realised that she'd voiced what she was thinking.

'See?' Rachel was semi-squatting with her tiny knickers banded around her knees.

'Your pussy. I'd like to see it.' Mel couldn't stop now.

'Oh. OK.' Used to obeying orders and reluctant to disobey Mel in case she complained to Hugh, Rachel stood up, opened her legs and gently pulled up her soft, lightly-haired pussy. She was fair with the palest pink lips although she felt them deepening to a rich rose colour as Mel drank up what she was showing her.

'Thanks,' Mel said genuinely. 'You're really pretty.'

'I am?' Rachel smiled and pulled up her knickers and trousers.

'Wanna see mine?' Then they both laughed because they sounded like experimental teenagers. 'Fair's fair,' Mel finished.

'Go on then,' said Rachel, again not wanting to cause trouble with Hugh. Then she gasped as Mel lifted her short red dress. For one, she wasn't even wearing any knickers and secondly, she had absolutely no hair down there at all.

'I shave it smooth every day,' she said, reading Rachel's wide eyes. 'It feels really nice. Like going about every day things without any clothes. It's my little secret. Makes me feel on-fire sexy the whole time.' Mel's face screwed up with delight. 'Wanna touch it?'

'Me?' Rachel said immediately. She hadn't realised it would go that far; had never thought she'd ever touch another woman.

Mel leant back against the vanity unit and parted her legs. 'Go on, just put one finger on it. I won't bite.'

Rachel tentatively reached out a finger and placed it on the cleft at the top of her lips. One touch, for only a second, and then she withdrew like Mel was electric. Rachel felt delirious. Happy forever that she'd done it.

'Is that it?' Mel asked.

'I touched you, didn't I?'

'I want you to do it properly. Let me show you.' Mel eased Rachel's trousers down again and then slowly snapped the thin elastic of her knickers around her thighs. 'Open your legs a bit.'

Rachel did as she was told.

'Like this,' Mel said, watching the reaction on Rachel's

face as she eased her lips apart with the tips of two fingers. She pushed back, knowing she'd find wetness, and then pulled forwards again dragging Rachel's juices up to her clit.

'Oh . . .' Rachel whispered, steadying herself on the wall.

Mel worked her fingers back again and allowed them to slip inside by an inch, feeling the soft, wet flesh part at her touch. It had been a while since she'd played girl games.

'You like?' Mel asked, already knowing the answer. Rachel's cheeks had turned pretty pink and her eyes were misty as if they had fogged from the steam residue in the bathroom.

'Oh yes,' she said quietly. 'But isn't it a bit naughty?'

Mel laughed. 'That's the whole idea, silly. There's no point coming away to an amazing place like this with one of the most powerful men in London and not getting up to some seriously dirty mischief.' Mel circled her forefinger around Rachel's clitoris, causing her to literally go weak at the knees. 'Come and lie on the bed. I want to work you right up for Hugh.'

'I think you have already,' Rachel said breathlessly.

With her fingers still latched on, Mel led Rachel to the four-poster. 'Take your trousers off. I don't want to crease them up.'

'Really?' Rachel said, still unsure they should be doing this. But then she imagined Mel pouting to Hugh about how his selfish PA refused to share her body and then Hugh firing her in a fit of rage and . . .

'Pull your knees up to your chest so I can get to you.'

'Oh God,' Rachel said, lying on her back with everything exposed. Mel's warm mouth came down on her sex, while her hands made sure her legs stayed up and spread wide.

Rachel's spine relaxed into the bed as Mel's firm

tongue pushed inside her. 'This is too rude for words,' she whispered to herself. And then it occurred to her that Mel would probably expect the same in return. Ever so gently, Rachel began to shift her hips to the rhythm of Mel's quick tongue and ever so gradually, she felt the first stirrings of climax building through the wetness.

Mel stopped and sat up. 'My turn.'

'But . . . I didn't –'

'And you're not going to, either. Neither of us will come until Hugh is here. I want us both to be desperate throughout dinner and have to race to the loos just to finger each other close again. But we mustn't come. That's the rule.' Mel grinned. 'OK?'

'Sounds fun,' Rachel giggled and her eyes went wide as coat buttons when Mel offered up her own hairless sex for the taking.

'I got you a dry sherry,' Mel said, winking at no one in particular. She sat between Hugh and Rachel and adjusted the hem of her flimsy dress so that whoever walked into the lounge bar would catch a glimpse of her neatly shaved packet. She was still wet from the licking Rachel had given her. 'And Hugh, I got you another Scotch.'

'Hugh has sniffed us out,' Rachel told Mel. 'He knows what we've been up to.' She took a long slow sip from the small glass and her eyes narrowed at the thought of another woman's sex pressed onto her face. She wondered why she'd never tried it before. 'And we really ought to eat soon as Euan Douglas will be here to meet us before long.' She tried to revert to the role of PA but just the mention of eating sent new-found tingles between her legs. 'And has anyone seen Mark?'

Rachel glanced around the lounge, which was now full of diners taking pre-dinner drinks. There was a mixed bunch of clientele, some old, some young but every one of them obviously very well off. And even though it was May, a log fire was burning in the huge stone fireplace. It truly was a magical castle.

'He told me he was going into Dundee to eat,' Mel confessed. 'I meant to mention it earlier. Maybe he fancies his chances with a local lassie.'

'Perhaps,' Rachel replied. She had rather hoped he'd join them for dinner, to tip the male/female balance even. She knew that Mel was Hugh's favourite. Both their favourites now, she smiled to herself.

'Shall we, then?' Hugh stood and offered an arm to each of his two women. He was ravenous and had an appetite that would take much sating.

Euan Douglas cruised politely from one circle of hotel guests to another. The fifty or so diners had returned from the restaurant and were taking coffee and liqueurs in the lounge. The only clue Euan had to the insistent Vandenbrink's whereabouts was the location of the pretty blonde who had come to see him earlier.

Rachel, wasn't it?

He paced confidently around the lounge, smiling, greeting, making pleasant chit-chat about the day's roebuck hunting. It had been a slow start with many high-quality heads coming later in the day. On the whole, he had a castle-full of content guests. Given a choice, he would have preferred to spend the day alone, bumping the Land Rover about the land, managing his estate followed by a cosy evening for two. Wine, dinner, an early night. Euan sighed, resigned to being single forever.

There she was, sitting by the fire. White trousers, sexy top. And a good-looking friend, too. It helped repeat business if there was an attractive girl or two staying at the castle. Briefly, he thought about marriage, about how he should be more proactive about finding a wife. He thought about heirs and then about his impossibly high standards.

Before approaching, he took a moment to size up the party. Vandenbrink was typical of his usual male guest. Loud, loaded and leering. The woman to his left, in the red dress, was well ... he swallowed. Not wearing any knickers?

He strode up to Vandenbrink and offered out his hand. Just get it over with.

'Mr Vandenbrink, I presume.' He wondered if he had any underpants on beneath the kilt. He balled his left hand to prevent a laugh.

Rachel smiled. He had got the name right.

Hugh stood and turned. A broad grin widened his face. 'Yes, Mr Douglas. How very pleasant to meet you.'

Hugh instantly disliked the casual yet confident air of a man who was obviously several years younger than him, several degrees better looking and with a hearty chunk of south east Scotland to his name. Not to mention that he was in possession of the stone statue.

Euan, on the other hand, reserved total judgement until he had got to know Vandenbrink better. He was a fair man by nature and intrigued by what Vandenbrink had to say.

'Please, call me Euan.'

Just a faint hint of accent, Hugh thought. 'And I'm Hugh,' he responded. 'Please, do join us.' He gestured to an empty chair.

Rachel had purposefully set aside a fourth chair in anticipation of Euan's arrival. She had made sure it was right next to hers. 'Hi again,' she trilled, wondering if now was a good time to inch her top lower. She was so hot it was unbelievable and now, with Mel sitting opposite and the gorgeous Mr Douglas to her left, she thought she might come right there and then. Plus, knowing that Hugh wanted to fuck her all night didn't do anything to calm her down.

'Good evening, Rachel. You're looking very –' He was going to say beautiful but in light of the patch of nipple he could see peeking from Rachel's top, he stopped. He didn't want to draw attention to her. The poor woman would be mortified if she knew her top had slipped.

'Very what?' she asked hopefully.

'Smart,' Euan finished, politely averting his gaze. He hoped her friend would signal a visit to the restroom.

'And I'm Mel,' Mel said, not bothering to shake hands. Instead she offered a wider view up her dress by crossing her legs loosely. Her sex was angled directly at Euan and Hugh would be delighted, she thought. What better way to make him putty in Hugh's hands than to distract him with a glimpse of her recently licked assets.

'Well, very nice to meet you all.' Euan's voice snagged on something in his throat. Who were these people? 'So … Hugh, what can I do for you?'

'You have something I want. Something that by rights should be mine.' Hugh leant forwards, forearms resting on thighs.

'Oh?' Euan took a sip of the pint the waitress had just left for him.

Hugh laughed, noticing how Rachel had gone pale and gooey-eyed gazing at Euan, while Mel was offering a private show. Good girls, he thought.

'The statue,' he continued. 'The stone carving you recently bought at auction in London.' Hugh stirred his coffee. 'Basically there was a mix up at the auction house and it should have been mine but the telephone bidder was … well, I can write you a cheque tonight and we can sort the whole mess out and –'

'You mean Druantia?' Euan's brow knotted and his shoulders tensed.

'The ancient stone thing with the huge breasts.' Hugh laughed. 'Bit of a silly folly really but sweet nonetheless.'

'Sorry,' Euan said seriously. 'She's not for sale.'

Hugh's eyes widened. His mouth glued into a plain horizontal line. 'Oh come on, Mr Douglas. Everything has a price. How much do you want?'

'It's not a matter of price and even if it was for sale, I couldn't help you, Mr Vandenbrink.' No first names anymore.

'And why would that be?'

'Because the statue is not in my possession yet, if you must know. It's quite worrying. I paid a fortune at auction for it, keen to have it returned to its rightful home. I even hired private transport to have it shipped directly here. It should have arrived yesterday but I've had no word yet from the wretched charter company I used. All the big names in the city were fully booked so I had to settle on some small-time barn-stormer. A woman pilot, would you believe.'

At this, Rachel's dreamy eyes hardened and she glanced at Hugh. Her mouth hung open.

'Look, I'll pay you ten per cent more than you paid at auction. Can't say fairer than that.' Hugh stirred his coffee so hard it spun into the saucer.

'You're not hearing me, Mr Vandenbrink. I do not have the statue. And when it arrives, I am not selling it.' Euan sipped his pint, wanting nothing more than to retire to his small quarters in the castle's east wing and watch a good movie. 'Long ago, my people fought hard to keep the statue. They believed in its powers of love and fertility. Really, I can't sell. It belongs here in the castle for the Scottish people to enjoy.'

'Do you really believe in its powers, Euan?' Rachel asked. 'And, if you don't mind me asking, what was the name of the company that you used to ship the statue?'

Rachel's tone was pleasant and Euan was only too happy to answer.

'Myths and legends and Celtic traditions are part of my heritage. I can trace my family's roots back centuries. I believe my ancestors lived on this land as far back as history is recorded and probably beyond. When a place owns you so comprehensively, when the hills and rivers are as familiar as your own body and the corbie take to screeching your past and your future as you work the land, fish the loch and hunt the forests, you can't help but believe in the magic of this place.' Euan downed half his pint. More than ever, he wished he had someone to share his heritage with.

'And the female pilot you mentioned?' Rachel felt it appropriate to hitch up her top. There was something about the look in Euan's eyes, something passionate about the way he spoke of his love for this place . . . and the statue . . . that being so provocative didn't seem right. Anyway, there'd be plenty of time for sexy goings-on later with Hugh and Mel.

'Let me see now.' Euan dug into his pocket for his phone and in a second he was able to recite a name. 'I used a company called Bright Charter. The pilot was called Jenna Bright. A one-woman company, I assume, and not big on customer service it would seem. She promised to call me the minute she arrived in Dundee so I could fetch her and the statue from the airport. I even invited her to stay the weekend and join the hunting party. To date, I've heard nothing.'

Euan watched three jaws drop, one spoon fall to the floor, one pair of legs fold primly beneath the table and two gasps of shock. It wasn't until later that night, when Rachel tapped lightly on the door to his private suite, that he learnt Jenna Bright was Hugh Vandenbrink's fiancée.

10

Jenna ran. They would be after her. She sprinted up the hill to the Saratoga, relieved to see that the statue was still there. She smiled briefly. The warriors had placed a circle of stones and flowers around it. It was certainly special to them.

Using all her strength, she heaved it back inside the cabin and retrieved the key, securely fastening the door and window. By its own fearsome appearance, the beast would defend itself. Jenna smiled nervously. Those silly warriors were scared of a plane.

Then she ran again. To where, she had no idea but before locking the plane, she'd pulled the map from the rear locker as well as a portable compass she always carried in case the aircraft systems failed.

'Right,' she said, squatting with the map, her hands shaking with fear that soon the entire clan would be hunting her. She glanced down into the valley and so far, everything was peaceful. 'I was heading here ... so, last known co-ordinates ... east north east ... four hundred, maybe four twenty...' She tapped a nail against a tooth. 'I reckon I flew at least four hundred miles before the storm. Perhaps more. I could be very close to Dundee and really close to the castle. If it even exists yet.'

She orientated the map and compass and checked and double checked the direction of the valley and the loch where she knew her client's castle was located. She'd been told it was only a twenty-minute drive from Dundee.

'I'm still in denial,' she panted to herself as she ran through the long grass. 'When I find Dundee, when I find my client and apologise and tell him where his statue is, everything will be back to normal and...'

Jenna froze. She heard voices. Fast as a rabbit, she darted to a clump of bushes, noticing for the first time that there weren't any hedges or fields. Just miles and miles of meadow flanked on either side by endless woodland and forest. She cowered in the undergrowth as the voices grew nearer.

'Singing?' she whispered, recognising the voices to be harmonising a tune. Women's voices. Careful not to expose herself, Jenna peeked out of her hiding place. A twig cracked beneath her foot just as a band of five women walked by only feet from the bushes.

'Who's there?' one asked.

'Come out,' demanded another.

Then, 'Look, she's hurt.' The women, all wearing similar clothing to the women in Brogan's clan, approached her cautiously. One drew a small sword from a belt.

Jenna raised her hands. 'Really, I'm not hurt and I won't hurt you either.' She glanced at the sword. 'I'm just trying to find Dundee. Before they catch me.'

'Before who catches you?' the fairer one asked.

'The warriors from the village in the next valley.' Jenna pointed to the direction from which she had run. The women gasped, their eyes widening. Several were carrying large baskets of fruit and flowers and nuts, which they placed on the ground.

'Dunlayth warriors are hunting you?'

'I guess,' Jenna replied, wondering just how serious this was. 'How far to Dundee?' Instinctively, she knew the women wouldn't know what she was talking about. She just wanted to stretch the vague thread of hope to infinity.

'Why? Which clan are you from?' the woman with

the sword said. She was about ten years older than the others although no more than thirty herself.

'I'm not from a clan. I'm from...' Jenna wasn't sure she wanted to go through the whole goddess thing again. 'I'm from the south. I'm lost. Is there somewhere nearby where I can rest, get food and –'

'Hide out?' another woman finished.

Jenna nodded. She glanced around, expecting to see Brogan and his warriors emerging from the forest. He was intent on keeping her as his own private goddess.

'We're from the Caravye Clan. If you like, you can come with us to safety. Our leader, Cathan will know what to do with you. He is a Druid and will advise your future from reading your past.'

'He will?' Jenna's heart skipped at the mention of Cathan. It also banged in her chest at the mention of her future and her past. Could he possibly help her get home? Brogan had told her more than once about Cathan's evil ways but these women seemed pleasant enough and if their leader could see into the future...

Jenna shook her head vigorously. What *was* she thinking?

Then, interrupting her doubt, she heard clanking of swords and male voices in the distance heralding the approach of Brogan's men. Jenna felt sick.

'Quick, get back in your hiding place. We will cover for you,' the older woman said.

Jenna did as she was told and crawled deeper into the thicket. Brambles and thorns and nettles scratched and ripped at her arms and a twig snapped back against her cheek. She stifled a cry as the men's shouts drew nearer.

The women started to sing again and Jenna could see that they had crowded around the bushes to shield her and were acting busy by picking flowers and leaves.

'Oh!' one woman exclaimed as she pretended to see

the band of four warriors for the first time. Gradually, the other women turned and cautiously greeted the men.

'Have you seen a woman fleeing through this area? A slim woman with hair the colour of fire?'

The women shook their heads in unison. 'We've only enjoyed our own company today. We are out gathering food.' A couple of the other women tripped into song again.

'Shut up,' yelled a warrior. From her hiding place, Jenna recognised it to be Brogan. The women continued to sing. 'I told you to be quiet. You're from Cathan's clan, aren't you?' Brogan laughed and Jenna saw his long feet approach the ground where the women clustered. 'No wonder he steals women from other clans. He has poor specimens of his own.'

Jenna heard the clank of metal and verbal protests from the woman who carried the sword but then she was silenced by another female voice.

'We want no trouble,' she said. 'If you find us unattractive, then so be it. We are not trying to gain your attentions. You may leave us to our business.'

Jenna screwed up her eyes and mentally screamed no, no, *no*! Even after only such a short time, she knew Brogan well enough to know how he would react.

'Take your clothes off and let me be a proper judge of your beauty.' That laugh again: gravelled, mocking, serious. 'All of you. Strip.'

Jenna heard whispering amongst her new friends. They were trying to protect her and had ended up endangering themselves. But if she came out from her hiding place, what good would it do? Brogan would simply capture her and most likely still demean the women. If she stayed hidden, who could tell how far he would go? Jenna decided to remain silent until absolutely necessary.

'No,' the women chimed one by one. They continued with the picking and Jenna heard Brogan talking in a low voice followed by outraged screams and cries from the women.

'Get off, you brute!'

'Leave me be ...'

'Hey –'

Jenna closed her eyes again as she heard fabric ripping in the scuffle. Brogan had ordered his men to force the women from their tunics.

'Better than I first thought,' Brogan laughed when the women were naked and still. 'Quite pleasing to a tired warrior,' he continued. 'You, bend forwards.'

Jenna breathed in sharply.

'Why?' the woman said.

'Because I want to see every part of you,' Brogan said and lashed what sounded like a length of willow on the ground. 'Do it!'

The woman leant forwards and took support from her friend. She pressed her terrified face into the other woman's soft belly. It was some comfort.

'It is pale, like the rest of you, and more inviting than I would have imagined. Cathan keeps quite an assortment of girls for his pleasure, I see.'

Then there was the sound of leather sliding across leather and the chink and clank of a sword and more gasps and low-voiced rumblings as Brogan did what Jenna suspected he would do all along.

He was going to fuck the woman. Right there. In front of everyone.

The game was up. Jenna had to come out right now to save the poor creature. Brogan could have *her* instead. After all, he already had.

About to emerge from the bushes, Jenna froze.

'Ohhh, yes,' came the woman's stretched moan.

'Deeper, please,' she begged as Brogan entered her from behind.

Having moved a little in the undergrowth, Jenna could now just make out the shape of Brogan from the waist down and she had a clear view through the leaves of his huge cock sliding in and out of the naked woman's sex. Her lips flowed back and forth with entry and exit, the edge of them framed by a white rim of juice. She had been wet and ready for Brogan.

'They're like animals,' Jenna whispered so quietly. 'They just get it on anytime with anyone. Dogs in the park, rabbits in the field, they're as highly sexed as . . .' Jenna's faint words faded completely and in her mind she finished the sentence

As Hugh.

Her fiancé's neediness hadn't occurred to her as being unusual before she'd left home the day before. Sure, she knew that he was a demanding lover, would bend her over anywhere they could find privacy for a quick dick-fix. Last week he'd even frog-marched her into the gents' toilets in a restaurant and took her in a cubicle, such was his need for immediate relief.

But it had never been a *problem* before. Not until she had heard him and Mel together on the phone. That he desired her so much was a good thing, she'd always thought. He wouldn't be getting it anywhere else because she was available pretty much whenever he wanted. Until yesterday, it hadn't occurred to her that she wasn't enough. That he needed other women as well, all the time, day or night. Jenna wondered how long it had been going on. All that fucking behind her back.

'Tell your Cathan that I had his woman today,' Brogan laughed. He was drawing close to orgasm as he pumped hard and fast against the woman's buttocks. One of the other women stroked her back while the one she was leaning on for support teased her hair. Jenna couldn't make out what the other warriors were doing although she could take a guess.

'Don't ... let ... me ... find ... you ... here ... again...' Brogan said to the rhythm of his climax. Then, as the woman obviously came too, judging by the squealing, Brogan lashed her buttocks with a length of willow. It seemed to make her pleasure go on forever and Jenna was ashamed that she wished someone would do that to her. Having Hugh make love to her, she realised, was only ever with his satisfaction in mind. If she came, it was a bonus. If she didn't, she usually sorted herself out later.

Moments later, the group of men were walking off into the forest. 'If you see a woman out here on her own, tell her Brogan's looking for her. Tell her that I'll take to her with my whip if I catch her.'

And only when the voices of the men had subsided, only when the snag in Jenna's throat had been swallowed away, did she come out and help the women dress in their torn clothes.

Cathan's village was similar to Brogan's in virtually every way except that it was closer to the banks of the river and there were more crops growing nearby. Jenna supposed it was the same river that wound through Brogan's valley although further upstream. By her reckoning, it would be the River Tay.

'You have nothing to fear,' said the older woman in the group as they entered the village.

They had been walking for what seemed like hours although they had probably only travelled a couple of miles across the undulating land. Jenna's feet were sore and ached in the primitive leather sandals that Iona had given her. As she thought of Iona and Cailla, she felt slightly saddened. However brief their acquaintance had been, she had grown fond of the sweet women. A brief flash of desire sparked through her body.

'I am fearful of Cathan. Brogan told me what an evil, angry man he is. He warned me away from your village.'

'Cathan is not evil,' the woman said with a smile. 'Let me take you to him so you can see for yourself.'

Jenna swallowed back her fear. Strangely, no one in this village paid particular attention to her as she was led between the thatched roundhouses. She supposed it was because she was wearing Celtic clothing and hadn't landed in a ball of flames.

She admired the way the primitive buildings were constructed; mud mixed with straw piled up around the support of locally grown trees. The roof sloped gently upwards to a central hole to allow the fire smoke to escape. In the winter, a constant fire in each home would be essential. They were simple, cosy and stood strong yet blended easily with the countryside. Jenna thought of London; of the river banks choked with brick and concrete. She listened to the other woman.

'Cathan can usually be found by the river. He spends much of his time meditating and looking for the best way forwards for his clan. He is a well-respected leader.'

Jenna was forming a new picture of him in her mind. Shorter than Brogan, she thought, perhaps even by a foot. Raggedy grey hair fanning around a wizened face, Jenna predicted Cathan to be old and wise. Maybe she was imagining the Druids at Stonehenge. Maybe Cathan would be the fierce warrior that Brogan had described.

'There he is.' The woman pointed to the banks of the quick-flowing river up ahead, some way outside of the village. Jenna longed to dip her face and take a drink. 'I'll leave you now. Go, introduce yourself. Don't be afraid.'

Jenna felt the woman's hand give her a gentle shove

in the small of her back. She stared at Cathan, an indistinguishable figure hunched over the water. When Jenna glanced at the woman again, she was gone. She had never felt so alone.

She walked closer, her legs trembling, and cleared her throat.

'Hush,' was his reply. Cathan, dressed in a long brown wool tunic, didn't move. Jenna couldn't make anything out about the man except that he was bent over the river.

Suddenly, in a flash of movement and spray of water, Cathan turned with a metal spear held high above his head. The largest salmon Jenna had ever seen struggled on the end. It was completely impaled and in a few more seconds, it gave up the fight.

'A good catch,' Cathan said using a rock to finally quieten the fish. He laid his dinner down and beckoned Jenna to him.

She could hardly move. It seemed that her feet were embedded in the earth. Cathan was not at all as she had imagined.

'Come,' he said in a voice that was levelled with gentleness and concern. 'Let me see who you are.'

Slowly, Jenna approached Cathan. As she had already ascertained, he was dressed simply in a brown cloth robe tied at the waist with a leather thong and he wore no shoes. He was a tall man too, over six feet, and his shoulders sat squarely over his lean body. Lightly haired forearms grooved with the lines of hardworking muscle leant on the rudimentary spear as Jenna approached. She noticed, too, that his skin was fairer than Brogan's and his essentially blonde hair was washed with a touch of red in the lowering sun.

'My name is Jenna Bright,' she began nervously. For some reason she felt like bursting into tears and sobbing into Cathan's deep chest. Perhaps it was relief that he wasn't the fearsome enemy Brogan had made him out to be or perhaps it was just sheer exhaustion and hope that perhaps this wise-man would be able to help her get home. But Jenna maintained composure and allowed her sobs to escape internally. 'And I'm lost.'

'We are all lost,' he replied with a smile that lit up the twilight.

Jenna was about to reply but stopped. It was the sort of thing Vic would say just to be cryptic. And thinking of Vic made her want to cry even more. How she longed for familiarity and a friendly hand to pull her back where she belonged. Then she wondered: if Brogan had such an obvious link to Hugh back home, then who was Cathan similar to?

Vic? she wondered but then dismissed this thought as speculation. Apart from the vaguely religious comment he had just made, there were no similarities to the vicar-pilot. Perhaps, she decided rationally, there was no link to anyone and she had even been imagining the similarities between Brogan and Hugh, although they were uncanny ... and then there was the mole.

'Really lost, I mean,' Jenna smiled back. 'As in I haven't a clue how to get home.' She refused to mention how her plane had crash landed, thought better of mentioning the statue. 'Would you know how far Dundee is from here?'

Cathan came close and put his hands on Jenna's shoulders. At once, she heard a whooshing sound and felt light-headed as if she was going to faint.

'I'm so sorry. I don't understand you.' He steered Jenna towards the river. 'Come and sit and drink the water. You look as if you have travelled far.'

If only you knew, Jenna thought, surprised she could think anything at all with her mind fizzing from the man's electric touch. There was a danger about him, for sure, but not in the way Brogan had forecast.

Don't give up hope, she told herself. You may yet get some sense from someone.

They sat side by side on the banks of the lively river and Cathan filled a clay pot with the coldest, most refreshing water she had ever tasted.

'Is it OK to drink?' she asked.

Cathan frowned and lifted the cup to her lips. 'And what caused a beautiful woman to be wandering the land all alone? Did you not fear the other clan warriors stealing you for themselves? Did your own clan leader not think to protect you?' Cathan scratched in the dry dirt with a stick as Jenna greedily drank the water. She wiped her mouth on the sleeve of her itchy wool dress.

'It's kind of hard to explain,' she began. 'You won't have heard of the place I come from. It's a long way from here and very hard to get back to.' Jenna plunged the cup into the water and drew it up towards her mouth again. 'Lots of people will be looking for me but no one will think to look here. That's my problem. And no one I've met here has ever heard of the place I come from and so can't steer me in the right direction.'

'I see,' Cathan said and Jenna gasped, hopeful that he did. 'And how much do you want to go home?' he asked after a moment.

Jenna was about to reply, *with all my heart*, but stopped. Did she really want to go home *that* much – with the prospect of facing Hugh and Mel, knowing what they had been up to together? Hugh probably had a dozen other girlfriends and that PA of his, Rachel, was most likely opening her legs daily. How could she ever trust him again? How could she marry him? What incentive was there to go home?

'Of course I need to get back home. There are things that have to be taken care of.' She thought of Vic, her business, her parents. They would all be crazy worried about her. 'My folks will be going frantic,' she said. 'They'll think I'm dead.'

'And what if you could let them know you're not? What if you could get word home?'

'You mean like a messenger?' She doubted he meant via email or a text.

'Something like that,' he grinned cryptically. 'But more complex. Something you don't need to understand.' Cathan eyed the catch lying behind them. 'Hungry?' he asked and Jenna realised that she was.

It was just the two of them and Jenna liked it that way. Whoever he was, Cathan made her feel safe, calm and totally content with her unusual situation. The sun had slipped below the bank of hills to the west and the lake was so flat and glassy in the light of the full moon, Jenna wondered whether she could step out onto it and walk on its surface to the other side.

'Mmm, it's good,' Jenna said, pulling chunks of salmon flesh off the pale bone with her fingers. 'It's hard to get it so fresh these days.' She grinned when she realised Cathan didn't understand what she meant.

The fire crackled and sent a shimmy of sparks out over the water. They watched, intrigued, as water birds flapped their way home for the night.

'Can you hear the music?' Cathan asked.

Jenna listened, smiled and nodded. 'It sounds like a celebration.'

'It is,' he confirmed. 'For you.'

'Really?'

'Yes, our clan always welcomes newcomers this way. They know you will hear their music. They believe it will draw you back to them in times of need. If you are ever lost.'

'But I *am* lost,' Jenna laughed, wishing Hugh had the

good sense to do something to draw her home. 'And it's a bit different to the reception I received at Brogan's village.'

A silence fell, as deep as the lake by which they sat.

'You have been with the Dunlayth clan?' Cathan stopped eating and his eyes widened.

'I ... er ... fell upon their village by accident, spent a short time there and then ran away. Brogan and several of his warriors were hunting me until the women from your village rescued me. They risked –'

'What did they risk?' Cathan demanded.

'They allowed their bodies to be ...' Jenna didn't know how to say it. 'Well, Brogan took a liking to one of the pretty young women and ...' She sucked her fingers, glanced at the rising moon, full as a dinner plate. 'He bent her forwards and, you know ...' Jenna pulled a face.

'Sadly, I think I do,' Cathan said thoughtfully. 'The man has no control of himself. Over the last year, he has laid claim to at least half the females in this village and will stop at nothing, it would seem, to get what he desires.'

'Brogan said that you steal *his* women away from his village. He told me you were evil.'

Cathan let out a laugh that was streaked with sadness as well as incredulity. 'He said that? Truth is, the women flee Brogan's village in fear of their lives. They run to me complaining of they way they are used for pleasure ... one woman suffered his body so long and so often that she never found time to eat and became perilously thin. A careless moment by the guard Brogan had put in place and she was able to flee to us, her nearest neighbours.'

'I see,' said Jenna thoughtfully.

'So you must understand, I am not stealing Brogan's women. They are coming to me of their own free will for salvation. Of course, he doesn't see it that way. And then there was the theft; an act so despicable that I thought not even Brogan would stoop to such measures.'

'Oh?' said Jenna, picking at the pile of seeds and nuts that Cathan had scattered beside the fish. Food had never tasted so good.

'It was many seasons ago. As Druid priest and leader of this clan, it is my job to forgive.'

'Forgive what?'

Cathan sighed and offered the drinking vessel to Jenna. 'Brogan's clan were having problems. Let's say that the women weren't blessed with children at a rate to satisfy a good leader. Brogan, of all men, wanted his women to produce every season but sadly this wasn't happening. He blamed his men, his crops, the gods, and even the women themselves were laden with guilt for not reproducing. And then he stole Druantia.'

Cathan stood and walked to the edge of the lake. Jenna thought he might step onto the silver path made by the moonlight and walk on the water. If he did, she resolved she would join him.

'Now where have I heard that name before?' Jenna half smiled, half wondered if she should tell Cathan that it was an ugly stone carving of the same unusual name that she was transporting when the freak tornado struck and she crashed ... but that would mean being revered as a goddess all over again because, it seemed, falling from the heavens in a metal beast was unusual and therefore goddess-worthy.

'Druantia is our earth goddess and provider of fertility and creation. She is very sacred to our people and we carved her likeness from stone and worshipped her regularly. But Brogan heard of Druantia's powers, he saw for himself the beautiful children our women were bearing and sent his men to steal the statue.'

'I think I could help...' Jenna trailed off. Did she

really want to help or did she just want to find a way home and leave these feuding clans to battle it out over their stupid lump of stone. 'I think I know where Druantia is.'

Cathan turned and wore the moon's reflection as a halo. His face was as calm as the water and his eyes as deep. He held out his hands for Jenna to approach. 'You do?' he whispered, trying not to betray his hope.

'Yes,' Jenna sighed. There was something about this man, something that made her feel safe, complete, as if she had known him for years. And she believed that he could possibly grasp the contortions of time and help her find a way home. 'I have Druantia but your statue won't be safe for long. It is locked inside my aircraft ... like a big metal casket ... and if Brogan's men find a way in, then they will take back your statue for sure.'

Jenna didn't believe that her cargo could possibly be Cathan's own statue but, because Brogan had recognised it, she thought that it would do as a replacement for Cathan too. She tentatively walked inside his outstretched arms and was swallowed up by his jade eyes.

'First, we have to send a message home so that your loved ones will not fear for you.'

'Thanks,' said Jenna, excited by the prospect of communicating with home, not to mention the proximity of the enigmatic Druid. She had never felt so safe with anyone, not even Hugh.

'I need you to think of the person you love most in the world. In your mind, tie a cord around them, pull them into your thoughts and never let them go.' Cathan swivelled Jenna around in his arms so that she was standing facing out over the lake. He stood behind her with his hands on her shoulders. 'Now close your eyes,' he instructed. 'And think of your loved one all the time.'

Jenna nodded, aware of the sudden prickle that spread over her skin as Cathan began to chant words that she didn't understand. She felt a gentle breeze skim over her face and heard the final flaps and calls as birds and other wildlife settled for the night. She was aware of the water lapping rhythmically at her feet and, of course, she could feel the weight of Cathan's hands slide down her arms, onto her waist and down her legs.

What she couldn't think of, though, was a loved one. Hugh just wouldn't stay still in her mind. However hard she tried to lasso him with her thoughts, he kept slipping away into the arms of another woman. Jenna was about to declare the task useless but Cathan's magical voice kept her from interrupting and now that his hands were drawing her woollen dress up over her head, she had no use for words anyway.

She felt the cool night air wrap itself around her naked skin as if Cathan had draped a silk sheet over her shoulders. She stayed perfectly still, allowing the strange words to work up the enchantment and get the message home.

Frantically, she forced her mind into overdrive in the hope that someone she knew would pick it up. How, she didn't know, didn't care, she just wanted someone to know that she was still alive.

Oh, very much alive, she thought, as her mind and body drowned in Cathan's touch making her feel like she was already home.

11

In the dream there was a moon as fat as butter hanging over the loch. Euan stood at the mullion window and gazed out across the still waters, mesmerised by the scene but invigorated by the magic blooming in the air.

As he squinted through his dream, fumbling to separate reality from delusion, Euan saw a woman standing at the edge of the water. The moonlight reflected off her red hair, making it glint as bright as fire flickering in the night.

He slung a robe around his body and trod the stone steps quietly. He left the castle without a sound and made his way to the loch. He found the beautiful woman still standing there, her back to him, quite naked, quite unaware of his presence.

He reached out a hand and mapped the length of her spine with his fingers. He pushed his face into her hair and breathed her scent. She smelt of the past and the future but Euan couldn't understand why she didn't exist now.

When she turned, her eyes stared right through him. When he pressed his lips to hers, she didn't respond. Instead, she whispered a name so silently – such a thin thread throughout time – that he couldn't possibly hear.

'Who?' Euan asked, desperate for her to speak again. But the woman's words turned to mist and dropped around his ankles.

Fearful that she might leave, Euan reached out and took the woman's wrists but his hands slipped right through her. He placed his hands on her shoulders, her arms, her breasts but the same thing happened. She was there but not for the taking.

Then the woman turned and began to walk away, as if she would continue into the loch along the runway of moonlight that made a path into the water. But before she finally left, she reached out a hand and placed it on Euan's chest.

He felt her touch.

His heart lost several beats and when it recovered, he was in love.

Mark 'Vic' Maloney knew what they were all up to. It was twelve-thirty, well past his bedtime, and as he stalked the castle corridors on the way back to his room, he paused outside the Cameron Suite and listened to the noises seeping under the door.

They were all in there and if he'd chosen he could have been part of their games too. When he'd returned from a very pleasant meal-for-one in Dundee, he'd taken a nightcap in the bar and been virtually accosted by the rowdy trio and press-ganged into playing their naughty games.

'To be honest, I'm tired.' What he really meant was he could think of nothing else but his good friend Jenna Bright. She didn't deserve this man even though their impending marriage had been recently announced all over London. That such a wealthy bachelor was marrying was newsworthy indeed.

Mark blocked Jenna's pale face from his mind as he imagined her reaction to discovering what her husband-to-be was up to behind her back. But this was nothing compared to learning of another, far worse fate that might have befallen her.

'Jenna didn't arrive at her destination,' Rachel informed him while downing another shot of tequila.

Mark froze, drink halfway to his lips. He recalled their chance encounter at the airport several days earlier. What was it she'd said? *Don't fly today. Watch the weather.*

'Well, has anyone checked with the airports, for heaven's sake?' Mark paced the bar and frantically dialled some contacts. It was all falling uncomfortably into place. He had heard Hugh talking about the statue on the flight up. He should have made the connection with Dundee and the castle that Jenna had mentioned at the airport. There was something going on that he didn't understand or like, especially when it involved Jenna's safety.

'Take it easy,' Hugh said confidently. 'The authorities are doing all they can to trace her. There were no reports of any aircraft going down. No wreckages found. Knowing Jenna she probably decided to nip over to Dublin to do a bit of shopping without telling anyone.' Hugh laughed and his arm grew around Mel's waist like a pernicious vine. 'She's an excellent pilot. Nothing will have happened to her.'

Mark made some calls – including one to Jenna's voicemail – and snapped the handset shut, not convinced that his best friend hadn't fallen out of the sky. He sat beside the fire sipping whisky, praying to God that Jenna was safe while Hugh and Rachel and Mel made one last attempt to coax him to their suite for games.

'I'm tired,' he reiterated and watched them stagger, arm in arm, out of the castle bar.

Later, in his small room, after he had paused for a moment outside the Cameron Suite, Mark lay on his bed and watched a shower of stars pass across the sky as the full moon arced over the loch.

It was as he was drifting into sleep that he wondered where the music was coming from; a primitive drumming, chanting, singing. Echoing through the hills, transcending time.

'Oh Hugh!' Rachel exclaimed, shocked that he should suggest such a thing. 'Aren't you even a bit worried?'

'Of course,' Hugh replied. Nothing, not even his fiancée's untimely disappearance was going to dampen his spirits for a decadent night with these two women. They looked ravishing – Mel with her show-off tendencies and Rachel bursting with ripeness and a need for exploration. If he didn't have each of them about ten times, he would be useless to Jenna anyway. Nothing worse than a frustrated fiancé.

'Jenna's a big girl. She would have called if she needed me. Don't let it ruin the night. I have plans for you both.'

Hugh threw his jacket on the bed and caught a glimpse of himself in the mirror. He liked the sturdy yet fit appearance that stared back from within the Scottish outfit. His private trainer worked him hard – when he wasn't fucking her over the saddle of an exercise bike that was. He deserved every inch of thick muscle and taut buttock. Something else caught his eye in the mirror too. The giant bulge rising behind the tartan fabric; an invitation to Mel and Rachel.

'Fetch me a drink, there's a sweetie,' Hugh ordered. Rachel busied herself at the drinks cabinet while Mel chose some music.

'I'm going to change,' Mel announced.

'Don't bother,' Hugh said. 'No clothes will be fine. You too, Rachel.'

The women looked at each other and stifled little smiles. Hugh took a seat in a large comfortable chair in the window after opening the heavy curtains. 'Wouldn't want anyone to miss the show now, would we?' And he settled down to watch them strip.

Rachel and Mel slipped easily out of their evening clothes. If they hadn't required full use of their mouths, Hugh would have gagged them immediately not wanting any female tattle to ruin the performance. Maybe later, he considered, wondering if he'd brought enough silk ties to bind them up. The naked women stood in front of Hugh on the thick rug.

'Do whatever you like,' Hugh instructed, lighting a cigar. 'Just as long as it includes a replay of your dirty foray into lesbian action earlier.' Then a laugh, a long draw of tobacco and a hearty leer at the two girls through squinted eyes.

Oh yes, he thought. I am a lucky man.

It didn't seem the same now that someone else was present. Rachel felt a shiver up her spine although the room wasn't cold. She knew that her body was responding to Mel's presence but she wasn't sure how to feel about performing in front of Hugh.

Mel on the other hand couldn't wait to wrap her legs around Rachel's slender shape and wind their thighs together in an entirely female embrace. That Hugh was on the periphery made it all the more exciting. She knew just how desperate he was to meld his body with theirs and be the governor of their lovemaking. But for now, he was content with fighting the desire to join in; that act alone a measure of blissful torture.

'Show yourself off to me again,' Mel suggested.

'OK,' Rachel agreed, glancing at Hugh. She turned a little so he could see too and then she gently pulled on the mound of her sex so that the pinkness of her lips was exposed. If she'd been alone, she'd have slipped a finger inside immediately.

'As pretty as ever.' Mel smiled and dropped to her knees. Slowly, she stuck out her tongue and inserted the tip in the soft grooves between Rachel's thighs. She tasted better than the dessert they'd just paid a fortune for in the restaurant. Rachel should be on everyone's menu.

Gently, Mel inserted a finger deep inside her and watched as her shoulders pulled back and her neck curved to that of a ballerina. Still with her fingers working up her new friend, Mel stood and trailed her tongue up Rachel's flat belly. She paused to harvest the scent and taste of each full breast, allowing her tongue to drift to near the point between curves and underarm. Rachel hummed with sex, oozing it from every pore.

'I wish I was a man,' Mel whispered into her ear. 'You would never sleep.' Mel imagined driving an erection into the soft, closed space between her legs. A space so intimate that it would only open for the right person after much coaxing and licking and teasing. A space that would provide them both with immeasurable pleasure.

Mel was drunk on desire and realised that she was fantasising about what she needed herself. Being with another woman – and she had done this several times before – was, for her, like making love to herself. It was an illumination of her needs and a reflection of her desires. She did as she would have done to her. And she loved every soft, warm, scented minute of it.

'Kiss each other,' Hugh ordered, shifting himself forwards in the chair. With his legs apart and his kilt drawn wide, he knew the waiting erection and heavy balls would be visible to the women should they choose to look.

Mel put her hands on Rachel's shoulders and drew her close. The women's breasts pressed together, almost perfectly nipple on nipple and each of them felt the new thread of pleasure waking undiscovered nerve pathways.

It was Rachel who made the first move on Mel's lips. She closed her eyes and opened her mouth a little, hardly daring to breathe in case she blew the moment away. Never before had she felt so invigorated, compelled or in need of a man. Mel was her appetiser, the morsel of taste that she so needed to whet her hunger for a hearty main course.

Her lips touched Mel's. Slivers of sweet fruit served with a tangy sauce that she could barely bring herself to eat. Just a tiny taste then, she thought, easing her tongue forwards.

In a moment, it was over, like the waiter had whipped away her plate before she'd finished. But it only left Rachel wanting more and before her senses levelled, she realised that the kiss wasn't finished, it had just moved.

Mel's mouth was on her neck, her ear, pushing through her hair, trailing between her breasts and chewing gently on her nipples. Then it was back at her lips again, carefully reproducing the fragile kiss that Rachel had started.

Then they fingered each other. Now oblivious to Hugh's presence, although in need of something else, too. It was as if they'd each lost something and a frantic search was beginning, not leaving any hiding places unchecked. That point of realisation: what if it's not found or lost forever or never existed? The point at which another person would be called to help.

Mel and Rachel's hands and arms, lips and cheeks and hips and thighs brushed and nudged together as they continued with the flurry of the search. Rachel felt the hot iron of pleasure draw her sex into a pout as Mel worked on her. Hugh, she noticed, was unable to keep his distance and was kneeling on the rug to get a close-up view.

When the women slid their four hands up his kilt, they knew they had found what they were looking for.

'Morning's going to come too quickly,' Hugh complained as long firm fingers took control of his explosive erection. 'I just need to get one out the ... way,' he said, not stopping to draw air before he buried his face in the nearest soft place. Judging by its musky scent, he had found Mel. Nuzzling in her wet folds, he sucked in her natural aroma and then passed it on to Rachel by kissing her on the mouth.

'Mmm, you taste good,' she whispered as Hugh's tongue left her mouth.

'I need to come,' Hugh said, almost begging although both women knew that was not a usual character trait. Hugh demanded, he fought, he kicked up and screamed and paid large amounts of money to get what he wanted, but he never begged.

Mel pushed him back into the thick pile of the rug. He was long in all directions, his legs and arms stretched wide and his cock straining to the ceiling. A fine sheen of sweat coated his face and neck. The need for it, the urgency, was almost too much to stand.

'Let's just swap about and see who makes him come first,' Mel suggested. 'You sit on him for a few minutes, then I will.'

Hugh moaned like he was ill when he heard what they were going to do. His head rocked and his legs turned to bars of iron as Rachel slowly straddled him and primed the tip of his cock with her juice. Then, slower still, she filled herself up by lowering herself down until the erection was invisible and his dark patch of hair merged with her paler covering.

Then she fucked him. She went at it hard for a couple of minutes and only when she sensed danger did she swiftly lift off him and allow quick transfer to Mel. The same thing happened and Mel allowed herself time to bring Hugh back to the boil before swapping again.

In the end, Hugh didn't even know – or care – whose body was clamped around his as long as he was taken up and over the edge that he needed. Then he would concentrate on working himself up all over and using those two naked women to the max.

He rammed home half a dozen times and came into one of them – could have been Rachel, could have been Mel – and at the eye of the storm, at the point where nothing mattered except the spasms in his groin, the full moon passed across the window and lit up the entire room. The white glow bathed his body and made him appear milky and pale. It seemed to draw out all his life energy, rendering him immobile and spent on the floor. As he lay, calmly gazing at the bright sky, Hugh noticed the regular pulse of a plane ticking through the night. He wondered if it was Jenna.

12

Cathan said he knew it was coming. With an expression-less face, yet wonder stirring in his eyes, he walked around the moonlit carcass of Jenna's Saratoga as if it was as familiar as his own reflection. And although Jenna was exhausted, night was the safest time to make the journey to the crashed aircraft. Brogan must not know of their presence.

'The visions, the dreams, they all make sense now.' Cathan smiled, breaking the solemn look that made Jenna wonder exactly what else he had seen coming.

'I've had her three years now. A damn fine aircraft and perfectly suited for short hop business flights to Europe, which is my mainstay these days.' Jenna halted herself. It was hope again, she remembered. Hope making her believe that she was back in modern Britain with a good-looking chap in fancy dress eyeing up her plane. Talking to Cathan about such things was useless although strangely, he seemed to be listening. Trying to understand, at least.

'I see things,' he said, sweeping his hand along the leading edge of the wing. He reached the tip, swung around and rocked the aileron. He knocked on the rear fuselage. 'Iron,' he said confidently. 'In the sky. Like in my dreams.'

Jenna nodded. She was impressed although she didn't bother to correct him about the iron. Had Cathan really predicted her arrival?

'And there was fire, too, and a great storm. I saw this on Beltane, our spring celebration. A celebration of new life.'

'That was when I arrived,' Jenna said, a drawstring of worry tugging at her brow. 'Brogan's people were having a big celebration and thought I was their Fire Goddess because I fell from the sky in a metal beast and I could have been killed and then he made his entire clan line up and they all –'

'Sshh . . .' Cathan had his arms around her. Her tears were absorbed by his long hair and her grief was swallowed by his embrace. 'All is well now,' he said softly. 'You are in the right place.'

Without looking up, without seeing the relief written on his face, Jenna knew he was right. Whether she got home or not, she knew that she could survive here. That roots were already starting to sprout from her predicament; that if need be, she would settle, love and be loved, and make a new home for herself here. With whoever loved her in return. She gripped Cathan tightly. Already, she felt at home.

'Look,' she finally said, sniffing and looking up at the Druid leader. He was a good deal taller than her, his body a long stretch of muscle wound around sturdy bone. Jenna could see that he wasn't a warrior type, like Brogan, but rather a swift hunter, a catcher of deer and fish – a planner and a thinker. On every level, the two men were different. Where Brogan would demand and take, at whatever cost whether financial or emotional, Cathan would coax and discuss, encourage and debate. And all this from knowing him such a short time. Already it felt like thousands of years.

'Look at what?'

'Druantia. See?' Jenna had already unlocked the aircraft and she lifted the lid of the wooden crate. 'Your beloved statue is returned!' She held out her hand and watched Cathan's face. He didn't smile as she expected, rather he looked puzzled.

'A container made of trees,' he remarked. 'But it is not my Druantia.'

Jenna turned and saw that the stone carving was gone. Perhaps the moonlight was playing tricks. 'Oh!' she gasped. 'It's been taken.' Futilely, she rummaged around the dark inside of the plane but knew she wouldn't find it. 'Brogan must have taken it!' And she knew that she'd probably never see it again. She slumped down and sat on the step. 'I'm so sorry,' she said, although really she should be apologising to her client in Dundee. If she ever got there.

'Don't be sad,' Cathan said. 'Druantia can look after herself. She knows she belongs to my clan and will return herself when she can. Whether it be now or in the future.'

'Such wise words...' Jenna stopped herself saying *from such a primitive man* because she truly didn't believe that he was primitive of mind. Not in the way that Brogan and his fellow warriors were ruled by their needs – whether their appetite was for sex or food or comfort or warmth.

'Come,' Cathan said, patting the side of the plane. 'Show me how this gets into the sky.'

'With pleasure,' Jenna said and it gave her an idea. What if she *could* get the Saratoga airborne again?

She walked around the aircraft, the lines of its body glinting in the silver light, hardly daring to mention the future, about how she had hit a freak tornado, about how her whole life had spun in a loose reel of film across the cockpit window as she hurtled to the ground through the vortex. Waking up on the hillside, taking her first breath of prehistoric air – although she didn't know it then – had made her the luckiest woman alive. If indeed she really was still alive. Maybe this was heaven. Or hell.

They sat inside. 'And this makes us go into the air. If

you push it forwards or pull it back, it makes the engine go fast or slow.' She felt like she was explaining to a five-year-old.

'Nothing happened.' Cathan had his hand over Jenna's on the throttle and had levered the stick.

Jenna laughed. 'The engine has to be running for it to work. And we have to be on a long flat piece of ground facing into the wind so that we can move forwards quickly before take off. Then, and only if we go fast enough, will we go up into the sky.'

Jenna studied Cathan's face. It turned through a kaleidoscope of wonder but there was no trace of him not understanding. She didn't know how an Iron Age man could find such a thing plausible. 'Well, that's assuming we have landing gear,' she added and got out to show Cathan the buckled metal and how the wheels wouldn't turn. 'No chance of going anywhere like that.'

Cathan dropped to the ground and cast his hands along the sheared metal. 'Arlen makes things from metal. He can mend this for you.'

'He can?' Jenna stiffened with hope. Would take-off really be possible? If she managed to get airborne, would she find her way home?

'But we will need to move your...' Cathan paused, frowning.

'Saratoga, aircraft, plane ... whatever,' Jenna said grinning.

'We will need to move your plane back to our village. It is heavy.'

'Very!' she replied. 'But look at Stonehenge. They managed that, didn't they, and that was several thousand years ago now.' Jenna noticed Cathan's blank expression. He obviously knew nothing of the stone circle at the other end of the country. 'We'll need long poles, from trees, and all the rope you have. Plus as many of your strongest men that are willing to help. It's not the weight of the plane that will be a problem, rather the uneven ground we have to pull it over.'

Cathan laughed again. 'Your excitement alone will move the ... plane.' He said the unfamiliar word like it was a rare treasure. To him it was. It had brought him Jenna.

'If Arlen can really fix it, there's a chance that I can get home. I *need* to get back. There are things to be taken care of.' Again there was that speck of doubt. A snowball at the top of a white hill.

'First, let me take you to my home.'

Jenna slumped onto the grass. She was exhausted and couldn't walk another step. She would bed down in the plane if necessary although that would be risky if Brogan and his men came back for more looting. 'I don't think I can walk another step,' she yawned.

'You don't need to,' Cathan replied and before she knew it, Jenna was hauled off the ground and was lying like a small child in the crook of his arms with her head nestling against his shoulder.

'You can't carry me back to your village,' she said. 'It's a long walk.'

'I'm not going to.' His lean body coped easily with Jenna's light frame. It also coped when her hair brushed against his face and her breast pressed against his heart. 'Home is wherever you need it to be.'

'Where the heart is, as they say,' Jenna mumbled as she felt her eyes closing.

She didn't know how long she'd slept but been when she woke she was lying on her side with a glimpse of the moon crazed through twigs and undergrowth.

'Where am I?' she said, not even remembering that she'd been with Cathan. The last couple of days mixed up in her mind like washing tumbling in the machine. Jenna tried to sit up but all her muscles ached.

'At home,' Cathan said softly and for a moment, Jenna

relaxed into a content state, truly believing she was in her bed in the flat in London.

'Home?' she said, finally managing to sit upright. 'No I'm not.' Looking around, all Jenna could make out were twigs and plants and mud and more twigs. 'Home to a rabbit or a fox perhaps but not my home.'

'Are you warm?' Cathan asked.

Jenna thought. 'Yes.'

'Are you hungry?'

'No.' Jenna recalled the salmon, the nuts and seeds.

'Are you frightened?'

Jenna shook her head. 'Not with you here, no.' It was the truth.

'Then indeed you are home.' Cathan wrapped his arms around her shoulders and eased her down. 'Your bed is soft and fragrant and I will keep you warm.'

It was true. The soft pile of plants that Jenna sank her aching body into smelt like the aromatherapy oil she put in her bath. 'Chamomile, rosemary, perhaps sage too?' She yawned and closed her eyes. She felt Cathan's body bedding down beside her and curl into the shape of her back so that he was wedged behind her like a warm protective barrier.

How can I be here? she thought. How can my life have changed so suddenly with no possibility of it ever being the same again?

'Cathan,' she whispered. An owl hooted from a nearby tree.

'Yes.'

'I come from a place a long way from here. Another time. I come from the future.'

'I know,' Cathan admitted. 'I have seen it. I tell stories to the children of our clan about creatures in the sky and great battles across the world and the bitter air that you breathe and that there are so many of you all living squashed in together.'

'You see all those things?' Jenna wanted to turn and face him but she was far too comfortable how she was.

'And more. The stories I tell are a warning. It is not a good place to live.'

Jenna smiled to herself. 'It's not that bad. I mean, we have running water and television and electricity and cars and pizza and cigarettes and because there are so many of us, you're never short of a friend.' She thought of her own assortment of friends. Mel had betrayed her and most of the others were too busy to see her very often. Mark was the only person she could count as a true friend. Always there, waiting.

'I still want to get back. It's my home, you see.' Jenna wondered at her reasoning. Did she really have warmth, food, comfort and safety in the modern world? Sure, she had food, as much as anyone could want. And for warmth, she only had to turn up the thermostat. But comfort and safety were hard to measure. Yes, she was comfortable – physically and materially – but did she have comfort in the truest sense of the word? And safety in the modern world was a lottery for everyone.

'Do you know how it happened? The time shift. Do you know how ... I fell ... over two ... thousand years ... through time?' But Jenna never heard Cathan's reply because she was asleep.

In the dream she was underwater. She was naked and she could breathe and her eyes were open. It was murky down there and so deep that even though she was trying to find the surface, she just swam and swam ever upwards, searching for a flash of sun, the silver ripple of the surface.

She looked back and saw the wreck. All crumpled on the bottom. No good to anyone now. She kicked her legs and swam on, not looking back. Only forwards, searching for what she knew was up there.

And there it was. A disc of silver shining like a coin through the skin of the water. The moon. The sky around it was indigo blue, turning the water into ink with its reflection.

One final kick and her face broke the surface.

She didn't gasp or splutter or scream or panic. Instead, she enjoyed the cool air on her wet head, the feeling of cutting across the water's surface to the edge. And she swam to where she knew he was waiting. Standing naked too, watching her as she pulled herself from the water. One body pressed against the other. The perfect fit as they locked together.

Even though she was drenched, the fire still burnt bright.

They took time to study their faces. Used the moments where clothes would have been removed to cast a spell, to map every detail, undressing their souls. He pulled his fingers through her tangled hair, separating every fiery strand so that it could dry. She grazed his body with her nails, memorising every bump and trail as if she was making a journey home.

They had never met in this life before.

She opened her lips to speak but when she did, nothing came out. Just water trickling from between her lips and when he kissed it away, he understood what she was saying.

I hear you, he replied from deep inside his head. And the narrowing of her eyes told him that she heard him too.

They walked hand in hand, soul in soul. They walked to a building. Its walls were tall and weathered and it was covered in moss and strangled by twisted ivy. The walls were hundreds of years old and had absorbed time and history. With their breathing urgent, they leant against the stone and blended in as if they were thousands of years old too. At first glance, the naked humans were nearly invisible – their skin wrapped in ivy and the colour of limestone. It was only the rooks that knew they were there, perched on the turrets a hundred feet above.

Her hands explored every inch of his body. He relished the feeling of her touch and grew in her fingers as she wound them around the part of him that couldn't hide his feelings any more.

He let out a deep moan and she saw it in his eyes. The green of them brightened as he lengthened.

'Do you want me?' she asked silently.

He didn't need to answer. He cupped her face in his hands and bent his head down to kiss her. It was a kiss that took away time. A kiss that restored all that was wrong in the world. A kiss that ensured, wherever they were, they would never be separated. Not even by thousands of years.

'Take me,' she whispered into his mouth.

Carefully and as if she was made of silk, he carried her inside the great building and up a winding stone staircase. There he placed her on a feather bed and rubbed scent on her skin. With her damp hair spread around her head like an orange veil and her skin as pale as alabaster, he pulled himself on top and slipped inside as if they were stitched together. The join was seamless.

A flutter of breath as he made the first exploration. As slow as time itself, he eased himself deeper until he could go no further. A little arc of her back told him he was home. A tiny twist of her lips told him she was feeling the same pleasure that ripped through him.

He pulled out. Just so the very tip of him hovered on her edge.

Then he fell deep again and lost his mouth on hers.

When they had finished, when they were a puddle on the feather bed, she opened her eyes just in time to see the rook flap off the stone window ledge. It had been watching them and now it had gone to tell the others.

Despite all the walking, Jenna's ankle was mending. The brisk walk back to Cathan's village seemed easy second time around, especially as they were to rally a team of strong, willing clan members to drag the Saratoga back to Arlen's fire. It was going to have new landing gear.

Jenna hadn't slept so well in a long time. The herb bed had seeped oils and smells that had transported her into another place. Her dreams had been wild. And her body ached not from sleeping in a thicket but from desire. A desire for something although she had absolutely no idea what.

She thought of her last night at her flat in London. It hadn't been a patch on the night she had just shared with Cathan. In fact, she could add up all the evenings of her life in London – pleasant and not so pleasant – and still the sum would come to only a fraction of the experience last night. The full moon, the lake, the hills, the salmon cooked on a fire, the breeze brushing her neck as she and Cathan sat with their toes cooling on the edge of the water – all of this was a small part of the few hours they had spent together.

He was an unlikely man in a bland wool tunic with hair that had probably never been cut but he had kept her entertained and enchanted for hours with his undeniable knowledge of the world. Anything more intimate had not been suggested yet she didn't think she could have got any closer to him.

'I have been travelling,' he said. 'To far away places and far away times.'

'Have you been to my time?' she asked. If she never returned, at least perhaps he could tell her what was going on back home.

'I have been through *all* times,' was his cryptic reply

and he told her of the trance state necessary before being able to travel.

'Can you teach me to go into a trance?' she had asked. 'That way, can I get home?'

It was the seed of a plan in Jenna's mind. A sceptic of all things supernatural and a strong believer in science – what else held her plane in the air? – over the last couple of days she had come to accept that almost anything was possible. If she hadn't, she would have gone mad already.

'To become a Druid, to be able to shapeshift and travel through time takes lifetimes of learning. It is something innate, a natural instinct although it can be aided by . . .' He smiled, trailing off, somehow unwilling to draw Jenna into considering shapeshifting.

'Aided by what?' she asked. 'You *have* to tell me. I am stuck, for whatever reason, over two thousand years back in history. I don't care if it's silly or doesn't work or is dangerous or even lands me in the Jurassic period. I just want to try.' Tears built again, like silver seeds.

Cathan sighed. 'There is a plant. We can make a drink. I give it to the younger Druids, when they are learning. It helps you to see where you are going.'

'Fine. I'll have some.' Jenna sniffed. 'Will it get me home?'

'It really is not that simple. You can't just drink it and wake up back in your familiar place. Besides, I think we will need the help of someone else.' Cathan stopped and stared directly at Jenna. She thought he was going to reach out and touch her. There was something in his eyes, something that suggested familiarity; similar to passing a stranger in the street and not stopping, even though there was a bond, unspoken.

'Who?' Jenna asked.

'Druantia. We need to steal the statue back from Brogan.'

13

Euan Douglas had lived his entire life at Carrickvaig Castle. As a boy, he roamed the estate first on foot and then, when he learnt to ride, he discovered new crags, new hills, new hideouts on horseback. Even now, as a grown man in his mid-thirties, he sometimes came across an undiscovered spot ideal for taking wildlife photographs – golden eagles, if he was lucky enough – or an uncharted spot for an autumn picnic to soak the last warmth from the sun.

If only he had someone to share it with.

These days, his home was continually full of people. Loneliness, in the truest sense of the word, was not an issue. Certainly a weekend never went by without the vast rooms of the castle being filled with the bubbling warmth of chatter, log fires and whisky. Guests came to the hotel from Britain, Europe and even as far away as the United States and Australia. Company was never scarce. Pick a nationality. Pick a look. Pick a size. Male or female? Chances were, someone would fit the bill.

But not for Euan. Not to fill the gap in his life that stretched as wide as the loch.

He urged his horse on along the track that wound around the edge of the water, the path sometimes dipping down to the shore, occasionally lurching into the deep woods that sat upon the east bank. The bay mare whinnied nervously as a crow flapped out of a tree and then continued on her steadfast path, carrying her owner to nowhere in particular.

Euan's mobile phone vibrated at his chest. Unusual, he thought. Reception was hard to come by away from the castle.

'Hello.' He held the reins in one hand. 'Hello?' The signal was poor. 'Rachel, is that you? Is everything OK?' He recognised the young woman's voice, her slightly turned-up London accent.

Euan pulled the reins gently and the mare stopped. She scuffed a hoof in the dirt and sidestepped as a rabbit darted from under a bush.

'OK, just calm down. I can't hear you very well so just sit tight and I'll be back at the castle in thirty minutes.' Euan snapped his phone shut and put it back in his shirt pocket. He clicked his mouth and turned the mare around, noticing her reluctance to go home so soon. 'Come on, old gal,' he urged. 'Something's up back at the ranch.' He nudged her sides with his heels and they were soon heading back to the castle at a gentle canter, as fast as the winding path would allow.

Hugh had Mel naked. It had been three hours, after all, since the sun had crested and he had eaten breakfast – how he had eaten! – and now, lying in the bath with Mel washing his balls, he was ready for sex again. It was a weekend away. He was allowed.

'Fancy a bit of deer stalking this afternoon?' He sloshed water over his face.

'Does it mean rolling around in the undergrowth with you?' Mel lathered up her breasts, paying particular attention to her dark nipples. Hugh couldn't take his eyes off them.

'Definitely. I'm up for a bit of outdoor activity.' She half-submerged her body in the huge spa bath and clamped her cleavage around Hugh's nearly full-grown cock. It was a perfect fit and with her arms fixed in place pushing her breasts forwards, Mel was able to slide back and forth and make Hugh's speech nothing but a useless slur.

'Something tells me you have a lot to get out of your system first, though.' She giggled as Hugh's face crumpled with every pull on his cock.

'I never want to stop fucking,' he moaned. 'I'm born to fuck.'

'Of course you are, darling,' Mel said, increasing the frequency. She wasn't sure whether to sit on him now or let him come on her tits. She could have asked Rachel to lick up the mess had she been around, but the inconsiderate girl had decided to go for a walk. She had looked quite distressed.

'I need to see more of you, Mel. Having you around on a more permanent basis would ... suit ... me.' Hugh's deep and quick breathing blew a waft of bubbles in the air. Imagine if he had her and Rachel both on-call during the day. He couldn't always rely on Jenna to be around when he needed relief.

'I'll be by your side whenever you need me.' It was music to Mel's ears and she blew an egg-white hillock of foam back at Hugh. She'd never come to terms with her best friend, Jenna, scoring one of the richest, best-looking guys in London.

Jenna. They had been at school together. Grown up together. Cried and laughed on each other's shoulders. Been to the same parties as each other. Snogged the same boys. Dumped the same boys. Borrowed each other's clothes. They'd even shared the same flat for a while. It was natural, it was right that they should share Hugh.

'It wasn't by my side that I was thinking of.' Hugh fumbled with the fleshy spread of Mel's breasts. They were perfect. 'On top of me would be better.' And as he imagined keeping Mel locked away in the small room adjoining his office, quite naked, quite ready and primed for action whenever he wanted her, he exploded a dose of semen almost as white as the bubbles onto Mel's neck.

'I'll get Rachel to draw up a contract, then,' he said and climbed out of the bath.

Rachel waited in the castle foyer. After fifteen minutes, when Euan hadn't returned, she walked outside and paced the large gravelled spread of drive that spilled out from the castle's entrance. Formal gardens stretched beyond with a central fountain spurting a greeting to visitors. She walked up to the circular stone ornament and peered into the water. A dozen or so Koi carp fanned easily around, one or two looking up, showing her their open mouths, expecting food.

'Rachel?'

She turned, hopeful, but her face betrayed her disappointment when she saw it wasn't Euan.

'Oh hello, Mark,' she said to the pilot. He wore jeans, a short-sleeved shirt and sunglasses pushed on his head. No sign of a uniform – pilot's or priestly.

'Nice to see you, too,' he chipped. 'Waiting for someone?'

'Mmm. Mr Douglas. Euan.'

'I saw him go off on a horse a while back. Is it urgent?' Mark dropped his glasses onto his face as the sun's rays spilled from the edge of a cloud.

'The receptionist gave me his mobile number and I called him. He's on his way back. And yes, it is urgent.' Rachel's face was a series of thin lines and she nibbled on the end of a forefinger. 'I'm worried about Jenna Bright. Hugh's fiancée. I'm certain that something's happened to her and Hugh doesn't seem to be bothered. He's more interested in . . .'

Rachel stopped herself. He was her boss. She was contractually obligated to him. She was his loyal PA and paid to be discreet. How could she tell Mark, a virtual stranger, about Hugh Vandenbrink's hobbies?

She continued. 'I went to see Euan last night in his private quarters. I explained about Jenna and how she's a pilot and also Hugh's fiancée. Euan found it hard to believe that Hugh didn't know Jenna was flying cargo up to Dundee and staying here for the weekend. It's a coincidence, I admit, but there's more to it than that, I'm certain.'

'Jenna Bright is a good friend of mine,' Mark said slowly. He was trying to piece this together. Why hadn't Hugh flown up to the castle with Jenna? Why had Rachel begged him so desperately to be their pilot for the weekend? What was Hugh up to with the two women and most of all, where was Jenna? 'The last time I saw her was at the airport and since then, no one's seen her. I spoke with traffic control in London and Dan said that Jenna left their traffic zone fine although he thought she sounded a bit stressed at one point but she denied this when questioned so he thought nothing more of it. Then his shift ended so he made no further contact.'

'I see,' Rachel said. Then, 'Call it gut instinct, whatever, I just feel that something's not right.'

'I'll do whatever I can to help. I'll check all arrivals with Dundee Airport but if she didn't land, then what?' Mark shrugged and linked eyes with Rachel. She was pretty, he thought, and determined – he remembered how she had secured his services when he'd spilled her coffee – and she was caring, in that she was obviously worried about Jenna. 'Maybe a prayer or two wouldn't go amiss,' he added but was interrupted by crunching gravel and a disgruntled whinny as Euan's horse reluctantly came to an impatient stop beside them.

'Rachel,' Euan said, sliding out of the saddle. He held the reins loosely. 'What's the matter?'

Rachel glanced at Mark and then turned to Euan. She

shrugged. 'I'm very concerned about the pilot who was bringing your statue to Dundee. Jenna Bright.'

'Like I said, Rachel, I'll check with Dundee this morning.' Mark spoke before Euan could reply. He placed a hand on Rachel's shoulder, making her turn abruptly. They both felt it: the little shock, the pinpricks in their hearts.

'Wait ... there's more than that. While I was eating breakfast earlier, I read this in the Sunday paper.' Rachel took a torn piece of newspaper from her bag and unfolded it. She handed it to Euan and when he had finished reading the story, he raised his eyebrows and handed it to Mark.

IRON AGE ARTEFACT WREAKS MODERN DAY HAVOC

An ancient stone carving, believed to be around two and a half thousand years old, has left a trail of disasters in and around London. Recently sold at auction for an undisclosed but substantial sum, the artefact listed in the catalogue as *Druantia* was offered for sale by its elderly owner after a series of mishaps that were believed to be related to the stone carving.

'The statue has no place in my home anymore,' explained the previous owner. 'From strange mists in the house to unexplained voices, illness and accidents, every phenomenon can be linked to the statue. My car was even hit by a truck when transporting the thing to the auction house. It's like it doesn't want to be owned by me. Besides, it's a vulgar object and I'm glad to be shot of it.'

Archaeologists believe that the stone statue is of great historical importance and would ultimately like to see the piece in a Scottish museum. Professor Gill Michaels, head of Celtic and Pagan Archaeology at the privately funded CRAIA Foundation in Edinburgh, said, 'Relics like this are rare. They are not for the super-rich to take a pot-shot on at auction. *Druantia* should be returned to her homeland of Scotland. She was an ancient fertility symbol worshipped by the Iron Age Celts and deserves the same respect that these people bestowed upon her.'

Druantia, the likeness of a naked woman in a provocative pose, stands approximately 24 inches tall and weighs around 25 kilograms. She is crudely carved from red sandstone, a rock commonly found in the Tayside region of Scotland. The relic was discovered in the nineteenth century and has been privately owned ever since.

Professor Michaels is sceptical about any remaining mystical powers of the statue. 'Iron Age man lived by the forces of nature. Fertility was as important to their way of life as eating and breathing. To believe that the statue has any supernatural residue would be a misconception. *Druantia* is a national treasure and as such, should be valued for the insight into Iron Age Britain that she gives us.'

Professor Michaels is keen to speak with the new owner about loaning the statue to a museum. The auctioneers refused to comment on the sale.

'Well, what do you think? They're talking about your statue, aren't they, Euan?' Rachel asked. 'Should we be worried?' She raised a hand to stroke Euan's mare on the white blaze that ran the length of her nose but the animal pulled away and snorted.

'God only knows. Literally,' Mark said, shifting from one foot to the other, unsure whether to be touched by the charge he felt when he put his hand on Rachel or moved by the article. In the end, he decided that both needed his attention. 'Let me make some more phone calls. We can't do anything until we know if Jenna arrived in Dundee.' He looked at Euan. 'Just what *is* it that you've bought?'

Euan shrugged and let his hands slap against his thighs. 'I only know that I had to have it. Druantia belongs here at the castle. I would never have known that it was for sale if my car hadn't broken down when I was in London a while ago and, while I was waiting for it to be fixed, I picked up some antiques auction catalogues. I had some extra rooms to furnish for the hotel.' Euan tightened his hold on the horse. She was getting restless. 'That's when I saw the statue screaming out at me to be bought. Whatever she cost, I wanted her back here.'

'Wow,' said Rachel. 'But what if it's cost Jenna's life?' She didn't particularly know her boss's fiancée. It was only from putting through phone calls that she'd ever encountered the streak of sincerity in her voice and it was only from the photo that used to be on Hugh's desk that she remembered the woman's pretty face, the intense eyes. Where the photo was now, Rachel hadn't a clue, but it wasn't on Hugh's desk anymore.

However, it was from Hugh taking possession of her body that Rachel knew most about Jenna. It gave her the most intimate insight into the other woman's life – having her husband-to-be on top of her, behind her, beneath her. Hugh was the common denominator and while in the beginning, Rachel was able to block Jenna from her thoughts, it was now becoming increasingly difficult to remain cold and detached about her duties.

Rachel didn't like the knot of guilt that was now firmly wedged in her throat.

'Hey, Jenna will be fine. She has to be.' Mark turned and walked a few feet away. He flipped open his mobile and dialled. As he spoke, he fiddled with the small silver cross that hung just below his throat. It was a gift from Jenna last Christmas.

Rachel and Euan waited while Mark made the call. The mare continued to scuff and Euan tried to figure out why his statue and its carrier might have gone missing.

'Finally,' Rachel said even though it had only been a couple of minutes. 'Well?'

Mark shoved his phone in his back pocket and sighed. 'It's not good news, I'm afraid.' He sighed, hardly having absorbed the information himself. 'Jenna didn't arrive at Dundee. In fact, none of the traffic control centres across the country have any record of her Saratoga entering their airspace that day. The only thing we know for certain is that she left London City.' Mark stared at the sky, as if Jenna might buzz overhead at any moment. 'After her last radio contact with London, it's as if she disappeared completely.'

14

Brogan was a happy man. He stood in the centre of his burgeoning clan and grinned proudly. Many of the women were with child, others were pairing off with the best of his warriors and he himself had spread his seed widely throughout the females. The celebration was building and would culminate with everyone taking part in a fertility rite with the reclaimed and powerful statue taking pride of place.

How Druantia had ever escaped their possession puzzled Brogan. True, he and his men had stolen it from the Caravye clan and guarded it fiercely when it wasn't being worshipped. Never before had his clan had such a powerful force among them – proven now by neediness and desire of his women. But how it had fallen out of their possession was a mystery. It was like the thing had a life of its own.

'Are you admiring your clan?' Iona came to his side. Brogan pulled her against him and felt the warmth of her ripe belly pressed against his naked torso.

'They are joyful,' he said. As he had instructed, Iona was wearing nothing but a slim piece of coloured cloth around her hips. Her breasts hung free and her dark hair fanned over them giving minimal cover. Brogan eyed her adoringly. All of the women in his clan were beautiful but none as defined and elegant as Iona.

'The women are ready,' she informed. 'Some of them have never been more ready.' She laughed softly and rested her head briefly on her leader's shoulder. 'Will I be with you tonight?' She stuck out her tongue and pressed it onto Brogan's nipple. Such a quick signal but one that warned his entire body of what was to come.

'Of course,' he confirmed. 'There is no one else.' Neither of them mentioned Cailla, who would, of course, be with Brogan but she would have to be prepared to share. What their leader wanted, he got.

As Iona went back to the women, to tell them that the procession could begin, she allowed the brightness of the fire – flames leaping high into the night sky – to burn the guilt from her mind. Stepping on Cailla's territory made her uncomfortable.

Drums kicked off the evening and two dozen of the most fearsome warriors danced and beat their way around the huge stack of blazing wood that lit the entire village from its heart. Painted up in indigo and orange and black dye, the pigments made from natural resources, the men were a formidable sight. The body markings – some depicting naked women, some reproducing sexual positions, some just abstract images that they had daubed on – rippled and flowed over the muscle beneath as they pounded out their desires to an increasingly frantic rhythm.

Brogan stood and watched as the women danced onto the scene. Horns and shrieks and excited voices blared loud, adding to the layers of music that flooded the village. He hoped all the neighbouring clans heard their celebration. If nothing else, he thought, Cathan would feel it in his bones; their celebration vibrating through the earth.

Laymar stepped into the heart of the spectacle. His face was barely visible beneath the thick woollen hood of the ground-length robe that he wore. He carried a length of twisted willow decorated with a hundred gleaming objects that spun and shone in the firelight. When he raised his arms in the air, the villagers gradually silenced and the only noise to be heard was the spitting of burning wood and the cattle scuffing the earth in their pens.

'We shall honour and seek the power of the north by calling upon the heavens and the earth. Hear our plea and bless us all.' Laymar turned half a circle and continued to speak. His voice resonated through the trees and blended with the forces that he called upon. 'I call to the south. To the heart of the great stag and the heat of the sun, I beg for your blessing.'

Brogan murmured similar words along with his clan. To his left stood Iona and to his right, dressed in a long pale dress, was Cailla. She wore tiny metal charms in her hair and had painted her arms and hands to match Brogan's body art.

Laymar completed the circle by requesting the blessing of east and west, of the hawk that hovers at dawn and the breath that delivers the clouds, of the fish in the sacred river and the power of the flowing water. Then, 'The harmony of our circle is complete.'

There was more singing and drumming and not even Brogan noticed the sleek line of Cathan and his men as they moved stealthily through the woods surrounding the village.

'I can feel it already,' Brogan said to the women by his side. Each of them looked up at him, questioning. 'I can feel the power of Druantia.' And instinctively he reached down to the knot of cloth that was girdled around his waist and thighs. He was growing hard already.

'May you take the hand of your loved-ones forever,' Laymar chanted. 'And may the gods bless you all with health from the wind, with food from the earth and passion from the fire.' Then the Druid bowed his head and made another blessing with the willow wand.

Brogan cocked his head and listened. A twig snapping nearby? A deer stepping cautiously through the forest perhaps?

More chanting and drumming led by Laymar and echoed by the villagers. They burst into further frenzied dancing and then there was silence again as Laymar progressed the rite.

The air hung heavy with expectation and Brogan was not the only male to have a hardness nestling beneath the cloth of his scant costume. The women's faces glowed from the orange light and their lips pulsed with anticipation. It truly was a powerful celebration.

Suddenly, Brogan turned. He glared out into the trees, now convinced there was something, someone, out there. His eyes were as sharp as a hawk's and his jaw clenched as adrenalin prepared his body. He reached to his side and slid the dagger from its sheath.

'Wait here,' he whispered to the women and he slipped off into the night.

Jenna watched Cathan ease his hand under his robe. She hadn't intended on spying although she'd suspected that he was as tight and pent up as she was. Trying to ignore the feeling that knotted between her own legs as she crouched outside his small roundhouse was impossible, especially now that she had stumbled upon this scene. She didn't think she should be watching but was equally unable to turn away. The way her body was behaving was inappropriate, out of character and likely responding to the primal lifestyle to which it was becoming accustomed.

Jenna knew that Cathan had also been tense all day, animal-like in fact, and it was the disappearance of the stone statue that had made him most anxious. Losing it twice to Brogan and his men was more than he could stand. And now he *needed* it back if he was to help her get home. It was the key to everything.

It was no wonder, then, that in the safety of his roundhouse, Cathan fell back onto a pile of furs and unhitched himself from the assortment of daggers and tools hanging from his waist.

He drank thirstily from a clay pot before finally sliding his palm under the thick cloth. It was at this point that Jenna had peered through the willow door to see if he was still awake. She'd wanted to talk. Despite her tiredness, she couldn't rest as she had been advised. There was an energy in the air, the promise of something powerful – perhaps even dangerous – about to happen. Being instructed to sleep when it was still perfectly light and with the impending assault on Brogan's village only a few hours away kept her as alert as a fox, even though her body wanted to fold in two and sleep for several days.

Jenna's mouth fell open as she saw Cathan delve under his clothing. She had never seen a man do this before – only Hugh when he was impatient and couldn't wait for her to undress. That was the thing with Hugh. It wasn't so much about *how* he made love to her as how quickly or how often.

Jenna refocused through the woven willow twigs and saw that Cathan had removed his clothing completely although the lower half of him was draped with an animal fur. Suddenly, Jenna's aching body – so tired from helping the men drag and roll the Saratoga back to the village – longed to lay down beside him; to curl herself behind him and bend to the shape of his back. The fur would reach across them both. The fire could be stoked for the evening. They could sleep in each other's arms. They could forget that she was lost and he was alone . . .

Jenna watched Cathan unravel his body piece by

piece and as his hand worked hard beneath the fur, she thought back to the very first time she had seen Hugh doing the same thing. It had shocked her.

It was a Sunday morning and they'd been out to dinner the night before. It wasn't a particularly entertaining evening, just some of Hugh's tedious clients, and it had ended with the expected fuck. Hugh demanding every inch of her body to service his needs. Hugh strapping Jenna's wrists together. Hugh taking her coldly from behind as if he'd just found her like this, waiting for someone to sink into the crease of her buttocks.

Jenna thought she enjoyed it – really, she did – but when she found Hugh early the next morning bent over a magazine, his entire body curved and tensed and pumped, she enjoyed that more.

He didn't know she was watching, which made her head spin way more than anything he could physically do to her body. Jenna could clearly see the magazine and its double page spread of naked beauties. Nothing that she could compete with in terms of implants and uplifts and airbrushing ... nothing that she *wanted* to compete with. But seeing her fiancé pulling himself hard, varying the length of his strokes as he turned the pages with his free hand, hearing the little grunts swell into louder growls as he came closer, was a bittersweet mix of excitement and anger.

Jenna, transfixed by the sight, wondered if this is how she would feel if she found him with another woman.

In another few seconds, Hugh was spurting over the pages. Large globules of semen dropped onto the breasts and faces and thighs of the posing beauties. From then on, if she was honest, Jenna knew that there would always be other women in their relationship.

* * *

She fell forwards, catching her hand on the willow door to steady herself.

'Who's there?' Cathan called. His voice was shaky from need.

'It's Jenna,' she said. 'I'm sorry to disturb you.'

'No, come in. I was just resting.'

Jenna went inside and stood at Cathan's feet. He was still wrapped in the furs but tried to appear as if he was on the verge of sleep. The hut smelled of wood smoke and musk – a man on the brink, a man holding back. Jenna looked away. 'Are you sure this is wise? To steal the statue back?'

Cathan sat up and beckoned Jenna to sit beside him. She did so tentatively but the closer she got to him, the more she realised how much she wanted . . .

She shook the thought aside. Hugh was her fiancé.

'It's too dangerous. Just for a lump of rock.' She sighed.

'Druantia belongs to my people. Brogan believes that he can take anything that he desires. He must learn this is not so. I have seen this day coming for many seasons now. Your arrival has confirmed my visions. We will make the attack tonight.'

Jenna sat thoughtfully on the edge of the straw bed, resisting the urge to pull back the fur; to run her hand up his slightly bent leg; to finish what he had begun. Again, she couldn't fail to see the similarities between Brogan and Hugh. Hugh took what he wanted without thought for the consequences just as Brogan had plundered Cathan's settlement.

'Besides,' Cathan continued. 'If you want any chance of finding your way home, you are going to need all the help you can get. It is my belief that Druantia brought you here so it's likely she will take you back.'

'You really think so?' Jenna looked around Cathan's hut. Mud, straw, willow, dust and fire. It needs a woman, she thought. Someone to share the straw bed. Someone to take the place of Cathan's hand.

She did want to go home, didn't she?

'Here,' Cathan gestured. 'Rest with me. I will need strength later.'

'I'm coming with you,' Jenna insisted. 'If it wasn't for me, you wouldn't be in this mess. I don't claim to understand what's going on here, with the statue and why it brought me here, but I want to help get it back and I think I have just the thing to secure its return.'

Then they slept. Jenna dreamt of Hugh, that he turned into Brogan, and she dreamt of herself, that she turned into a bird and flew home.

The shot rang clean through the night air and Cathan's men dropped to the ground. Jenna lowered the barrel and smiled. With this, she would be invaluable on the assault on Brogan's clan.

'What is it that makes such noise?' Cathan was by her side, running his hand along the slim metal and polished wood of the Browning.

'It's a shotgun,' she said. 'It belonged to my father. I was going on a shooting weekend so thought it would be good to try it out. I have a licence and...' Jenna stopped. Cathan had no idea what a shotgun was. He knew nothing of its potential and it was pointless explaining the chaos it contained. 'Taking me with you tonight will assure Druantia's return.'

She bowed her head briefly and felt guilt as Cathan stared directly down the barrel. Its danger was invisible to him as it would be for Brogan and his men. How would they know what it was until it was too late?

'Ready?' she said and Cathan nodded solemnly, signalling to his men that they should proceed.

The thin line of warriors – five of the best plus Cathan and Jenna – cut a brisk walk out of the village and into the night. If it wasn't for the moonlight, their passage across the undulating land would have been near impossible. As it was, the trek through the many forests slowed them down. And Jenna was exhausted from having made the journey several times already. Supervising the removal of the Saratoga from the hilltop had exhausted her just watching. But Cathan's men had been determined and finally hauled the Saratoga back to the village. Now, Jenna wasn't sure her legs would make the walk again.

The aircraft had initially refused to move – the landing gear having dug firmly into the ground on impact – even with over a dozen men harnessed to its body by thick, handmade rope. Then slowly, as they pulled, as their muscles tightened to hard bands and their teeth clenched white against their faces, the plane loosened its hold on the earth.

'Mind you don't damage the wings!' Jenna cried out in dismay as she witnessed several Iron Age men crawling over the body in order to secure more rope. It was like a scene from a movie set – the incredible disparity between semi-naked, prehistoric men and the grounded aircraft with its instruments and radio and new Sat-Nav system.

Then, with the assistance of wooden rollers cut from the straightest trees they could find, the clansmen manoeuvred the strange metal object back to their village. The promise of discovering what it actually was drove them on, as well as the warmth of the spring sunshine on their aching backs.

Now, covered in branches and leaves, the aircraft sat camouflaged ready for Arlen to heat and shape and fashion new landing gear for the Saratoga. Then, and only then, with the help of Cathan and Druantia, would Jenna have any chance of getting home.

'Listen,' Cathan whispered into the night. The men

stopped dead in their tracks. The core of the valley below them glowed orange from dozens of fires burning in the Dunlayth village. 'They are celebrating because they have the statue in their possession again.' He pulled his dark wool hood up over his head and his silver-green eyes flashed from beneath.

Cathan urged the men forwards; their stealth second only to a wildcat moving in for the kill. Jenna followed at the rear of the group, gripping the shotgun tightly, its barrel pointing at the stars. She trailed the scent of the men – their painted bodies virtually invisible as they skirted the undergrowth around the camp – until the drumming and the singing and chanting grew to a deafening stew of revelry and danger.

'You men create a disturbance when I give the signal. I'll locate the statue and we will carry it away.' Cathan gave his instructions.

It didn't sound like much of a plan to Jenna. She crouched in the trees and thick bramble growth and, as her gaze filtered around the scene, she caught her breath as Brogan came into view with Cailla and Iona standing beside him. They were watching the celebrations but for a moment, Brogan glanced around, as if he had heard or seen something in the trees. Jenna held her breath and only released it when he looked away again.

Then, as they waited for a chance, while Jenna watched the increasingly crazed dancing and antics of the Dunlayth people, Cathan and his men scattered silently around the village perimeter, each intending to storm the camp from a different angle. How so few men planned to overcome so many fierce warriors, Jenna didn't know and she was considering using the shotgun as a diversion when . . .

. . . the hand over her mouth stifled the scream that would have otherwise stalled the celebration . . .

Jenna thrashed and beat her fists on whatever had

taken her firmly from behind. The gun fell from her grip and she was unable to resist the force that sent her reeling backwards into someone's iron arms.

'You have come back,' the bitter, taut voice spat.

Brogan, she thought. Her mind was a battle-zone.

If she didn't escape, she would ruin everything. She prised her lips apart and bit down on the fleshy part of his palm. For a second, he loosened his grip and Jenna took the opportunity to scream for Cathan. Then in another second, Brogan had spun her round and forced his mouth down upon hers so that no noise except deep moans that he mistook for pleasure travelled up Jenna's throat.

She lifted her knee to drive into Brogan's groin but he caught it and wrapped her leg around his thigh. Strangely, it remained there and the will to fight back lessened with every plunge of his tongue into her mouth. Jenna glanced sideways at the shotgun, wondering if she could hook it into reach with her foot.

Then what? Would she shoot Brogan?

She felt her breasts being pummelled by rough hands and when one hand then traversed her leg, climbed up under her wool tunic, skimmed the tender flesh on the inside of her thigh and entered her without warning, the internal scream that deafened her mind was outdone by the loudness of pleasure that tore through her body.

'Lie down!' Brogan demanded and while Jenna was at the crossroads, where she could take the ram raid of her body, where she could endure the fierce invasion, she also remembered why she had come.

She obliged, lay down in the leaves, moss and dirt and spread out her arms. Her right hand was only inches from the gun.

'Tell me why you're here,' he demanded, pulling cloth away from his groin. Brogan's urgency was palpable, his determination as rigid as what sprung from beneath the cloth. Then he laughed. 'Appropriate then that you return during our fertility rite. Laymar's magic is so powerful that it has brought you to me.'

Brogan hovered over her, the glans of his erection dancing on the edge of her body as if it had its own sense of direction. Jenna felt the warm silk, the only tender part of him, nudge the moist entrance between her legs. Her muscles fought in a push-pull battle of wills between body and mind. Should she let him in?

In a flash decision, Jenna reached for the gun, dragged it across the ground and raised it in the air. Brogan, unaware of the danger, continued easing himself inside the reluctant woman.

The gunfire silenced everything. Brogan froze just as he had forged inside; the drumming stopped and the chanting turned to frightened murmurs as the echo ricocheted throughout the village.

Jenna fired again.

In a flash, Brogan had rolled off Jenna and was running for his life, stumbling through the leaves with his clothing dragging around his legs. Jenna stood and saw the clansmen all fleeing similarly.

She approached the centre of the celebrations, feeling the heat of the bonfire increasing and as she drew close, she gasped. There, standing upon a shaped lump of stone beside the fire was Druantia, her legs still wide, her mouth open and her crudely carved breasts poking up to the sky.

Jenna launched an assault of one shot after another, reloading when necessary and forcing Brogan's clan from the vicinity. Cathan took the opportunity to rally his men and recapture the statue while Jenna spun round and round with the gun, aiming at the stars, laughing wildly, wishing that she was firing at Hugh.

15

A ghost was no good, if that's what she was. Her transparency would make a thin veil of a wife and her whisper words rendered useless at making him smile when they cooked, watched a movie, rode through the glen.

This ghost would not make a good wife.

Euan woke suddenly, again, the pain of his erection more fearful than the woman who caused it. Reaching below the blankets, he felt his penis. Hard and hot, it stared back at him wondering where she was.

'Oh hell,' he said, flopping back onto his sweat-soaked pillow. 'Not again.' Euan stared up at the ceiling, foxed again by his own imagination.

The first time she had come to him was the night he had won the stone statue at auction. This was easy to recall because, in celebration, he'd had an evening of wine and friends and then, when they were gone, she came.

He thought someone had stayed behind but he didn't remember any of the female guests wearing such a crude sackcloth garment, least of all with rough sandals strapped up their legs. No, of the three women who had shared in his joy at winning Druantia at auction, none of them had dressed like that.

It was only a glimpse at first, maybe a reflection, a refraction, something in his eye or the lingering effects of the wine. The figure that stood in the bathroom doorway glanced at him briefly before disappearing inside. When he followed her in, she was gone. Just a faint hint of herbs in the air, which he put down to perfume from one of his guests.

That same night he stripped, cleaned his teeth, splashed water on his face. He looked in the mirror, noticing the flicker of a smile left over from the good news – at last the statue was returning to its homeland – and then he saw her again, standing behind him, pulling off that dress like she was glad to be free of the itchy cloth.

When he turned, his heart thumping, she was gone.

In the night, she came again and stood at the end of his bed. This time, he smiled at her and she stayed a while longer. Euan's erection hurt and she seemed to know this. Silently, weightlessly she approached him, the gossamer veil of her body gaining intensity as she came near. Up close beside him, he could see that she was completely naked.

'Shhh,' he thought he heard her say. Maybe it was the finger she touched to her lips that stopped him asking who she was. Maybe it was the narrator in his dream that told him not to speak.

The woman, her red hair seeming ablaze even in the dim room, pulled the blankets off Euan's naked, terrified body and clambered in beside him. The bed didn't move as she nestled against his goose-bumped body; no dipping of the mattress or waft of air from the disturbed covers. But the grip of her hand around his shaft was as firm and warm and tantalising as if she had been real. And really, who was he to say she wasn't?

Euan came in many paralysing spasms of relief. Every clench of his body was accompanied by a soft kiss or a whisper from the woman lying beside him. When it was over, when he lay still with sweat cooling his body and the moon passing across the ancient leaded window panes of his castle bedroom, he turned to kiss her but she was gone.

He sat up quickly and scoured the room through squinted eyes. This time, he thought she had been his for keeps but as usual, she was only the woman of his dreams.

Now, praying she would come again, Euan went to the kitchen. He stood leaning against the sink and drank the soft mountain water. She was coming more often, for sure, yet her visits seemed thousands of years apart. Euan's longing for the woman matched any he had for a real-life female. Love, marriage, company, children – all priorities high on his list until recently; until *she* started visiting. She was a distraction – she was *driving* him to distraction with her tantalising appearances. Euan was finding it hard to concentrate on anything else. And the permanent need his body had for the wisp of hers frequently stirred his penis at the most awkward times.

Unable to sleep, Euan put on his robe and went outside. The night was still, the air disturbed only by a gentle breeze that rolled down off the hills. The loch was still, too – a big black skating rink reflecting the sky above.

Then, without warning, there was a disturbance out on the water, as if something was struggling beneath the surface. Euan squinted through the night, relying on the moonlight to illuminate the strange scene.

His mouth fell open in shock as he saw her cut through the water in a clean stroke to the shore. When she reached the shallows she stood and waded to the edge, her path intent on him. Her naked body shimmered silver in the blue-grey light, her nipples standing proud of the gentle rounds of her breasts. The tiny patch of hair at the top of her legs glittered with water droplets.

She approached Euan and pressed herself against him, as if she was trying to walk through him. They were a perfect fit as her soaking body melded around his; around his heart.

Euan stared into her face, hardly daring to look at her in case she vanished again. He mapped every detail of her with his hands, undressing her soul, easing his fingers through the fiery hair framing her face.

In return, she dragged her hands over his body, reading and memorising his shape as if it held the key to his past and perhaps their future. When she opened her mouth to speak, nothing came out except water and when Euan kissed it away, he understood her perfectly.

'I hear you,' he told her in his head and he knew that she had heard him when her eyes narrowed and her lips upturned.

Then he took her hand and led her to the castle. He wanted to lock her away in the tower so he could keep her forever. But he didn't make it inside without stopping for another dose of her beauty. With breathing as urgent as the heat in his groin, he eased his mouth over her transparent mouth and for the first time, he thought he felt the warmth of her skin, the softness of her plump lips.

Their limbs and thoughts became as intricately entwined as the ivy that curled on the castle walls, their skin blending to the colour of the weather-faded stone. It was only the watchful crows perched keenly on the turrets above that even knew they were there. To the rest of the world, their coupling was an invisible folly.

'Do you want me?' she asked silently.

Euan didn't need to speak his answer as he lengthened against her thigh. He cupped her face and bent his head down to kiss her. It was a kiss that took away time. A kiss that restored all that was wrong in the world. A kiss that ensured, wherever they were, they would never be separated. Not even by thousands of years.

'Take me,' she whispered into his mouth, at which

Euan picked up the lightness of her body and carried her inside the castle. Once in his room, he put her on the bed and, moving so carefully in case she broke, he pulled himself over her alabaster body. As he slipped inside, they both knew that it was as if they had been stitched together for eternity. The join was seamless.

The flutter of her breath on his shoulder caused his back to tense as he eased deeper still. Her own back arced as he neared the top of her channel and her lips mirrored the pleasure she was feeling.

Then he pulled out almost completely and watched her face drop a couple of degrees to the brink of torment as the tip of his erection sat on the edge of her welcoming lips.

A second later, he fell deep again and lost his mouth on hers.

When they had finished, when they had come so that the ghostly pulsing of her delicate body pumped him as if she had been real flesh and blood, Euan noticed the rook flap from its perch on the stone window ledge. Then the woman dissolved into the bed and disappeared like ice melting in his hot embrace.

When he saw her again, even making allowances for the mismatch of her blue eyes and blonde hair, Euan instinctively knew that it wasn't Rachel or even her obvious desire for him causing the ghostly appearances. He'd rather hoped she was the one and he'd just overlooked it due to all the fuss about the missing plane and his statue.

Yes, Rachel was attractive, apparently available, alluring yet not overly so. She wasn't forcing herself upon him – as his ghost woman did – although he knew the offer was there, the door left a little ajar, just by the looks she gave him and the angles of her body towards him as she tried to hold the shotgun level.

'Like this,' Euan instructed. He could have wrapped his arm around her shoulder or brushed the strand of straw-coloured hair from her cheek. He could have widened her stance so that her thigh brushed against his or levelled his face so that their cheeks touched with the merest hint of sensation between them. 'Now squeeze the trigger until –'

The gun fired and Rachel staggered back. Euan caught her.

'Oh,' she scowled, gunshot still ringing in her ears. 'I didn't expect it to be like that. I really don't think I can do this.' She handed the gun back to Euan and slapped her hands on her thighs in defiance. 'Plus my mind's on other things. Like Hugh's fiancée disappearing and...' She trailed off.

'I've told the police everything I know about the woman including what I know about the auction house and the statue. It's up to them now to track her movements and locate her.' Euan sighed then raised his binoculars. Two roebucks stood perfectly still within a thicket after fleeing from the gunshot. The only sign of movement was the urgent flare of their nostrils as they breathed heavily from their flight. Four eyes glinted within the darkness of the trees.

Euan was hunting a human now, it seemed, as well as deer, and felt ashamed that he was possibly more concerned for the whereabouts of the priceless statue than its careless carrier. If he'd known how capricious the owner of Bright Charter was going to be, he would have never used the company. It was some consolation that the artefact was insured but to have lost something so precious before he had ever been able to hold it...

He breathed in heavily. Was it not the same with his ghost-woman?

Hugh and Mel blustered through the undergrowth, Hugh apparently in a fit of rage. Mel glanced at Rachel and shrugged. Both women knew why he was in such a foul mood. It had been nearly three hours.

'Bloody stupid deer struck off through the woods before I could even raise the barrel.' Hugh swung his gun precariously as he spoke.

'Best to keep it down,' Euan instructed, levering the barrel to the ground. Mel giggled and Rachel sighed.

'Not much chance of that, is there my darling?' Mel latched on to Hugh's arm which afforded a slight change in mood. The promise of something, perhaps.

'There were two deer here a moment ago but I scared them off with a useless shot. Thing is, I don't really want to kill them. They're so beautiful with their little furry horns and –' Rachel turned away. Shooting wasn't going to heal the hole in her heart. It would only make it worse.

'Maybe we should head back then. There could be news of the pilot and my statue.' Euan gathered his equipment. He had been out long enough with this amateur party and Callum, his estate manager, had taken another larger, more experienced group of hunters out into the hills. Besides, he had other things weighing heavily on his mind; things that haunted him with every turn of his head, every flicker of his eye or brush of the wind on his skin.

Euan was obsessed with a woman who didn't exist.

'So,' Rachel said as they walked back to the Land Rover. 'Are you or have you ever been married?' She didn't know why she said it. Probably a reflection of her own internal stew and Euan seemed as good a person as any to tell. She didn't mean for it to be such a leading question, rather a brief glimpse into the man's life than whining about hers.

Hugh and Mel lagged behind, dropping back several paces for every one that Euan and Rachel strode forwards.

'No,' Euan replied, nervously glancing over his shoulder. The others were almost out of sight. 'No, I've not met the right woman yet.'

There. Was that her? Crouched in the hawthorn? Her pale skin blending into the foliage like a spread of flowers?

'Sorry?' Euan knew that Rachel had spoken again. He just hadn't heard her. Something about failed relationships?

'Oh, nothing.' Rachel scuffed the rich earth as they walked. Looking for love was futile, she knew. It darted out of sight quicker than the roebuck at the first sign of a hunt. She'd be stuck with servicing Hugh for the rest of her life. 'Where *have* they got to?' Rachel asked, stopping so that Euan paused too. 'Hugh!' she called but there was no reply.

'Come on,' Euan smiled, taking Rachel by the arm. 'Let's go hunt them.' He grinned, determined not to let his obsession cloud every aspect of his life. Something was brewing, he felt sure of it, but spending all his waking hours thinking about it was only going to drive it away or him mad.

But Euan didn't get a chance to think any more about the mystery woman. Rachel had retraced their steps and was peering into a mossy thicket with her hand clapped to her mouth, presumably because what she was witnessing had caused her great shock.

'What?' Euan called out but he was silenced by Rachel flapping her arm up and down. When he approached, she turned to him wide-eyed with cheeks the colour of strawberries. She couldn't help the grin that worked from behind her hand.

'Oh my God,' she whispered slowly. 'Just look at him. Or actually, you'd better not.'

Euan peered through the hedge and brambles that separated a small enclosure from the track they had been following through the glen. He half expected to see a roebuck for the taking, as if Rachel had spotted one with a target ready imprinted on its rump. But the rump in question was not that of a deer. It was Hugh's and it was pumping for all it was worth up Mel's own behind as she bent over a tree stump.

Euan turned away. His eyes strained wide at the sight too, preventing him from speaking. He'd never seen anyone do that before. In fact, he'd never witnessed another couple actually having sex, let alone like that.

'Huh,' Rachel said indignantly, crossing her arms. 'He didn't ask me if I wanted to play.'

Euan raised his eyebrows. 'Wanted to play?' He wasn't sure what she meant.

'It's my job. Until *she* came along.' Rachel had tried to keep her bitterness concealed. 'But now, with Jenna disappearing and Mel on the scene, it doesn't seem right anymore.' She sighed but in spite of her feelings, she still turned back for another look. She noticed Euan's fascination, too.

'Good God, look at him.' Euan glanced at his watch. 'And you said he's getting married soon? I pity his fiancée then. No wonder she's disappeared!' Euan laughed but then silenced himself as he saw the length of Hugh's enviable erection draw slowly in and out of Mel's accommodating arse.

Rachel pouted then kicked herself for being so brazen in front of a virtual stranger. She'd blown it now with Euan anyway, she realised, so she might as well reveal her true feelings. 'I'd never been with another woman before we came here. Mel was my first.'

Euan frowned. 'You mean, you and her . . .' He pointed between the two, catching sight of Mel's breasts squashed in Hugh's demanding hands. What if the other hunting party stumbled across them? His business would be scandalised. 'Will they be long?'

'Doubt it,' Rachel replied. 'Hugh has this need. If he doesn't get it every few hours he's a complete sod. It's always been my job, as his PA, to satisfy his desires. I believed that I'd been saving his fiancée, Jenna, the trouble so she could enjoy the other, more loving side of him. But he doesn't seem to have one.' Rachel sighed. 'Now I realise I've just been a bitch. The poor woman needs telling. That's her best friend he's fucking.'

They both turned just as Hugh came in the clean-shaven seam between Mel's buttocks. Then, dutifully, he knelt down to lick up the mess he had made. Within a few minutes, Mel was writhing on the log as she somersaulted through orgasm.

Euan walked away as Hugh zipped himself up. Rachel followed and they heard Mel's frivolous giggles in the forest behind as they marched back to the car, each of them caught up in their own private thoughts about ghosts and true love.

Mark was tetchy. His nails curled into his palms as she spoke. She stood prettily outside his door so that arguing was futile. He'd bent over backwards to help them and now he was being tested to the max.

'He'll pay whatever you want plus your room can be upgraded now that some of the hotel guests are leaving.' Rachel gazed at Mark Maloney. He was dressed in his pilot's uniform and his overnight bag was packed.

'Dundee and back, you said. For the weekend. It's Monday tomorrow.' Mark's face was blank. 'I have other work to do, you know.'

'I thought he was all-forgiving?'

'Who?'

'God,' Rachel said, wishing she hadn't. It was hardly Mark's fault that Hugh wanted to stay another night.

'Look, come in and let me make a phone call or two. I

might be able to get someone to cover.' He pulled his phone from his flight bag. 'Any news about Jenna yet?'

Rachel shook her head. It might help him decide to stay, she thought. It was a coincidence that they were good friends. Surely, if by staying another night, Jenna was found either in Dundee or at the wrong castle then it would be worth the inconvenience.

As an afterthought, Mark dialled Jenna's mobile number. It must have been about the tenth time that day.

'Strange,' he said, glancing at the phone's screen. 'I've been getting her voicemail but it crackled with static this time, as if it was trying to connect but couldn't quite.'

'Must be poor reception here.' Rachel shifted from one foot to the other, glancing up and down the pilot's long, lean body.

'Nope. Full reception. Look.' He handed the phone to Rachel but she didn't take it. She was too busy staring at Mark and his undeniably sexy uniform. He felt uncomfortable from her intense stare. It was as if her eyes didn't belong to her, the way they pored over him.

'I just don't get it,' she said slowly, tipping her head to the side and licking her lips. Hugh would kill her but she couldn't help herself. Too long she had been his plaything. Too long she had ignored her own feelings and desires. What if she used all her experience to take what she wanted – another man who was willing to succumb to needs that she was gradually realising had never been satisfied.

'Anyway,' he continued, removing his jacket. 'Staying another night won't be a problem. You can tell Hugh we'll fly back tomorrow evening. I'll let the airport know.'

'Wrong thing to do and say,' Rachel suddenly blurted, advancing on Mark with her eyes still boring into him.

'How come?' He sidestepped the woman and ended up sitting on the bed.

'And wrong place to sit, too,' she said, diverting to the bed. 'Why not just admit that you're attracted to me. That's why you *accidentally* spilt my coffee at the airport last week. Just to give yourself a chance to speak to me.'

Rachel eased Mark's legs apart with her knee and wedged herself between them, leaning on his shoulders so that her breasts were level with his mouth. 'Really, you shouldn't have taken your jacket off or mentioned that we have another night in the hotel. And as for getting on the bed . . .' She smiled, wanting her desire to seep slowly over Mark although she had a feeling her forwardness was already flooding him out.

'Oh, no, really. You've got the wrong idea about –'

'I don't think so,' Rachel said. 'That's your other uniform talking, the robes, the collar . . . I want Mark the pilot, the sexy man with his gold-trimmed cap and aviator sunglasses and –'

'Whoa,' he said, raising his hands to halt her. They landed on her hips and Rachel took this as a sign to lower her mouth onto his. Mark gave a little push with his hands but somehow all his strength was lost.

'You see, you like it,' she teased, planting little kisses on his chin.

Rachel felt giddy from the power of her own assertion but the best bit was that she could take him guilt free. Aside from God, Mark Maloney belonged to no one.

16

Jenna drew in the dirt what she was trying to explain to Arlen. He didn't understand many of the words she was using let alone technical terms referring to the aircraft. But, having scratched out a crude diagram of how the Saratoga was now and how she wanted it to look, Arlen nodded and stoked the fire with charcoal that had been previously made in a soil and turf clamp.

'That's it,' she guided as Arlen chopped and hacked at metal bolts on the landing gear. 'You need to remove this part here in order to access . . . yep you got it!'

Jenna admired Arlen who seemed to instinctively know how to work the metal, whether it was glowing red from the furnace, or cold, painted and cast in a factory two and a half thousand years in the future. His fingers worked intricately yet there was plenty of muscle available when it came time to lift the heaviest part off the aircraft. Arlen and several of the village's strongest men had previously shored up the plane on a wooden rack to hold it steady during the repair.

'I have never seen anything like this,' Arlen commented. It was the first thing he had said about the aircraft or indeed, Jenna's arrival. Had Cathan primed them and explained enough that they accepted her presence? She could only assume this was so.

'You wait,' Jenna grinned. 'When it's all fixed up, I'm going up there in it.' Jenna pointed to the sky through the chimney hole in the roof. Arlen briefly glanced upwards then continued heating the fire in the roundhouse furnace until Jenna could no longer stand to be inside. She went out into the daylight.

'It's so hot in there,' she said to herself. Her spirits were good, especially since the successful recovery of Druantia. Home was flickering on the horizon.

Cathan approached her, a serious look to his face. 'My clan are grateful to you. The women are joyous that Druantia is among her creators again. Our ancestors carved the goddess's likeness from stone. To lose her forever would be like losing one of our own. Thank you.'

Cathan placed a hand on Jenna's shoulder. They both felt it. Not the warmth of his palm or the gentle curve of bone beneath her rough tunic. Instead, they felt the link that surged between them, as if they had always known each other and always would.

'Lift the veil and you will see what I do,' Cathan said cryptically. 'There's nothing to be scared of. Everything is as it's meant to be.'

'I don't understand,' Jenna confessed. Her life may have been filled with technology and over three decades of fast-paced living but when it came down to it, she realised she understood little about the universe.

'It's simple. I know you. I have always known you.'

'Really?' She looked up into Cathan's unbearable green eyes, framed by golden eyebrows and skin that had been dappled by the elements. 'How can you be sure?'

'We are together in my dreams, my travels. I knew that you would come to me one day.'

'Whoa,' Jenna said, stunned. Could he be right? She would believe anything now. And what of the twinge in her heart that connected to the tips of her breasts and the little nub between her legs? Was the ache she felt there anything to do with what Cathan had told her?

'And one day,' he continued. 'We'll get it right and

meet in the same life.' His hand still rested on Jenna's shoulder.

'Why, I mean, how ... will that be getting it right?'

'You don't know?' Green eyes hard and glassy against the cerulean sky.

But Jenna knew. As the swelling in her heart displaced her other organs, her thoughts, her rationale, Jenna knew exactly what Cathan meant. 'Maybe we will,' she suggested. 'But how will we know if we walk past one another in a supermarket or I accidentally bump your Toyota while parking or –'

'We'll *know*,' Cathan assured. 'Trust me.'

And she did.

It puzzled Jenna all day. She went with the women – several bursting with child – to gather nuts and seeds and nettles and root vegetables growing wild. In the end, she asked one of the women.

'Why is Cathan alone? Why doesn't he have a wife?'

They glanced at each other. It seemed as if they knew but didn't want to say. They carried animal skin pouches over their shoulders, which bulged with wild garlic, nettle and dock leaves. Jenna had promised to show them how to make a special kind of unleavened bread. It seemed they hadn't considered using garlic and wild herbs in their dough. She thought of her own diet, suddenly ashamed that it frequently consisted of take-outs and meals for one microwaved in the box. The health of these people shone through their skin.

'Cathan is waiting,' a pregnant woman called Evina told her.

'For what?'

'We think –'

Another of the women gripped Evina's arm to silence her.

'You think what? Tell me.' Jenna placed her bag of food on the ground. She wiped her face on her sleeve. It was hot today.

Evina sighed, pulling away from her friend. 'I think that Cathan has been waiting for you. That's what I believe. He has described your visit for many years now. It means much to him that you have come.'

'Really?' Jenna was stunned. If there was reason behind all this, it would help her come to terms with what had happened to her: that she may never actually go home again. She wafted the skirt of her thick dress. She was sweltering.

'Shall we go to the lake to bathe?' It was Evina's idea.

The great expanse of water was cool satin on Jenna's skin. The four women stripped and waded into the depths, taking their dresses with them to wash. The cloth would soon dry spread out on a rock.

Jenna let her shoulders slip beneath the dark water. A shudder ran up her spine and not entirely from the spring chill of the water.

Had Cathan really been waiting for her? It rang true with everything he had already told her, based on his dreams and visions. One thing was for sure, Jenna wanted to know more about his precognitions.

The other three women laughed and splashed with Evina being carefully floated in the water so that her round belly protruded into the air. They took turns to hold her while the others caressed her stomach.

'It won't be long now,' one said. 'I can feel your baby is ready.'

Jenna smiled. She dearly wanted children in the future. She sculled on her back, staring up at the deep blue sky, wondering what mini-Hughs would be like. That was when she went under and came up coughing with a disturbing vision of her future.

'Oh no!' she cried out. It couldn't happen. Then she

felt the firm hands on her shoulders. She was being pulled deeper through the water.

'Relax,' Cathan said and so she did. 'See the island out there?'

Jenna turned and squinted to the centre of the lake. 'Uhuh.'

'Let's swim. There's something I want to show you.'

With Hugh fresh in her mind – however far away through the ages he was – and Cathan's wet eager face beside her, the dissimilarities between the men were enough to illuminate her mind.

Jenna did not want to marry Hugh.

They reached the island after a gentle twenty-minute swim. Jenna was grateful of the sessions she allowed herself at the sports club otherwise she wouldn't have been able to keep up with the naturally lean man who cut an easy passage beside her.

'It's beautiful here,' she said, walking heavily up the pebbled beach.

'It is my retreat. The others know not to come here. They respect it as my private thinking place where I dream of my clan's future and well-being. I ask the gods and goddesses for inspiration.'

Jenna walked up to a miniature hut made of hazel and turf. She peered inside and smiled at the straw bed, the fire pit filled with the remnants of a blaze, metal pots of herbs and smoked meat hanging from the low roof. Even two and a half thousand years ago, a man liked to have his own shed.

'Everything was floated across on a raft. Sometimes I stay here for days. Just thinking.' Then Cathan went into the little house and, to Jenna's surprise, he came out naked.

She gasped and turned away. 'You, you ... haven't got anything on.'

Cathan came right up to her and looked her up and

down. 'Neither have you.' He laughed out loud when Jenna's eyes went as wide as the pebbles underfoot and she grabbed for the wet cloth Cathan had set out to dry. She pressed it clumsily against her front and even though she was shivering as the water evaporated off her skin, something warm swelled inside her. Cathan had laughed.

Jenna felt silly, happy, angry and sad all at once but most of all – and this confounded her the most – she felt so at home with Cathan, as if she had lived in Iron Age Britain all of her life and that her memories of the modern world were nothing more than drug-induced fanciful visions. The belief was starting to become her reality.

'You are cold.' Cathan saw the goose bumps on Jenna's arms. He stepped forwards, arms outstretched, as if to hug her but when Jenna glanced at his groin, the stirrings of which gave his intentions another meaning, Jenna retreated. For him, being naked was as natural as eating.

'Come inside and let's make a fire.' Cathan led the way into the small hut and they both sat on the straw and fur bed. There was no room to stand.

'That's better,' Jenna said, trying to make light of the crackle of electricity that bounced between them. Already she felt warmer, as if she was nestled next to his heart. In his hut, she truly felt as if she was.

Cathan raked the ashes in the pit with his fingers and then worked a stick and twine and dry grass to make a fire. Jenna was fascinated. Everything she had ever learnt in history lessons or seen in films and documentaries was here in front of her. Perhaps she would write a book about her experiences when she got home. If she got home.

'Cathan, there's something I don't understand.' Jenna

pulled a fur around her shoulders. She was still chilled from the swim, despite the warm day. 'If I take Druantia in my aircraft and I do manage to fly into the future, then you will have lost your statue again.'

'That is where you are wrong.' Cathan's shoulders and arms rubbed hard and fast and in seconds the grass caught light, spreading to the surrounding twigs that he had fanned around. 'Because I am coming with you and I will be able to bring Druantia back when I return.'

'You're coming with me?' Jenna had hardly dared suggest such a thing and her heart skipped with joy although quickly saddened at the thought of him returning to his time. 'If we make it, why don't you stay with me? I could show you so much and –'

'To speak of such things, to change the narrow passage of time as it slips between the ages would be to throw all of our lives out of their true path. Just remember, sweet Jenna whose mind is faster than the wind, that everything is as it should be. Remember my words whenever you doubt the strength of the universe. The power of nature will pull us together and everything will be, as always, as it should.'

Jenna didn't speak a word for nearly an hour. She sat, staring into the flames, seeing visions that if she blinked, would burn and be replaced by others.

She saw Hugh and Mel, their naked bodies hungry and ravishing and wet with desire as soon as her own back was turned. She saw female clients and Hugh's PA and even a delivery woman all with their legs spread and their neat little packages calling her fiancé to take a taste.

Jenna saw herself, alone, flying her plane. She saw Mark, thankfully happy and ... married? She squinted with sadness as the flames dished up yet another vision of her crooked and unsatisfying life back home.

It was only when Cathan handed her a small metal cup of something he had brewed on the flames that she blinked out of her reverie and took a deep breath.

'I was miles away,' she said, realising she should have said centuries away. 'I want to go home but I want to live like you,' she admitted, wondering why her mind was screaming *with you* instead of like you. 'My life seemed good when I was in it. I loved Hugh, honestly I did. But being here, away from him, with you and your beautiful clan . . .' She trailed off and took a sip of the brew. It tasted bitter, caught on the back of her tongue. But then she took another sip as the aftertaste appealed to her. 'I can see what's wrong. I can see what I should do except . . .' Another sip, searing her throat and mind. '. . . except you're here and this is your home yet why do I see us together, even though we never can be?'

Jenna wanted to cry – tears of relief – but she couldn't. Her eyes were dry and her mouth was, too. 'What is this?' she asked, holding the cup out.

'It is an infusion of the plant that I told you about. The one that can help you to travel. You will fly, if you are fortunate.' Cathan drank the same brew from another vessel.

'Let me see the plant.' Jenna's heart started to race, not from worry because she trusted Cathan's knowledge of herbs and plants. No, something else caused her heart to flap and beat behind her ribs as if was about to jump from her throat.

'I steeped the leaves in water and simmered it on the flames. Just relax.' Cathan held up a bunch of wilting leaves. He had obviously picked them on a previous visit to the island.

'*Deadly nightshade,*' Jenna whispered, fear constricting her throat as she recalled her mother warning her of the plant as a child. She had grown up in the countryside and it had been her job to check the hedgerows for poisonous plants so the horses didn't get sick. 'This is such a poisonous plant...'

She was about to tip the drink onto the ground but her vision went hazy and her eyes transformed into those of a crazed animal. 'What's happening?' she whispered.

Jenna was aware of Cathan talking to her but all she noticed were his huge black eyes set in a thin halo of green. His pupils had dilated so much she thought they would burst. And when she stared at the bright flames, she squinted and looked away. Her pupils had become fixed open and sensitive to the light.

'Don't be scared. Here, hold my hand.' Cathan reached out and took both of her hands in his.

'Oh!' she gasped as his touch needled through her. All of her senses were on red alert and so quickly after tasting the drink.

'The amount is so small your body will survive the effects. I will not poison you.' Cathan's voice was as warm as the flames and Jenna trusted him completely. What else could her dissolving body and mind do?

She sipped more of the liquid, eventually draining the cup. Following her instincts, she ventured out of the hut where the fierce sun made her eyes screw into slits. Aimlessly, she wandered around the tiny island, circumnavigating it in a few minutes. The cloth she wore around her hips had come loose and fallen off but Jenna didn't notice or care.

'Where am I?' she sang, squinting through the brilliant blue day, pretending she was a bird.

And indeed she was, lifting off in a familiar trajectory, watching the earth fall away as she rose through the wind. Her controls were her feathers and her compass her nose. She soared way above the little island, watching the familiar dot of Cathan staring up at her, before allowing herself to swoop within feet of the lake's surface before pulling up high again.

This time, Cathan was beside her, his strong arms powering him through the air. Silently, in their heads, they talked of all the times past and all the times to come. Cathan told her that the future would be theirs and their love would always be in the present. For he did tell her of his love – as if she didn't know it – and she sent back hers, enough to last them thousands of years.

'Whoa,' Jenna said, curling onto the wet sand where the ripples from the lake lapped at the island. 'Get that . . .' She didn't understand her own words. All she knew was that her heart was ticking like a bomb and her head was filled with all of her life at once. 'We were flying.'

'Indeed we were,' Cathan confirmed. He seemed calmer, more experienced, and lay down beside Jenna, the sun on his shoulders, his hands on her flat stomach.

Somehow it was entirely natural for them to be lying there, naked, peaceful yet excited by all the potential the universe contained. 'It is a good sign. You respond well to the drink. Soon, we will take more. Our journey has only just begun.'

'Will I be able to get home?' Jenna heard these words but didn't recognise them as her own. She saw hands sweep up her stomach to her breasts but didn't know that they belonged to Cathan. In her mind, she was being touched by the hands of her lover – the lover she had always had, throughout life after life after life. In her heart, she already was home.

'I think with Druantia and your plane of the sky, we will re-create the perfect conditions to try. The rest is up to you. How much you want to get home.'

Jenna felt the stirrings of confusion in her hazy mind. No, she didn't want to go home because that would mean leaving Cathan. But he belonged here and she belonged there. Besides, she wanted to tell Hugh face to face that she wouldn't marry him in a thousand lifetimes. She was being torn in two . . .

Cathan's mouth came down upon hers and she had no idea what the soft probing of her mouth was until she registered the same feeling between her legs. It was like her mind and body had a time lag; she saw one thing and felt quite another.

But what she saw, she liked. And what she felt, she wanted more of. This man, this intelligent, sacred, trustworthy man, approximately two and a half thousand years younger than her, was adoring her body as if he had never seen a woman before.

'It was you in my dreams. I knew you would come.' This was his mantra and he used it over and over as he devoured Jenna's body. No part of her was left untouched and their union felt as natural as the way they soared in the sky.

They were eagles again, riding the thermals above the undulating hills. They skimmed over glassy lakes and followed the glittering snake of a river until they reached the sea. They perched on a rock, wings brushing and their eyes locked in a knowing tangle of understanding. Then off again, covering the land at a speed that stole their breath.

When they landed back on the island, he was inside her, her face a portrait of pleasure and agony that this would be their one and only time. She engulfed him, vowing never to let him go, trapping him in her body greedily like a wolf would guard its prey. And she bared her teeth, her eyes flashing orange at her mate as he plundered her body. Her claws dragged down the thick fur of his back, ravaging the skin beneath. He howled as she turned, broke free and ran, glancing back only to check he was following.

They ran through the forest, their noses close to the ground, ferns whipping their long faces. Side by side, they tore across the countryside, leaving a trail of their needy scent that would linger for lifetimes to come. Finally, she came to rest and he mounted her again, feeling the curve of her spine, the undulations inside her as he rode his female.

Jenna felt the sand grinding against her face as Cathan heaved her buttocks into a position that allowed him to reach the very core of her. Before he entered, he pressed his lips against the soft periphery of her sex, mapping her folds, memorising her taste so that it would last him through the years. He nibbled carefully on the bud that he would soon work with his fingers, making her want to escape from the unbearable pleasure yet demand all he had.

The water lapped around Jenna's legs and stomach as Cathan entered her body again. They were swimming, following the warm currents to oceans they had only dreamt of. They were silver and sleek, their tails a mass of power as they coursed through the black water. They swam in formation, him curling over and around her while she flicked him gently with her tail, making him hers forever.

Finally, at the end of the ocean, they came to rest, knowing this was where their journey finished. They flippered out of the water and lay together on the coarse sand and pebbles, drying, sweating, panting in the hot May sun.

'I love you,' Cathan whispered into Jenna's soft auburn hair. 'I will always love you.'

Jenna turned and sank between her lover's thighs, allowing the warm skin to brush her cheeks. She took him in her mouth, deep at first then lightly, hardly touching, her head spinning and her eyes rolling from the strange drink.

As Cathan slipped inside her once again, Jenna found that she could see into his mind. She wondered if he could see into hers. That's when she saw the storm, a vortex of swirling grey, tucked right at the bottom of his thoughts – so similar to the storm that brought her to him. Had he masterminded her time-travel? Had Cathan longed for the woman of his dreams so much that his yearning had bridged thousands of years?

Her belly ached first, a deep, intense pull that drew her stomach inwards. She opened her eyes and gradually focussed on the face above her. By the look in his eyes, he'd been trawling the depths of her mind too.

Then her sex fastened around Cathan's hardness, causing him to stop briefly as he worked himself to their one and only climax. From this moment on, every fibre in their bodies entwined, joining at cell level to ensure their connection lasted for lifetimes to come.

As he emptied hot bursts of his soul into the woman that had haunted him throughout the millennia, he pulled her close to his heart. 'I will be with you always,' he whispered as Jenna wavered through the final hold of her climax.

Then, as they lay side by side, Cathan took off one of two rings that he wore. 'I had Arlen make this for you. To match my own. Take this home with you and then you will always remember me.'

Jenna allowed him to slip the ring onto the finger where soon Hugh would be placing the gold band that had been custom-crafted by one of London's top jewellers. It was nothing compared to the intricate bronze ring that she now wore – a delicate spiral atop a circle of Celtic script.

'It's beautiful,' she said and kissed him on the lips.

Before they fell asleep, they held hands; Jenna gazing at each of their rings, studying them intently.

And when they awoke, Cathan said the time was right for Jenna to go home.

17

The sex was the best ever. Admittedly, Rachel's experience revolved around Hugh and the couple of lovers she had had before working for Vandenbrink Holdings were unmemorable. But this was unique, as if she'd discovered something she suspected existed all along but was never quite sure.

Hugh, if he found out, would kill her.

Mark's body made her wonder if she was in a dream and his tentative, unsure mannerisms lit a fire deep inside Rachel that Hugh's overbearing lovemaking had doused regularly. With Mark, Rachel was in control, deciding what went where and for how long. The highlight was dressing him up in his church robes – he'd brought them with him so he could change at the airport once back in London – and telling him to pull himself off with the tapestry curtains wide open so that anyone outside would get a wonderful view of the vicar and his compliant cock.

Rachel had never been more excited. She masturbated as she sucked him off, taking ripples of pleasure as he tried to stifle moans of passion. A man of God succumbing to her!

But the part that Rachel would always remember was binding his wrists and ankles to the bed, something she had only ever been the victim of rather than the perpetrator of, and watching the fear in Mark's face as she chewed and bit and licked and tickled and rubbed off all over his stretched-out body.

And he was nice, too. He asked her on a date when

they returned to London and promised they would hook up with Jenna – if they ever found her – with a guaranteed passage to redemption and forgiveness where Hugh was concerned. They both agreed Jenna was better off without the man and both promised to dissuade her from going through with the wedding.

After Rachel had come four times and Mark nearly as many over several hours, they washed, dressed and decided to file a missing persons report.

'She always calls me. Always replies to my text messages and voicemail.' Mark tied his shoelaces and put on a black jacket to go with his black trousers, black shirt and white dog-collar. He thought perhaps the police would take more notice of them if he was dressed like this.

They found Hugh and Mel having drinks in the bar. Mel was sitting provocatively and, judging by the way Hugh wrestled with the bulge in his trousers, she had been speaking provocatively too.

'We're going to the police to lodge an official missing persons report,' Mark said. He didn't like Hugh one bit but owed him this. Jenna was his fiancée after all.

'Well make sure they find her, dammit. I hate losing things. Stupid selfish woman's probably gone off on one because I didn't get the right prawns or cutlery for the wedding reception. You know what women are like.'

'I know very well what Jenna's like,' Mark retorted. 'And she wouldn't do this. She wouldn't disappear without telling anyone. I'm concerned her plane's gone down.' Mark sighed and they turned to go.

'Tell her I'll spank her botty when I find her,' Hugh called after them, winking and grinning.

'Check the details and then sign the report.' The desk sergeant slid the form across the counter and glanced wearily at the room full of people waiting to be seen.

'It's been several days since she went missing. Did you not think to come sooner?'

The same had occurred to Mark and now it had caused a lump of guilt in his throat. 'We were hoping she'd turn up OK. She's a grown woman after all.'

The sergeant looked puzzled. He studied the report briefly. 'And you travelled up to Scotland independently of Miss Bright, her fiancé included?'

'Yes.'

'I find it odd that you, Mr Vanden –'

'Vandenbrink,' Rachel assisted.

'– that you and Mr Vandenbrink didn't know Miss Bright was coming to Dundee herself at pretty much the same time. A bit of a coincidence, don't you think?'

'What are you implying?' Rachel asked. Suddenly, they both felt like they were being accused of something.

'It *is* a coincidence, sergeant.' And Mark himself was left wondering why they were all gathered together in a Tayside castle – just the place where Jenna was sup-posed to be.

'You're making it sound spooky,' Rachel said as they walked down the road from the police station. 'Like some weird magical force has brought us together. Or worse still, taken Jenna away.'

'Rachel, you really are quite clever for a blonde.' He smiled and gripped her round the waist. He'd only ever considered loving Jenna before and she'd always been taken. But now he realised that Jenna would always just be a friend. Besides, Rachel made him feel at ease, welcome in his own body. He would see where it all went; take it steady when they were back in London.

The next stop was the airport authorities but being dressed as a vicar, Mark's day job uniform was more of a hindrance than a help.

'Really, I am a pilot,' he confirmed, flashing his crew licence and other identification.

Mark wasn't familiar with anyone at this particular airport and logs and flight plans were confidential. But the department manager promised to be helpful to the police, when they carried out their investigation.

'Back to the castle then,' Rachel suggested, hoping that Mark would invite her for dinner and then an early night. How she would escape Hugh's clutches, she didn't know. She only hoped he was distracted by Mel, who seemed only too happy to keep Hugh for herself.

Euan slowly packed a bag. He needed to get away. Part of him, though, was reluctant to leave her, while part of him hoped that she was packing too and would come with him. Besides, the trip to London would give him a chance to visit the auction house, check into Bright Charter – he was beginning to think that this was possibly a scam and Hugh Vandenbrink and Miss Bright had set up some kind of sting to steal his statue – as well as visit the insurance company to lodge a claim for the missing artefact.

He'd briefed his housekeepers, estate managers, waiting and bar staff, cleaners and his secretary and all had smiled confidently, assuring him that everything would be well at the castle while he was away. He was a lucky man to have such loyal staff, he realised, as the cook delivered a tray of food to his private suite.

'If I didn't know better, I'd say you had woman troubles,' she smiled. Euan had known her since his childhood and had always adored her. And how she knew his heart!

'There is no woman in my life,' he lied. He wondered if cook could see her right now, standing by the window in a tartan tunic, her hair as wild as the wind, staring out across the loch. She seemed forlorn today and Euan assumed it was because he was going away.

'It's not for long,' he told her although she didn't turn. 'I just need a break. To sort a few things out in my head.'

When cook heard him apparently talking to himself, she left his suite, shaking her head.

Euan had hoped for a quick exit. A silent passage to his Land Rover, a drive with classical music to the train station and then the long, rocking journey to London where he would become anonymous. After everything that had happened, he didn't fancy flying.

But he had business he needed to attend to briefly at the reception desk and he thought he might as well take his bag down and leave via the main entrance. It was sheer bad luck that Hugh Vandenbrink spied him from the bar as he was dealing with the receptionist.

'Euan, my man,' he greeted with a hand on Euan's back. It made him shiver but not more than seeing *her* standing at the top of the grand staircase. She was watching him leave. 'Any news on the statue? Or Jenna, come to think of it.'

'No, sorry,' he said vaguely. 'I believe your pilot, Mr Maloney, has been to the police to inform them of her disappearance.'

And I'll be doing the same myself shortly, Euan thought, only I'll be reporting fraud. The more he thought about it, the more he reckoned the whole thing was a set up and that the auction house, Hugh Vandenbrink and his elusive fiancée Jenna Bright, had taken him for a fortune. How he set about proving it all was quite another matter. The Bright woman was probably waiting in London for her fiancé to return so they could sell the stolen statue and enjoy the proceeds.

'Yes, quite,' Hugh said when it was obvious the castle owner was lost in a dream, staring up the staircase.

'Now, about the statue thing. My offer still stands you know, when the damned thing turns up. I do hope it gets found. Be a shame to lose it.'

'And a shame to lose your fiancée also,' Euan said slowly. He walked out of the castle but his gaze was transfixed to the top of the stairs.

She was smiling at him now, playing with the hem of her dress and winding her hair around a finger.

As he left, Euan heard the words *I'm coming home* in his head over and over, until the castle was nothing more than a grey blur in his rear view mirror.

18

Jenna stalked around the Saratoga incredulously. Arlen had done a marvellous job with his furnace and tools and ironwork. True, it wouldn't pass any Aviation Authority tests but this was different. Jenna just needed to get airborne, re-create the right conditions and then ... well, see what happened. It was the flimsiest flight-plan she had ever dreamt up but at least she didn't have to submit it to the authorities. She pushed the questions of fuel levels and where she would land again if she didn't make it back to modern Britain firmly to the back of her mind.

Get airborne, get home.

'Thank you,' she said sincerely to the craftsman who stood proudly beside his work. Mending something when you didn't have much of an idea what it should look like in the first place was no mean feat, yet Arlen had used prehistoric common sense and workmanship that was rarely seen in the twenty-first century. 'The landing gear looks stronger than it did when I bought the plane.' And a good deal heavier, she thought, considering the burden of extra weight on take-off.

'It will not break now,' he said gruffly. He was a man of few words, content only when sweating from the heat of his furnace and hammering glowing metal into tools, weapons, farming instruments or jewellery for the clan. Arlen wore one of his own creations around his thick, veined neck – a torc twisted and shaped so that the joining ends looked like animal heads.

'Will your chariot fly?' Cathan's arms wrapped around her waist like the torc she had been admiring.

'Arlen has done an amazing job.' she smiled. She wanted to kiss him, welcome his body against hers but somehow that made things too permanent, as if she was only going out to work for the day and would return in time for dinner. 'I'm sure I will get home in no time.'

'No time is what it will take,' Cathan replied. 'Arlen,' he called. 'Instruct ten of our strongest men to drag the aircraft to the flat plain beside the river.'

'It will give me the best chance of getting up to speed,' Jenna confirmed.

'*Us*,' Cathan corrected. 'I am coming with you.'

Jenna was torn. Leaving Cathan behind was the hardest thing she had ever done. Even though she had only known him a couple of days, it felt as if they had spent lifetimes together. Every extra minute with him was a bonus, even if it was within the dangerous confines of the cockpit. And of course, if they made it to modern Britain, there was every chance he wouldn't make it home again. She would have an Iron Age man all to herself in London. The idea thrilled her.

'You need me to help with chanting and entering the trance. And I must to bring Druantia back to my people.'

Jenna rested her head on Cathan's rough clothing. She could hear his heart beating and hers fell into the same rhythm. She would have to trust him; she would simply have to believe that in some spiritual way, they would be together forever. She doubted, though, that thinking about him each day would be recompense for not feeling his body against hers.

'I'll worry about you getting back and what if –'

Cathan silenced her by placing a finger over her lips. She wished it was his mouth but Arlen returned announcing that the men were coming to move the aircraft.

Jenna stiffened. This was it. Time to be brave and let go of what she should never really have had in the first place.

'I ... I ...' She spun around in circles, her bare feet twirling in the grass. None of this was ever meant to happen. 'Just think of it as a bonus, a perk of the job, a freak occurrence. He's not my lover or ... or ... soul mate ... or ...' Jenna was muttering to herself like a mad woman.

'Stop!' Cathan cried. He took her by the shoulders and pushed his honest, wise, yet primitive face as close as he could to hers without them actually kissing.

With a haircut, a shave, maybe a pair of designer glasses and a business suit, he wouldn't look out of place in any of the office buildings surrounding the Vandenbrink Holdings block, Jenna thought as her mind still raced at a thousand miles an hour. She stared deep into his eyes until she couldn't draw breath.

'What are you talking about?' Cathan didn't understand her words but he did understand her anxiety.

'What I mean is,' she said quietly, 'that even though I don't want to go home and away from you, I know I have to.' She bowed her head. It was easier if she didn't look at him.

'Then come back and visit,' Cathan laughed.

'Visit? It's not like I can hop on a bus or take a long weekend to the Iron Age. I don't claim to understand how this happened – just a fluke, a freak, whatever – but re-creating it at will ...' Jenna shook her head. However appealing the thought of it was, she doubted it would occur.

'If you learn to shapeshift, enter a trance at will, perhaps make a drink like the one I made you, you can travel to the higher planes.' Cathan cupped Jenna's face in his large hands. 'We can meet. We will recognise each other's form. We will never be apart.'

Jenna sighed, her heart bleeding. The longer she was held close to him, the harder it would be to say goodbye. In her work, she saw farewells every day as lovers, families and friends were torn apart at the airport departure gates. Some would be reunited the same day, others in weeks or months. Some never.

'I understand things beyond my time,' Cathan confirmed. His persistence paid off.

'OK,' Jenna said, pulling away and grinning. 'You win!' She ran after the men who were now pulling the Saratoga towards the river's flood plain. The tears in her eyes blurred her vision as she gained speed over the rough grassland. She bunched her hair back in a ponytail and prayed that by the time Cathan caught up with her, her tears would have dried.

'Whoa!' she called out to the clansmen. 'No, you're going to have to pull it back as far that way as possible. I need as much of a run as I can get.' Jenna's chest heaved in and out between words. 'And angle the nose round so that it's directly pointing into the wind.'

To check what she already suspected, pretty much a westerly, Jenna held up her wrist and allowed the coloured fabric tied there to flap in the breeze. Fifteen, twenty knots maximum. She would have preferred more. She fingered the tatty, handmade fabric and smiled. Then more tears came, which she quickly wiped away. Cathan had found the cloth in his island hideout and had tied it around her wrist after they had made love. It was their hand-fasting, he had said. It sealed their union forever.

Next came the gathering of all the villagers and the procession of clansmen carrying their precious Druantia to the makeshift airfield. Jenna tried not to look because she was sure she would cry again or, worse still, never leave, but the generosity of the men and women, their unconditional giving of their prized statue touched her more than anything ever had. Nearly anything.

'Careful, now,' Cathan instructed as two men placed Druantia back in the wooden crate inside the plane. He approached Jenna.

'We're all packed,' she joked. 'They'll have to move,' she continued quietly. Dozens of villagers lined the runway, cheering, drumming, waving brightly coloured cloth. It was a sight to behold. 'It's too dangerous, especially with the makeshift landing gear.'

Cathan addressed his clan and dispersed them to safer ground. He and Jenna climbed inside the Saratoga – Jenna on the left, Cathan to her right – and the silence, the fear that crackled between them was enough to power the plane.

There are so many things that can go wrong, Jenna thought, just let us get airborne. Her silent prayer begged that they be allowed this chance; this one attempt for her to get home. She wouldn't even think about the possibility that if they didn't make it, she would have to crash land again. The landing gear would barely survive take-off.

The women of the clan brought them supplies of food and drink, including the special nightshade brew that had previously sent them tripping.

'I'd have my licence taken away in a flash if it was discovered I'd been flying while under the influence of atropine.' She knew Cathan didn't understand.

'Atro . . . ?'

'Atropine. It comes from the plant that you make the special drink from. We use it in medicine, although respect its incredibly poisonous qualities slightly more than you do.' She grinned, partly through fear and partly because she was sitting beside the man she loved. She didn't believe that had happened before. 'Take too much and you're dead.'

'The gods protect me,' Cathan replied, not understanding her doubt. 'And Druantia will care for us both during this great journey.'

Cathan trailed his fingers over the dials and instruments set out in front of him, while Jenna ran through some basic checks although, with the plane the way it was, most were futile. She turned on the radio but allowed it to crackle quietly, the absence of channels and air-speak confirming her unusual time zone.

'Right,' she said. 'Fingers crossed.' Then she muttered, 'Clear prop,' and turned the ignition key. On the third try, the Saratoga's engine juddered to life and thick, black smoke poured from under the cowl. Jenna's heart raced. No one in their right minds would fly an aircraft in this condition.

'Ready?' she asked and Cathan nodded, brushing the back of his hand across her cheek.

'Whatever happens now, we will always be together.'

It was some comfort, Jenna thought, as she increased the throttle and prepared to release the brakes. The Saratoga shuddered and shook, as if it was glad to be alive again after lying defunct on the hillside.

Cathan placed his hand upon Jenna's as she worked the throttle, increased the propeller speed and gradually drew the plane forwards. Everything creaked and crunched and, as their speed increased, so did the terrible noise.

'What's that?' Jenna shrieked fearfully. She knew the sounds of aircraft and that wailing certainly wasn't one of them.

'I can hear nothing except the din of this air ... aircraft and the noise of Druantia.'

'Then it's Druantia!' Jenna squealed in excitement. 'That's just the kind of thing that happened to me on the way here. All these things and the weird smoke and ... oh ... !'

Jenna hadn't noticed that the aircraft had approached take-off speed and was trying to lift itself off the bumpy grass. She turned to concentrate and within seconds of pulling back the stick, the nose wheel lifted off, followed by the main landing gear.

There was instant peace. No more rattling from the semi-wrecked plane trundling along the meadow. Now, it was just the straining whine of the engine – thankfully without the thick smoke anymore – as they continued to climb.

'Welcome to my kind of trip,' Jenna yelped with excitement. She trimmed the ailerons and steadied the drift with the rudder. 'Oh it's good to be back in the skies again.'

A sudden updraft caused the plane to lurch to one side and Cathan instinctively grabbed the nearest thing to steady himself – the control stick.

'Hey!' Jenna cried, correcting the sudden descending turn that he forced them into. 'You'll have us nose-diving into the village. Look, can you see it down there?'

Both of them stared five, six, seven hundred feet below as they continued to climb. The cluster of round thatched roofs looked like brown pebbles and Cathan marvelled at his river and lake.

'I am truly with the gods,' he remarked. 'Our land looks like it could be swept away with one angry hand. Our people will worship the gods more than ever before.'

Then they entered the cloud base and continued to fly blind until they pulled clear and levelled at several thousand feet.

'It is so beautiful,' Cathan said, his face pressed against the glass. 'Yet, I feel as if I have been here before.'

'Shall we take the drink?' Jenna asked. She would have loved nothing more than to give Cathan a pleasure flight but under the circumstances, she thought it best to begin what they had come to do.

'Oh, that's strange,' she said. 'All the instruments have packed up at once. We must have blown a fuse although I know they're all on several circuits.' Jenna tapped a finger on the altimeter, the artificial horizon, the engine gauges but none of them were functioning and the compass was spinning wildly on its axis. 'According to this, we're flying upside down, at zero altitude and going in every direction at once.'

She shrugged and watched as Cathan retrieved the covered pot of water that one of the village women had tucked beside Druantia. Some of it had spilt but there was enough to make the drink. He pulled the nightshade leaves from his pocket and dropped them in the clay pot, mixing them round with his finger.

'It is warm enough to infuse lightly,' he said, breathing the vapours.

'I'm scared,' Jenna admitted. Losing control of her mind and body while in control of the aircraft was not something that came naturally but she took the drink and sipped the familiar tasting liquid. 'Here,' she said, offering it to Cathan. 'You must have some, too.'

The pair shared the drink over the next few minutes, neither of them speaking, neither of them noticing the thin wisp of smoke that bled around the rear of the cabin. And this time, Jenna wasn't surprised by the initial effects of the drug. When the sun seared a hot line to her brain, she knew it was because her pupils were as big as saucers and when her lips tingled and her heart raced like it was powering the engine, she knew that she would soon be flying free with Cathan.

'Are you OK?' she whispered although her face didn't feel like her own.

Cathan simply nodded in reply. He was chanting; half singing and half reciting words that Jenna did not recognise. Somehow, though, she knew their meaning. Cathan spoke of his love for her through all time; that they would never be apart.

'Did you hear that?' Jenna asked, turning up the radio even though her hand missed the button first time. 'Maybe we're back already and I can hear an airport or control centre.' She listened as best as her buzzing head would allow but soon realised the voices on the airwaves didn't sound anything like air traffic control.

'The voices of the gods,' Cathan said, breaking from his chanting. 'The time has truly come.'

And it was then that Jenna saw the curling white smoke wrap around Cathan's face like a veil. When she looked behind her, she saw that the rest of the cabin was filled with the same smoke. In the midst of the strange vapour, she could see Druantia sitting proudly in the crate, her body vibrating slightly, her skin seeping the mist.

'Cathan?' she whispered, reaching out to touch his face. 'What has happened to you?' She could see the changes taking place and recognised that he wasn't the man she knew or loved but she couldn't see *what* he was becoming.

Then there was a sudden darkness followed by an abrupt surge upwards of the aircraft. With pilot reaction slow, it was moments before Jenna realised she should guide them back to straight and level safety. Her green eyes narrowed, desperately trying to focus on the controls. She glanced out of the cockpit window to get a visual orientation but what she saw caused her mouth to open in a long silent scream.

The whirlwind was directly in front of them and only seconds away. Jenna reached for the stick and tried to bank but there was no turning away from the grey swirling vortex that raged ahead of them.

'It's like before!' she wailed but no words came out.

The stick banged and pulled in her hands as the little aircraft became caught in the outer skirts of the giant funnel. 'We're being sucked in,' she screamed at Cathan but he was lost in trance and unable to hear her words.

'Concentrate, concentrate, concentrate,' Jenna chanted over and over. The Saratoga was suddenly spinning, being pulled round and round the circumference of the whirlwind. 'Concentrate, straight and level, concentrate,' she continued, fighting to control the stick and throttle. Truth was, her efforts were having no effect on their passage. The aircraft was spinning out of control and even the most skilful pilot would have admitted defeat. 'Concentrate, concentrate . . .'

Then there was silence. Total and utter stillness and a light so bright it dazzled Jenna's sensitive eyes. It seemed like both she and Cathan were floating, not flying, and their dance through the air was neither up nor down, left nor right. They simply existed; flotsam on an unknown tide.

'Cathan . . .' Jenna looked to her right and saw that Cathan was unfastening his harness. She frowned. Every movement she made was in slow motion. 'What are you doing?' Her mind said the words because her voice wouldn't work.

'Taking you home,' he sang back at her. His head was surrounded by a halo of ice-white light streaming in through the windows. Jenna thought that they were in heaven; that they had crashed and burnt and their souls were being sucked out.

'We're going home?' She knew the answer, of course, but her thoughts were fuzzy and slow, as if her mind had been dipped in toffee. A big grin overtook her face and she copied Cathan by taking off her seat harness.

Suddenly her breath was stripped from her lungs as Cathan opened the door of the cabin.

'*No!*' she screamed but nothing came out.

Everything in the tiny cabin banged and flapped or was sucked out. Only Druantia stood her ground firmly, still emitting bursts of white vapour.

Then Jenna realised. Cathan was a bird. His lean, muscular body had shifted into that of a defiant eagle and she could see he had to spread his wings.

Open your door, too ... he told her.

Jenna wrenched the door open. She couldn't breathe and felt that she might fall into the void at any moment. The light was dazzling but so inviting and pure and not as terrifying as the whirlwind into which they had flown.

She looked down at her own body and saw that she was the same as Cathan. They needed to be free, to be soaring, so with one quick join of their hands, a lifetime's worth of love seared between them, they sat on the edge of their seats and let themselves go.

Total peace and lightness. As if her body had blended with Cathan's and they formed the perfect soul. She could see him beside her, flying with wings so strong that only sporadic bursts of power were needed to keep him in flight.

Jenna copied Cathan and found herself riding the air currents. They soared and dived and plummeted through the eye of the whirlwind before climbing high again.

Seeing that Cathan had closed the piercing circles of his eagle's eyes, she did the same. Instantly, they were human again, naked and falling. She screamed until her throat burnt but no one heard. Suddenly, she was in Cathan's arms – she didn't know where or how because the light was still so bright she couldn't see anything beyond the beautiful lines of his lean body.

'Come to me,' he said, pulling her closer.

Jenna absorbed his body heat, thankful that it stopped the uncontrollable shiver. She felt her breasts press against the light covering of hair on his chest and wondered how, as they were falling through an unknown void, he could burn a sexual path to her brain.

'I'm here,' she whispered back. It didn't sound like her voice anymore, as if her soul had been lost in time and she was making use of a stand-in. Jenna didn't feel like herself in any way at all.

Everything was quiet and still around them. It wasn't even clear if they were falling now; more like hanging, suspended in limbo where dreams collide to make reality.

'I can see the real you,' Cathan told her. 'And you're as beautiful as I suspected.' His eyes adored her although it wasn't just her visual beauty that he admired. Jenna felt that she was being turned inside out by all of his senses – smell, touch, taste, sound.

'I ... I ... can see you but you're not like you.' Jenna ran her hands over Cathan's upper body. She felt his skin, warm and human-like, smelt the gentle scent of him as she breathed against his skin. But there was more. She sensed his soul, the very core of him, as if he had been peeled and laid out before her. And he was more stunning than she had ever realised.

True, Jenna loved the way his lean legs ended in compact, muscular buttocks; adored the way his narrow waist gave way to a ridged abdomen and splayed out at the shoulders in an awesome yet dependable form. She never stopped thinking about his wild hair, the way it caught the evening sun or tickled her face as she kissed him. And the hardness at his groin was the height of magnificence, a proud tool as essential to his existence as fire, the earth and food.

But Cathan now, Cathan lost in the ether, Cathan on an equal evolutionary level ... he was magical and spiritual and wise and essential and, what struck Jenna most as their pseudo-bodies wove around each other, was that *of course* they had known each other forever. It was obvious now that the weight of life on Earth had been temporarily stripped away.

'When I say I love you,' Cathan whispered. 'I mean I love *you*.'

'I know,' Jenna replied, understanding everything now.

In fact, she understood it so much that she knew for certain that when they returned to their lives, in whatever time that would be, all comprehension would be erased. It was memory loss after an accident, post-traumatic stress disorder, her body's way of protecting the soul. Jenna would remember nothing – snippets if she was lucky – unlike Cathan, more evolved spiritually, who would be able to cherish their time truly alone forever.

'Kiss me,' she said and he did. Her thoughts screamed pure pleasure as the lightness of his mouth blended into hers. His tongue searched for hidden treasures while his hands danced lightly on her skin. He was everywhere at once, his exploration of her new form more exciting than anything she had ever felt. She wished they could stay like this forever.

Not lying or standing or having anything for support, they enjoyed the weightless freefall. Cathan moved his kisses down Jenna's body, knowing he had all the time in the world – for where they were there was no time – to explore and taste and remember every mole, every downy hair, every curve and every tiny mark on her body. As a Druid, he had travelled to this place many times before and seen many souls but none as honest and pure as Jenna. And none that he knew so well.

When his lips were lightly touching her most sacred place of all, Cathan put out his tongue and sent her soul curling at the edges. As he licked, she twisted and turned through the void, devouring the heightened feelings that her body couldn't feel in real time. She wanted it to last for eternity.

'You taste sweet as clover.' Cathan pressed his face deeper into Jenna and even when he focused his attention on her back, her buttocks, her neck and breasts, she could still feel the lingering wetness of his mouth; still feel the flick of his tongue.

Their skin and hair and limbs and faces mingled and entwined so that it was like they were one entity. Anyone caught looking would not have recognised them as two separate souls with male and female bodies. Instead, their indistinct flesh merged into a beautiful creature with double the intelligence and love, forming a never-ending being. They truly were Yin and Yang, winter and summer, day and night, water and fire.

Their love would go on forever.

Cathan entered Jenna because there was no other way. His physical body did what it knew, while Jenna's female need pulled him deeper until she clenched so tight it almost hurt.

But greater than the rhythmic beat that their joined bodies, bigger than the feelings swelling inside them, was the heightening pleasure in their minds. It wouldn't be long before their souls split in an atomic-like explosion.

Then they felt themselves falling. Before, they had been floating, suspended by time and space. Now they experienced the freefall terror that, as they gained speed, turned into bliss and excitement that something was happening. The wind sped over their skin like the flow of air across the wing of a bird. Sounds of the earth filtered into their ears with a great rushing as they gathered speed, and shapes and colours seeped into their light-seared eyes.

'What's happening?' Jenna called from her mind. Both

her body and soul were on the brink and she was hardly able to hold back the life-changing climax that was about to grip her.

'You are going home,' Cathan told her as he thrust deeper into the woman that he never wanted to lose.

And then Jenna screamed.

It was a scream to split time; a scream to pierce thousands of years. A scream from her body and soul, silencing the universe as a climax jack-knifed her existence. Jenna had never known such painful pleasure.

And Cathan's body, growing more human-like as they fell, was gripped by surge after surge of pure energy as he came in raw lust deep inside the woman he was about to lose.

It was as they hit the water – with metal grinding and cracking, the smell of oil and burning fuel, the flash of an explosion, flames, thick black smoke – it was as they first cut through the dark green depths of the ice-cold lake that Jenna knew he was gone.

The water promised to keep their secret forever.

Without a glimpse of the landscape, Jenna was engulfed and dragged down to the muddy, murky depths. She was naked and she could breathe and her eyes were open.

Something pulled in her mind, as if her memory had snagged on a barb. Had she been here before?

Jenna swam ever upwards, her breath a ball in her chest and expiring with every pull of her arms. She glanced back and saw the wreck. All crumpled on the bottom. No good to anyone now. She kicked her legs and swam on, not looking back again. Only forwards, searching for what she knew was up there.

And there it was. A disc of silver shining like a silver coin through the skin of the water. The moon dropped light onto the water like giant net curtains flapping in the breeze.

One final kick and Jenna's face broke the surface. She breathed the air deeply and knew that she was home.

It was where she had come home *from* that she couldn't remember.

19

It was dirty sex. The kind that ignorance or alcohol or drugs or lust couldn't excuse. She stood in the doorway, watching them, unsure of how many bodies were wrapped in the mess of sheets and pillows. The air smelt of sweat and leather and perfume and something that she recognised but couldn't quite place.

Since the accident, her memory had been poor. The doctors had said it would recover in time.

There were three women and one man, she deduced. On turning her head sideways, Jenna counted two women and two men but had she really seen two cocks or just the one swapping places regularly to satisfy all those in need?

It did nothing for her, to see them at it. One was strapped up and had evidently taken a lashing from the red stripes across pure white buttock. Yes, that one was definitely a woman with her slit poking swollen and pink from between her cheeks as she pushed it in the air, desperate for attention.

'Sit on me,' he said in a voice that she knew but which struck the same emotional chord as a supermarket carrier bag. Useful and once thought essential but now a waste of resources. Now defunct. Now shameful to be seen with.

Hugh fucked his way through three women and one man – an extra player, it turned out – completely unaware that his fiancée was watching. Eleven holes between them and Hugh filled them all up, swapping from one to the other, sometimes accepting the other man's mouth on his, a woman's mouth around his explosive balls, two female tongues pressing around the base of his cock, someone's strong hands dragging down his back, forcing his buttocks in deeper.

Jenna swallowed. Mel was there, her dark hair stuck to her face with sweat that wasn't necessarily her own. Her big tits bounced as she impaled herself on Hugh. She was crouching above him, the muscles in her legs powering the surges that whipped up yet another climax.

'*Hugh sends his love*,' Mel's voicemail message had informed her, when she had finally managed to access her mobile phone account. If she was honest with herself, Jenna had known all along.

She couldn't watch the orgy anymore. Jenna stepped into the core of the heated room – the room in which she and Hugh were to spend their married life – and slipped her engagement ring off her left hand. Without anyone even knowing she was there, except for stray fingers that slid adoringly up her thigh, Jenna chucked the solitaire into the human cocktail on the bed.

Then she left.

'I've been given the all-clear by the medics.' Jenna smiled and squinted into the bright sun. It was nearing the end of May and the month had provided an early heat wave.

Now, every time she met with Mark, he couldn't stop staring at her. It was like she had risen from the dead. 'Just silly things left now like stiff muscles, a couple of cuts and...' Jenna trailed off, unsure whether to reveal this in front of the new love of Mark's life. '...And surprisingly sore feet,' she finished. 'As if I've been wearing ill-fitting shoes for the last week.' Then, 'Anyway, enough of me and my post-crash ailments. Tell me more about how you two met. I can't *believe* you were at the castle when I was meant to be there. I'd have flown more carefully if I'd have known we were going to have a party!'

But then she remembered that they'd told her Hugh and Mel had been at the castle too and suddenly her plane going down seemed like the preferable option.

'And you really can't remember anything?' Rachel sipped her cappuccino as they sat outside a café. Knowing Mark for a few weeks had cleansed her of the guilt she would have otherwise felt facing Jenna. Moving on was easy with Mark to guide her.

'Only bits and pieces. The storm and occasionally other things. I remember the cabin filling with smoke and then the tornado hitting and then . . .' Jenna screwed up her eyes as if searching for the memory actually hurt. 'Stuff comes back when I'm least expecting it. Like the other day when I ate fresh salmon. It's the first I've had in ages but boy was it evocative!' Jenna beamed at the recollection.

'In what way?' Mark asked.

'It tasted so good I almost felt like I was sitting at the edge of a Scottish loch eating it, as if I'd just caught it.' Jenna sighed. 'I don't know. Maybe my brain has been switched to a different frequency. Don't laugh but I feel . . .' Jenna stopped. It was impossible to say without sounding stupid. 'I feel older, wiser. It's like I've lived through thousands of years.' She laughed and finished her drink. 'Oh, and now I am completely lonely.' She forced a fake sniff. 'Which, I hasten to add, is a *good* thing.' She meant ditching Hugh, of course, but didn't mean to sound quite so convincing about the loneliness part.

'You'll find someone,' Mark replied earnestly. 'Or they'll find you.' And he squeezed Rachel's hand to accompany the silent prayer he said for Jenna.

* * *

They'd told her not to fly for a few weeks, if ever. They worried about what it would do to her psychologically although physically she was cleared for take-off. The thought of being grounded, to Jenna, was abhorrent.

As a child, she was passionate about horses and had grown up surrounded by them. She'd lost count of the number of times she'd taken a fall and got straight back on. It was the only way.

'This is golf bravo hotel juliet echo to the tower. Again.' She laughed into the headset. 'Sorry, Dan, but my client's still not arrived yet. I've had a message that he's just going through security so I'll just sit here and twiddle my thumbs if that's OK with you guys.' Jenna was tempted to turn over the aircraft's prop but withheld.

'You can twiddle whatever you like, Miss Bright,' Dan said cheerily. 'It's just nice to have you back.'

'Thank you, Dan. It's nice to *be* back.'

A bright light seared through Jenna's mind as she thought *no it's not*.

Then she saw him striding across the tarmac. A lone figure – tall, lean, purposeful and hair to match a golden sunrise. Even from a distance, his eyes shone like liquid jade.

Jenna pushed her sunglasses onto her head and followed his passage to her new Piper aircraft. For a moment, he looked lost as if he didn't know which plane to board but then he saw Jenna through the cockpit window and, strangely, recognition guided him to her.

In a second, Jenna was beside the Piper and welcoming her client.

'Good morning,' she said. The wind whipped her words away as fast as she spoke them. 'It's a pleasure to welcome you aboard my aircraft.' She stared at him and squinted her eyes.

There was something about him . . . something . . .

'And a pleasure to finally meet you, Miss Bright. You've caused quite a media stir.' The man stowed his small bag in the rear of the aircraft. 'But tell me, is it safe to fly with you or should I fear the worst and expect to go missing for several days only to be found alive and well when everyone had given up hope of finding a wreckage or a body?'

Jenna grinned although wished she hadn't. 'You shouldn't believe everything you read in the papers, Mr ... um ...' Hell, she'd forgotten her client's name. 'Mr ... er ...'

'Mr Douglas,' he finished. 'Euan Douglas.' And he held out his hand.

If their palms hadn't clasped together, if the rings hadn't clinked metal on metal and cast a spray of light through Jenna's bruised mind, it might have gone unnoticed. But would she really have overlooked his good looks and charm *and* that he was single in favour of returning to London? She doubted it. He'd invited her to stay at the castle and she had accepted.

Jenna hadn't ever believed in fate or synchronicity or whatever it was that had made Euan Douglas become her client for the *second* time. But now she did. That she had never met him first time round, that he had seen fit to book her services again despite her now shaky reputation as a cargo pilot, was proof enough that their meeting was meant to be. Where it led was now up to them.

'I made a point of not reading the papers or looking at the pictures when I was recovering. I would have found it too upsetting. Plus the press always get it wrong. They'd have had a field day with me. BRIDE TO BE DITCHES MILLIONS IN FAVOUR OF DITCHING AIRCRAFT or some other headline like GRIEVING FIANCÉ CONSOLES HIMSELF WITH THREE GIRL ORGY.'

Jenna finished the wine in her glass. 'I'm sorry,' she continued. 'I didn't mean to bring that up. But you are inextricably linked to all of this. In fact, if it wasn't for you and your statue I'd be walking down the aisle with Hugh today, signing myself up for –'

'Don't apologise. Ever. About anything.'

Euan had listened, cooked for her, given her wine, touched her only once on the shoulder when he thought she might cry. But he couldn't bear the brief connection again. His arm still tingled from the shock.

'Anyway,' she confessed. 'There's nowhere I'd rather be tonight. Your castle is stunning. You are a lucky man.' Jenna laughed at the irony. She'd been to the castle before, of course, but hadn't seen a single stone of it. Her recollections consisted of the taste of loch water being pumped from her lungs and a dozen faces staring down at her as the life surged back into her. No one knew what had truly happened following the crash. Not even Jenna.

Euan didn't reply. He just looked at her and wondered how, why ... Then he realised that yes, he was the luckiest man alive.

Later, they sat in the drawing room, listening to music, talking, tasting fine whisky and snacking on junk at midnight.

'It really is very kind of you to have me as your guest.' Jenna could hear her words slip sideways from the whisky but then she guessed that Euan's probably were too so she didn't make excuses. She'd not relaxed in ages. 'If I were you, I'd throw me back in the loch for losing your big stone thing.' Then she exploded in giggles and immediately apologised.

'It's not lost,' Euan declared. 'Would you like to see it?'

'You have it? Oh God, not that blessed thing. It'll put

a hex on me ... like it already hasn't!' But Jenna found herself on her feet and following Euan through to his study.

There, in a glass case, was the stone carving.

'Druantia!' Jenna exclaimed and ran up to it as if it was a long-lost friend. Then she stopped and turned to Euan. 'Druantia?' she questioned. 'What's that?' She rubbed the side of her head as if using the strange word had hurt.

'That's the name of the ancient goddess. The Scottish clans worshipped primitive deities and Druantia was a local clan's fertility goddess. She's about two and a half thousand years old. That's what the experts think anyway, and I like the story. It feels good to have her back on her home territory. Things like that mean a lot to me.'

'I see,' said Jenna. She felt dazed. 'Well, it's lovely.'

'Lovely and lucky,' Euan said. 'It could have been destroyed in the crash.' He came up to her and put his hands on her shoulders. 'Like you,' he continued. 'Lovely and lucky.' The likeness, at close range, was unmistakable.

Jenna was his woman from the loch. Jenna was his woman at the window. Jenna was the woman in his bed. Jenna was his ghost. Jenna was the woman of his dreams.

'I love you,' he said like a teenage kid might blurt out at a girl he hardly knew.

'Me too,' Jenna snapped back. She felt time was short. That their needs be shown in an instant; that if they didn't, millennia would separate them. She felt dizzy.

They laughed.

'Sorry,' he said.

'Me too.'

Their eyes held fast, delving and discovering, learning and remembering. 'That's a nice ring,' she commented although it was inappropriate. The kiss that was headed her way was diverted to answer.

'It's very old,' Euan confessed. 'And do you know, I can't remember how I came by it. But I like it.'

'Me too,' Jenna said again and held up her hand to his so that their rings were side by side.

They matched.

'If you put the script together, like this...' Euan joined the rings together. 'It says *love burns bright like fire*.' Euan surprised even himself. 'I didn't know that,' he admitted. They both studied the text that circled the bands. 'That's very strange.'

'Strange indeed,' she said and that's when the kiss came.

Someone had built a bridge; a gossamer thin, brittle and fragile bridge between two times, between two people. Yet the bridge was strong enough to stand the changes of several thousand years and promised to hold strong for centuries to come.

'What's happening?' he whispered.

It was definitely *her* but, unusually, he could now really *feel* her. No more the vapour-thin body and whiff of love. Gone were his glimpses of her at the top of the stairs or a streak of her scent left hanging in the air. This was real woman; flesh and blood with the same look and touch of the one he adored.

'I don't know,' she confessed. 'Since the crash, I've felt ... different. And now, coming here, meeting you, I feel like...' She stopped, unable to say the words.

'Go on.'

'I feel like I've come home. That someone was sending me home. Does that sound silly?'

It took him less than a second to answer. 'No.'

Their mouths matched like they had eroded through time together. They were a perfect fit with no gaps and no missing memory. All that was left was to decide that there was no uncertainty; that however much they dissected their situation, it would come full circle to the same conclusion – that they had always been together and would always be together.

His palm fitted neatly round her breast. 'We made it,' he said, without knowing why.

'Yes,' she replied breathlessly although she didn't understand what he meant.

'I've been waiting for you,' he told her.

'And here I am,' she replied, drawing her leg up so that it wrapped around his thigh.

A fire flickered behind them, a suitable backdrop to the grand castle room in which they stood. Druantia watched on, her twisted pose exposing and unwrapping everything masculine about the feminine form.

'I thought you'd died,' Euan confessed. The earthly side of him speaking now, someone that knew of their past but couldn't quite capture it. Why had he been so interested in the fate of a woman he didn't even know?

'I don't even recall trying to die,' she joked. 'Just a job, a flight and then a whole load of missing time.'

'That's how I feel,' Euan suggested. 'That without you, time was missing. Like it didn't exist. You were in my life but not in it.'

Both hands on her breasts now, gently moulding the shape to fit his palms. He kissed her mouth, her neck, her ears, her cheeks and nose. His lips dropped to her breast and then below, while his fingers loosened the crisp white shirt that she had worn to fly him home. It was his idea that she stay; his idea to never let her go.

'I followed your story over the last few weeks,' he confessed between mouthfuls of scented skin. She was smooth and pale and tasted of spun sugar. 'I have the clippings and the pictures.'

Jenna felt like he was trying to colour in her life. Only a few days had been missing and yet the whole country had tried to find cause for her disappearance. Some speculated that she had wandered the Scottish hills with memory loss following the plane crash; others deduced that she had been abducted by aliens, which accounted for the time loss. One newspaper reported that a strange phenomenon had cast her body into suspended animation and she had been preserved in the peaty waters of the loch, only reanimating when she had floated near the surface.

After all, weren't ancient bodies found virtually intact after thousands of years in the peat bogs?

The next morning, when they hummed from their union, when Jenna had climaxed so intensely she felt transported to another place, another time, the couple went for a walk by the loch. They stood at the southern edge, staring out like others had done through the ages. Only the people had changed, not the land.

'There's a little island, look.' Jenna pointed far out into the glassy water. The sky was reflected on its surface.

'There's a story about that island,' Euan began. He placed an arm around Jenna's shoulder. He liked the feel of her body wrapped up in his. 'Many, many years ago, when the Celts and Picts farmed the land, it is said that a hermit lived on that island. Once a great leader of a peaceful clan, the hermit took to a life of loneliness when he lost his loved one. The legend says that if you swim out to the island and spend a day and night there, you will be blessed with your true love that same season.'

Jenna laughed. 'And have you ever swum out there?'

Euan turned, wide-eyed, not sure how to answer. His shoulders still ached from the effort of cutting through the chilly water. 'Come with me. There's something I want to show you.' And Euan led Jenna back to the castle.

Fresh coffee and croissants accompanied the spread of newspaper clippings that Euan set out on the table. 'Take a look,' he offered. He leant over and kissed Jenna's neck.

'Really, I . . . I . . . can't. It's too pain . . .' But the pictures and the headlines called out to her and once she saw a black and white shot of the wrecked Saratoga being dredged from the loch, she couldn't help but look at the rest.

It still didn't feel like her in the pictures. 'That one's the worst,' she said. 'It can't have been very long after they found me. I still look half dead.' She smiled, ever thankful that she had survived. Ever thankful for fate. 'And no one's really explained how or why or when I actually crashed.'

'You're a mystery all right. Listen to this.' Euan took a gulp of coffee and then read. 'Jenna Bright, a 31-year-old pilot from London, narrowly escaped death when her Piper Saratoga aircraft came down fourteen miles west of Dundee sometime over the weekend. Guests at Carrickvaig Castle Hotel discovered Miss Bright early Monday morning at the edge of the nearby loch. "The lass was in a right mess," a witness stated. "I gave her the kiss of life but never expected her to start breathing." Authorities have determined that the aircraft crashed into the loch and will begin dredging for the wreckage tomorrow. Experts state that the time or cause of the accident is as yet unknown but early speculation has thrown up some inconsistencies about exactly when the accident occurred. Miss Bright was admitted to a hospital in Dundee and is as yet too ill to be questioned.'

Jenna didn't move. Inconsistencies? She thought. Yes, there were inconsistencies, she knew that. But what? The words were in her mouth, the thoughts in her head, all ready to say but nothing would form coherently.

Nothing that could explain the feeling that the crash wasn't an accident.

Everything was as it should be . . .

'Wow,' Jenna finally said although flatly. 'I made the second page, look.'

'Anyway,' Euan said taking her hand. Their rings touched again. 'They dredged the loch and recovered most of your aircraft. I watched as the divers and machinery hauled it all up. I knew Druantia was down there somewhere and didn't want her damaged.'

'Talk about door to door service,' Jenna joked. 'You didn't even have to come to the airport to pick her up. I should charge extra!'

'Interestingly, Druantia wasn't the only thing they found in the loch. You'll never believe it but I'm going to have a team of archaeologists staying at the hotel for the summer.'

'How come?' Jenna raised her eyebrows.

'Turns out that the area around the castle was once the site of an Iron Age settlement. They found ancient artefacts preserved in the peat at the bottom of the loch when they brought up your aircraft.'

'Amazing,' Jenna said. 'It'll be fascinating to watch.' And she truly meant it.

'The divers brought up a couple of swords and a belt buckle but the most unbelievable thing is this.' Euan pulled another newspaper clipping from his file. He gave it to Jenna.

ANCIENT BOG BODY FOUND UNDER PLANE WRECK. Jenna whispered the headline. Her heart raced then slowed, as if she wasn't sure how to respond. 'I didn't know any of this.'

'That's because you didn't read the papers. It didn't make much news, just one or two articles. You were the main media focus for a few days.'

Jenna slowly read the column. Her eyes danced forwards and she had to slow them purposefully to absorb every word. She knew this story meant something to her but she didn't know what. Her temples pulsed as she read.

'A two-and-a-half-thousand-year-old man has been lifted from the bottom of a loch after police divers found him while searching for debris from a recent plane crash. *Carrickvaig Man*, as he has been named, is well preserved and experts say possibly the most perfect specimen of the Iron Age period to have yet been discovered. "Many bodies found in the peat bogs seem to have met a gruesome death either through human sacrifice or ritual torturing. This body, a healthy fit male seems to have met with a peaceful end," said Jim McAndrews, Paleobiologist.

'*Carrickvaig Man* will be on display to the public for a short time before studies commence. "Much can be learnt from the body about life in the Iron Age from diet to social habits and even the climate. His hair still shows its blonde-auburn colour and much of his clothing is intact. We suspect he was a clan leader judging by items found on the body and also by his elaborate jewellery, especially a bronze ring." The owner of the property, Mr Euan Douglas, has kindly agreed to a full archaeological study of the site commencing this summer.' Jenna leant back in her chair. 'Wow again,' she said. 'Just look at him.'

And they both did.

As they leant in so that each of them breathed the other's scent, as they held the newspaper clipping between them and their fingers entwined, as they studied the brown, wrinkled man in the photograph, each of them – just for a flash – remembered everything.

Visit the Black Lace website at
www.black-lace-books.com

FIND OUT THE LATEST INFORMATION AND TAKE ADVANTAGE OF OUR FANTASTIC FREE BOOK OFFER! ALSO VISIT THE SITE FOR . . .

- All Black Lace titles currently available and how to order online
- Great new offers
- Writers' guidelines
- Author interviews
- An erotica newsletter
- Features
- Cool links

BLACK LACE – THE LEADING IMPRINT OF WOMEN'S SEXY FICTION

TAKING YOUR EROTIC READING PLEASURE TO NEW HORIZONS

LOOK OUT FOR THE ALL-NEW BLACK LACE BOOKS – AVAILABLE NOW!

All books priced £7.99 in the UK. Please note publication dates apply to the UK only. For other territories, please contact your retailer.

VELVET GLOVE
Emma Holly
ISBN 978 0 352 34115 0

Audrey Popkin realises she has bitten off more than she can chew when she gets embroiled with icy-cool banker, Sterling Foster. His ideas about how to have fun are more bizarre than any English Literature graduate should have to put up with! One morning she packs her bags and walks out of his luxury Florida apartment, heading back to Washington DC in search of a more regular deal with a more regular guy. But, for a girl like Audrey, this is not as easy as it sounds.

   When Patrick Dugan, the charismatic owner of an old-world bar with a talent for mixing the smoothest cocktails, fixes Audrey in his sights, some strange alliances are about to be formed. Within a week Audrey talks her way into a job at Patrick's bar and a room in the apartment he shares with a drag queen jazz singer called Basil – who has a great line in platinum wigs. Audrey soon realises that Patrick is not all he seems. Why is he pretending to be gay? And what is he covering up for his father, a pillar of the local community? Audrey is so besotted with the enigmatic barman that she doesn't realise they are connected by a mutual adversary – a steely, cold-hearted son of a bitch who will take them all down if he doesn't get his little plaything back.

Coming in June 2007

SUITE SEVENTEEN
Portia Da Costa
ISBN 978 0 352 34109 9

When vibrant, forty-something widow Annie Conroy spies her new neighbours having kinky sex in their back garden, she decides it's time that she too woke up and smelt the erotic roses. And where better to begin her daring adventures than the luxurious Waverley Grange Country Hotel, and its hidden den of iniquity, the chintz-clad but wickedly pervy Suite Seventeen? Under the stern but playful eye of exotic master Valentino, Annie quickly discovers the shocking hidden depths of her own sensuality, and surrenders herself body and soul to his outrageous games of power. But when the Waverley's entire future hangs in the balance, and Annie has the means to help save it, dare she gamble on going one step further . . . and giving her heart to the mysterious man who's come to control her?

IN THE FLESH
Emma Holly
ISBN 978 0 352 34117 4

Surely there has never been a woman more sensual, more irresistible, than svelte dancer Chloe Dubois. She is a heady combination of innocence and sultry seduction, and Japanese-American businessman David Imakita will risk everything he has to keep her: his career, his friends, even his integrity, such is her power over him.

But who is this temptress and what does she want? Is it money, prestige or just love? David's ex-Sumo bodyguard, Sato, believes Chloe will cause havoc in their ordered lives, and turns up information on her that is far from pretty. The warning signs are there, but it is already too late for David, who is under her spell and besotted. Will this unrepentant temptress overturn her wild ways and accept the opportunity to change her life for the better, or will the dark family secrets of her past resurface and destroy them both?

Coming in July 2007

THE TEN VISIONS
Olivia Knight
ISBN 978 0 352 34119 8

The moment she starts her doctorate in Oxford, Sarah is beset with mysteries. An old portrait in her rented house bears an uncanny resemblance to her. Her new lover insists he's a ghost. Her attractive, sinister supervisor refuses to let her see manuscripts on witchcraft. An ordinary hill on the meadow fills her with fear – and not just her, but also the man with whom she falls in love. Every time she has sex, she hallucinates strange places and other times.

Through sex magic and orgasmic visions, she must fight betrayal to learn the truth behind the secrets.

LEARNING TO LOVE IT
Alison Tyler
ISBN 978 0 352 33535 7

Art historian Lissa and doctor Colin meet at the Frankfurt Book Fair, where they are both promoting their latest books. At the fair, and then through Europe, the two lovers embark on an exploration of their sexual fantasies, playing intense games of bondage, spanking and dressing up. Lissa loves humiliation, and Colin is just the man to provide her with the pleasure she craves. Unbeknown to Lissa, their meeting was not accidental, but planned ahead by a mysterious patron of the erotic arts.

Black Lace Booklist

Information is correct at time of printing. To avoid disappointment, check availability before ordering. Go to www.black-lace-books.com. All books are priced £7.99 unless another price is given.

BLACK LACE BOOKS WITH AN HISTORICAL SETTING

BLACK LACE BOOKS WITH A PARANORMAL THEME

BLACK LACE ANTHOLOGIES

To find out the latest information about Black Lace titles, check out the
website: www.black-lace-books.com or send for a booklist with
complete synopses by writing to:

> Black Lace Booklist, Virgin Books Ltd
> Thames Wharf Studios
> Rainville Road
> London W6 9HA

Please include an SAE of decent size. Please note only British stamps
are valid.

Our privacy policy
We will not disclose information you supply us to any other parties.
We will not disclose any information which identifies you personally to
any person without your express consent.

From time to time we may send out information about Black Lace
books and special offers. Please tick here if you do not wish to
receive Black Lace information.   ❏

Please send me the books I have ticked above.

Name ....

Address ....

....

....

....

Post Code ....

Send to: Virgin Books Cash Sales, Thames Wharf Studios, Rainville Road, London W6 9HA.

US customers: for prices and details of how to order books for delivery by mail, call 888-330-8477.

Please enclose a cheque or postal order, made payable to Virgin Books Ltd, to the value of the books you have ordered plus postage and packing costs as follows:

UK and BFPO – £1.00 for the first book, 50p for each subsequent book.

Overseas (including Republic of Ireland) – £2.00 for the first book, £1.00 for each subsequent book.

If you would prefer to pay by VISA, ACCESS/MASTERCARD, DINERS CLUB, AMEX or SWITCH, please write your card number and expiry date here:

....

Signature ....

Please allow up to 28 days for delivery.